THEIR ARRANGEMENT

DIAMOND TIES SERIES
BOOK 1

A.K ROSE

This book is not soft.
It's not safe.
And it sure as hell isn't clean.
Their Arrangement drips with violence, obsession, and control.
It features morally corrupt billionaires who don't ask. They take. It includes scenes of coercion, blackmail, stalking, emotional manipulation, and psychological warfare—all wrapped in a dynamic where consent blurs, submission is demanded, and no one walks away unchanged.
Expect possessive antiheroes.
Expect depravity disguised as protection.
Expect one girl caught between the memory of a dead woman and the men who would break her just to see if she'll crawl.
This is a dark mafia romance that does not flinch.
If you're here for safe spaces, turn back.
If you're here to be *claimed*, kneel.

1

———

CLOE

I ALMOST DIDN'T COME.

I stood on the other side of the street for thirteen full minutes, watching the Lawlor Diamond tower shimmer like a monolith of glass and power. The kind of place that made people pause. The kind of place that didn't just reflect light—it reflected judgment. I counted the minutes, not the breaths, because the breaths were too shallow, too frantic, too fragile to matter.

The building loomed over me, elegant and sterile. Built by men who never had to beg, who bled only on their own terms— and here I was, about to beg.

My heels wobbled as I stepped off the curb. The right one had lost its cap, so it clicked louder than the left. It sounded like a countdown. Every step echoed in my skull. My blazer was too tight across the shoulders. My skirt was too short to be decent. And under it, sweat clung to my skin despite the cool morning. I'd spent twenty minutes in a gas station bathroom trying to dab my bra dry with toilet paper. It didn't work.

I adjusted the hem of my skirt and felt the snag in my stocking stretch higher. Like a ladder I couldn't climb.

God, I looked ridiculous.

The front doors loomed above me, polished chrome and obsidian glass. I hesitated for a beat, long enough to catch my reflection. My curls frizzed wildly from the humidity, under-eye circles deep enough to be bruises, and a purse strap frayed so badly it looked like it might snap under pressure. I looked like a girl who didn't belong.

And worse—they would know it the second they saw me.

I pulled my phone from my bag and opened my bank app. A habit now. A compulsion.

$6.72.

That was it.

That was all I had left in the world.

Well—*money-wise.*

Dignity? That had evaporated weeks ago. Somewhere between the collection agency voicemails and the moment I pawned Camille's necklace. When I started sleeping with the lights on. When I picked up the phone and told Selene Lawlor that yes, I'd listen to her offer.

I was in this mess because of men.

But the Lawlor brothers?

They weren't just men.

They were legacy.

I hadn't seen them in over two years. Not since the funeral. Not since Barron Lawlor placed a single white rose on his sister's casket and walked away without a word.

And now I was walking back into their world with a run in my stocking and shoes I couldn't afford to replace.

The security guard barely looked up as I stepped through the revolving glass doors. My heels echoed across the marble floor—sharp, anxious, uncertain. Eyes tracked me. Not for long. Just long enough to weigh me. Measure me. Dismiss me.

They already knew I didn't belong.

Maybe they were right.

The elevator opened with a soft chime, and I stepped inside, hands trembling as I pressed the button for the top floor. The doors slid shut and caught my reflection again—wider hips than I remembered, a soft belly under my blouse, lipstick too dark for my skin tone, eyeliner smudged.

I didn't look like the women who belonged here.

I looked like the reason they locked the doors.

The elevator rose.

Ticked upward floor by floor.

And with every passing second, the ghosts crept closer.

I closed my eyes.

And I saw her.

Camille.

Her laugh. Her lipstick-stained coffee cup. The way she used to lean against my side like I was something permanent.

The last time I heard her, she said, *Go rest. I'll cancel. You're sick*

But she didn't cancel.

She went out.

Alone.

And she never came home.

The elevator doors opened with a hiss.

The top floor welcomed me with silence. No background music. No warmth.

Only the hum of wealth.

Only the weight of expectation.

The receptionist sat at her desk, immaculate in her bun and pearl earrings. Her lipstick was the kind that didn't smudge. She typed with long, perfectly manicured nails.

I cleared my throat.

She didn't stop typing.

"I... I have an appointment," I said, too softly. "I mean, I'm here to see Barron Lawlor. Or... any of them. My name is—"

She held up a hand, as if silence was something she owned.

Her fingers tapped across her keyboard, eyes never leaving the screen. "Your name?"

"Cloe Woods."

A pause. A flick of her gaze. Not recognition. Just recalibration. A name she had filed incorrectly.

"Take a seat," she said. Already moving on.

I turned and sat slowly on the leather couch. It hissed beneath me as my thighs stuck to it. My skirt rode up again—I tugged it down, cheeks flushing. The run in my stocking had grown longer. A second one had started on the other leg.

Across the lobby, two women exited one of the executive offices, laughing. They were stunning—tall, blonde, surgically perfected. The kind of beautiful that came with a retainer and a publicist. One of them glanced at me. Not cruel. Not curious. Just indifferent.

Like I wasn't there.

Like I wasn't anything.

I waited.

Ten minutes.

Then fifteen.

Then twenty-seven.

No one spoke to me. No one offered water. My phone stayed silent. The cracked screen lit up once with a calendar notification I didn't remember setting.

My back ached. My feet throbbed. And I started to wonder if this was the first test. If this humiliation was step one in their evaluation.

I stood and walked back to the receptionist.

"Excuse me," I said, voice barely holding. "I've been waiting a while, and I—"

She looked up, mid-call. Annoyed.

"Name again?"

"Cloe. Cloe Woods."

Her eyes sharpened slightly. Not with familiarity. With realization.

"Oh." A pause. "You're expected. Go ahead. Last door."

She nodded to the far end of the hall. No apology. No warmth. Just a flick of her fingers.

I walked.

Each step dragged like it was being pulled from my bones.

And when I reached the door, my hand trembled as I curled my fingers around the handle.

Barron. Wolfe. Royal. Loyal.

They were on the other side of this door.

The last people in the world who had loved Camille.

The only people left who remembered me.

The men I was about to beg.

Then I turned the knob and stepped inside.

The hush met me. Sharp and immediate. Not the kind that welcomed you into stillness—but the kind that warned you, the kind that bristled like a live wire.

The office was cavernous, drenched in mid-morning light pouring in through floor-to-ceiling windows. Glass stretched behind them like the wall of a cathedral—only instead of stained glass, it was clean and cold, offering a sweeping view of the skyline. There were no signs of clutter. No hint of softness. Just hard edges and white walls and the weight of quiet like judgement thick enough to drown in.

And at the center of it, like kings at a war table, sat the four Lawlor brothers.

They were as beautiful as they were brutal. And every one of them looked at me like I was a memory they'd tried to bury.

Barron sat at the head of the desk, a throne more than a chair, a statement more than a seat. Black-on-black suit, no tie. His storm-gray eyes were the same—unblinking, unreadable. He didn't look surprised. Didn't look angry.

He just stared like I was a risk he hadn't decided whether to take.

Royal lounged across from him with one ankle propped on his knee, drink in hand. He wore his grin like armor, all sin and teeth. His eyes dragged down my body in a slow, deliberate pass—from my worn shoes to the curls pinned too high on my head—like he was already bored by the sight of me and was daring me to try and change his mind.

Wolfe stood apart, leaning against the far glass, arms crossed. His dark shirt strained at the shoulders, sleeves rolled to his elbows, exposing forearms lined with tension. He didn't look at me at first. Didn't have to.

Because even from the corner, I could feel him watching.

Loyal was the only one who moved.

He stood as I stepped in—too quickly, like reflex—and then froze. Sat back down. His jaw clenched, his throat bobbed. His eyes flicked to mine and away again, like the sight of me cost him something.

For a heartbeat, none of them spoke.

The tension filled the air like a pressure system, like gravity itself shifted.

Then Barron said it.

"Cloe Woods."

Not a greeting.

A verdict.

My name landed like a slap, sharp and familiar. Like he'd waited to say it just to see how I'd flinch.

I opened my mouth. No sound came. My fingers tightened on the strap of my purse until I felt the fraying leather cut into my palm.

"You're not on our schedule," he added, voice smooth and flat.

"I—I know. I'm sorry. I just..." My voice cracked like glass. "I was hoping I could talk to one of you. Or—" I swallowed hard. "All of you, I guess."

Another beat of silence. Royal arched one dark brow, his smile deepening. Wolfe didn't move. But I felt him turn. Like a wind current. Like a tide.

Barron didn't shift. But the way his body leaned forward slightly—like a shadow lengthening—told me everything.

Loyal's voice broke the stillness. "What's going on, Cloe?"

His voice wasn't cruel.

But it wasn't kind either.

It was distant. Hesitant. Like he was trying to remember something he used to feel about me.

"I need a job."

The words dropped like a stone. Naked. Humiliated.

"*A job,*" Barron echoed, tone unreadable.

"I'm not asking for favors," I rushed. "I just—I'll do anything. Admin. Phones. Filing. I'm good with people. I can learn. I just—"

"You want to work here," Royal cut in, his voice a lazy drawl, "at *Lawlor Diamonds.* The girl who ghosted after our sister's funeral. Who disappeared for two years and comes back with scuffed shoes and a sob story."

My cheeks went hot.

"I didn't disappear."

"You didn't come back," Wolfe said from behind me. His voice slid down my spine like smoke. "Same thing."

I turned toward him—and it hit me.

His eyes weren't just dark.

They were void.

Observant. Detached. Dangerous.

Wolfe Lawlor wasn't just angry.

He was remembering.

And remembering me didn't look like a good thing.

"I was nineteen," I said, throat tight. "I didn't know how to stay."

"No," Wolfe said. "But you *knew* how to leave."

The silence turned razor-sharp.

I looked back to Barron. His stare didn't shift. But something in the air did.

The temperature.

The charge.

"I'm sorry," I said. "I know I don't deserve anything. I just— I'm out of options."

"You're not asking for a job," Barron said, rising slowly from his chair. "You're asking for mercy."

He came around the desk, walking slowly, deliberately. A hunter, not a CEO.

His presence filled the room.

The air thinned.

He stopped just short of me—close enough that I could smell his cologne. Something dark. Clean. Expensive. It wrapped around me like a snare.

"What exactly are you offering, Cloe?" he asked.

My throat went dry.

"I'll work. I'll stay late. I'll clean the floors if you want. I just—"

"That's not what I asked," he said.

Royal shifted in his seat, setting his drink down with a soft clink.

"You said you'd do anything," Wolfe added, still from the shadows. "*Anything's* a big word."

I swallowed.

Held my ground.

"I meant it."

That made Royal smile. "Now that's dangerous."

Loyal said nothing. But he looked away.

Barron studied me like he was trying to see beneath my skin.

"To be clear," he said, "we don't *need* you. We don't want your apologies. We don't want your grief."

"I'm not offering grief," I whispered. "I'm offering my work. My hands. My time."

Barron stepped closer. Just half a foot. But it felt like stepping into the blast zone.

"Why here?" he asked. "Out of every company in this city, why *this* one?"

"Because," I said, voice shaking, "no one else will even look at me."

And there it was.

Laid bare.

The silence that followed wasn't cruel.

It was calculating.

Like they were all turning the idea of me over in their hands.

"Let's say we said yes," Wolfe murmured. "Let's say we did. What would *you* do for it?"

"I told you," I said, lifting my chin. "Anything."

Barron didn't blink.

Behind me, Royal's voice was softer now. "That's a *dangerous* word, sweetheart."

Barron held my gaze.

Then turned to his brothers. A silent message passed between them.

When he looked at me again, his voice was colder.

"Be here tomorrow. Eight a.m. Sharp."

"I—thank you," I breathed.

"I didn't say you *had* the job," he added. "I said we'd see."

Wolfe pushed off the glass wall.

And as I turned to leave, I felt his eyes trail the length of me. Slowly. Deliberately.

I walked out of the office on legs made of glass.

And I didn't breathe until I hit the elevator.

Everything inside me wanted to run. My body remembered the kind of danger these men carried, even if my pride didn't. The scent of them—cologne and control—wrapped around my lungs like a noose. My feet didn't move, but my resolve did. It cracked, just slightly.

But when the elevator doors closed behind me, I wasn't sure if I'd just been hired...

Or claimed.

My hands were trembling. I didn't realize how much until I missed the button for the lobby and had to jab it twice.

I swallowed back the taste of shame and sweat.

The moment the doors opened at the bottom. My feet moved, but the rest of me didn't. Not really.I didn't glance at the receptionist. I didn't look at the polished women who glided across the marble floor. Or the sleek men in perfect suits who barely noticed me.

I kept my head down.

Out the doors. Onto the street.

Into the chaos of car horns and smog and heat.

And that's when I cracked.

Just a little.

A breath stuttered out of me. Not quite a sob. Not quite a sound. My eyes burned. My chest ached. But I didn't cry.

There was no space left for softness.

I stopped on the corner, hand gripping the edge of my purse.

Then I reached inside.

And pulled out the envelope.

The one I'd stuffed into the lining that morning.

The one I hadn't shown them.

The one I couldn't bring myself to take out upstairs.

The paper was thick.

The name at the top?

Bold. Cold. Precise.

Selene Lawlor.

Barron's ex-wife.

And the woman who'd blackmailed me into coming here.

Inside the envelope was everything she wanted me to deliver.

Photos.

Financial records.

Contracts.

A single note, handwritten in slanted ink:

Make him bleed, or I make you disappear.

My fingers trembled as I folded the envelope shut.

Zipped it back inside.

I couldn't breathe.

They thought I came for a job.

But I came carrying a threat.

And whether I wanted to or not...

I'd just stepped into the fire.

2

____

CLOE

The elevator dinged.

I stepped out onto the same floor where I'd been humiliated less than twenty-four hours earlier—and the air felt colder.

It wasn't just in my head. The lights seemed dimmer. The marble under my heels sharper. The silence heavier. Like the whole building had shifted itself one inch farther from me, like it had decided I didn't belong and was now adjusting itself accordingly.

I clutched my bag, my knuckles whitening. Heels scuffed softly against the polished floor, not bold enough to echo like they had yesterday. I didn't want to be heard this time. I just wanted to survive the next eight hours without bleeding all over someone's designer carpet.

Today I wore the nicest thing I owned before last night. I looked down—and winced. That alone said everything. An off-white blouse that wrinkled no matter how many times I ironed it, with a seam that puckered awkwardly under my right shoulder blade. A navy pencil skirt that clung too tightly to my hips, climbing higher with every step.

The elastic in my stockings was tired. I could already feel it giving up on the left side, inching up, stretching higher. Cool air caressed dimpled skin pushing through the gaps. But there was nothing left to replace it with. I couldn't afford another run. Couldn't afford another mistake.

Not after yesterday.

Not after what I said to Barron. What Wolfe had seen in my face. What I offered—whether I meant to or not.

Jesus, had I really said that?

I reached the reception desk and forced a breath into my lungs. The receptionist today was different. Younger. Polished. Cold.

She glanced up from her screen with the kind of precision that meant she'd been trained not to smile unless it was necessary.

Her foundation was matte. Her liner perfect. Her bun flawless. She didn't offer a hello.

"Name?" she asked.

"Cloe Woods."

She blinked once. No flicker of recognition. She typed my name like she was logging a complaint.

"New hire?"

The way she said it made it obvious she didn't believe me.

I nodded anyway, trying to sound steadier than I felt. "Intern, I think. I'm supposed to be meeting with..."

I trailed off.

Because the truth was—I didn't know. No one told me who I'd be reporting to. No welcome email. No folder. No first-day checklist.

I was a stray someone had let in through the side door, and now everyone was pretending not to see the dirt on my shoes.

The woman typed something else. Her nails clicked against the keys with tiny, deliberate stabs.

"Go through," she said. "Office C. Third on the right."

That was all.

No badge. No instructions.

Just a direction.

Great. I mumbled a thank-you and turned, heels wobbling slightly as I moved.

The hallway stretched longer than yesterday. Too white. Too bright. Too fucking clean. This place felt like a hospital trying too goddamn hard to be an empire.

I passed two glass offices—each one sleek, occupied, silent. I didn't look too closely. I didn't want to see who was inside. I didn't want to see who was watching me.

I stopped in front of Office C.

It wasn't an office.

It was a storage closet with a desk shoved inside.

Wow.

Nice.

The light above flickered. The chair squeaked. One wheel was stuck, driving it sideways when I pushed. The desk was pushed so far back into the corner that my knees hit the metal lip every time I tried to sit. And there were no drawers—just hollow shells, stripped clean like someone had emptied the whole thing out for me without thinking I'd actually need it.

Like someone didn't expect me to last long.

My cheeks burned with desperation.

A sticky note had been slapped crookedly to the top of the monitor:

CLOE WOODS.

Not printed.

Handwritten. Black Sharpie. Block letters like a warning.

No title. No department. No designation.

Just a name.

Just my name.

Naked. Unclaimed. Floating in a place where nothing belonged to me.

I dropped my bag beside the desk and lowered myself into the chair. It groaned in protest, the back tilting at an angle that made me feel like I was on the verge of falling.

Everything smelled like toner, dust, and old coffee. Like broken promises and bureaucracy.

I pressed the power button on the computer.

The screen lit up. Loading.

And loading.

And kept loading.

They really did want me to break, didn't they?

I shook my head and looked up. The Lawlor empire had cameras in every corner. I bet someone somewhere was watching this and taking notes. Seeing if I'd curse. If I'd give up. If I'd start crying.

My middle finger itched to rise.

I thought about it...*hard*.

But I didn't do it. I didn't do *anything*.

I just sat.

Waited.

Pretended I knew what I was supposed to do.

I pulled my notebook from my purse and laid it gently beside the frozen screen. Opened it to a blank page and clicked my pen, the sound echoing too loud in the silence of the office.

Fingers twitched, write a heading—my name, the date, a vague attempt at looking productive. But then my hand stopped. The words didn't come. And the screen didn't change.

I leaned back slowly. The chair gave another pathetic squeak, tilted too far. My heart leapt as I thought the damn thing was going give out under me.

But it held.

Just barely.

Was this a test?

A punishment?

Or maybe a goddamn joke?

That seemed fitting.

Heat raced through my cheeks. My body felt hot and clammy like I was shrinking into the vinyl seat. A ghost already halfway out of the building, and no one had even needed to push.

I sat in a world apart.

No one poked their head in to check on me. No one welcomed me. No one handed me a schedule or login credentials or a flimsy plastic badge.

I had no tasks. No assignments. No guidance. Just a name taped to a monitor and a screen that refused to load.

I shifted again. My skirt rode higher. I tugged it down, or tried to. It caught on the edge of the chair, dragging fabric against skin. Nerves got the better of me. I touched the hem like it mattered. But it was already as far down as it would go.

The office wasn't quiet. It was full of noise. Phones ringing. Printers humming. Footsteps. Conversations that turned to whispers when someone important walked by.

But none of it touched me. It passed right over me. Around me. I wasn't a part of it. I was background. I was exile, right?

After twenty minutes of pretending to be busy, I gave up. The screen was still spinning. The fan inside the CPU clicked twice—soft, broken. Like it was tired of trying, too.

I pushed back from the desk and stood. My knees cracked too damn loud. My legs were stiff. My back ached from holding my posture like a shield. And I couldn't sit there any longer.

I needed to breathe. Or scream. Or disappear. Or all fucking three. So I wandered. A ghost in kitten heels.

Hallways stretched endlessly. I drifted like I had no weight, no anchor—just a body moving on autopilot through a world that didn't want to acknowledge I existed. Glass walls shone as I passed conference rooms, each one gleaming with polished furniture and people who fit into this world with ease. Not me. I kept moving.

Marble counters. Gold-trimmed plaques. The walls were lined with magazine covers and business awards. Their name was everywhere. Their legacy encased in glass.

The Lawlor brothers in every frame.

Barron's stare on the cover of *Forbes*—cold, unwavering.

Royal on *GQ*, grinning like he'd stolen something and dared the world to take it back.

Loyal—softer, in a way—caught in a candid photo from a charity gala. Smiling with someone who looked like they belonged.

And Wolfe?

Always in the background.

Always shadowed.

A shape just beyond the light.

And then I saw her.

The photo stopped me like a slap.

It was framed in silver. Smaller than the others. Mounted delicately in an inset alcove across from the executive elevator —subtle, easy to miss unless you knew where to look.

But I saw it.

Her.

Hair swept to one side. Shoulders bare. The sapphire gown clinging to her like it had been painted on. Her mouth wide with laughter, her eyes squinting like she couldn't contain her joy.

Alive.

So blindingly alive it made something in my chest split open.

Camille.

Her name hit me like a breath and a blade.

My best friend.

My *almost*-sister.

God I wanted her to be my sister.

The ache of that slammed into me so hard it took my breath. I stared and stared...*and stared,* as though I could conjure her from the image itself.

Camille was the girl who once swore she'd never leave me behind.

And did.

Or maybe... *I was the one who left her.*

The last time I saw her, we argued.

Over nothing.

She wanted to take me out—some party, a rooftop lounge opening. Something loud and ridiculous and beautiful in the way everything she touched was.

I had the flu. Couldn't keep down water. Couldn't sit up without shaking.

I told her to stay. To skip it.

I'll stay, she said, brushing my curls back from my face. *It's not important.*

But I told her to go.

I told her I'd be fine.

She kissed my forehead. Laughed.

One drink. I'll be careful.

That was the last thing she ever said to me.

I reached out without thinking. My fingertips grazed the edge of the frame. Cold glass. Warmer metal. I didn't touch her face. Couldn't. I pressed my fingers to the background, to the shadow behind her, like maybe I could absorb the moment she existed into my palm.

A lump built in my throat. Thick and useless. I wanted to

press my forehead to the glass, to say something—anything—but the words wouldn't come.

What could I say?

I'm sorry I didn't make it to the funeral until the last minute?

I'm sorry I left the reception without a word?

I'm sorry I couldn't face what you became—ashes and memory?

I swallowed it all.

Like I always did.

I didn't hear the footsteps behind me until they stopped just a few feet away.

A pause.

No movement.

Just presence.

Then—

"She hated that photo."

I turned slowly.

Loyal stood with his hands in his pockets. His tie was half-loosened, his hair slightly rumpled, like he'd run his fingers through it one too many times today. He wasn't smiling.

"She said it made her look too polished," he added. "Said she looked like she belonged to someone else's life."

His voice cracked a little. Just a hairline fracture.

He gave a bitter smile. "I liked it. She looked happy."

I nodded.

Too hard. Too fast.

"She was," I whispered.

The air shifted between us.

Not heavy. Not cruel.

Just... sad.

The kind of sadness that lives in the walls of old places and old grief.

We stood there in silence.

The hallway pulsed around us—phones ringing, laughter behind closed doors, the distant hum of an espresso machine—but none of it touched us.

Loyal shifted. "You okay?"

I could've lied.

Could've said yes.

That it was fine. That I was just tired.

But my voice cracked when I whispered, "No."

He didn't flinch.

Just nodded.

Short. Quiet.

Not unkind.

But not warm either.

"She wouldn't want you here," he said after a moment.

I flinched.

He caught it and winced. "I mean—this place. This world. She tried to keep you outside of it."

"I know."

"She used to say you were the only real thing she had."

My breath caught.

Loyal's gaze dropped to the floor. "She was right."

We were quiet again.

Then he turned and walked away without another word.

I stood there, in front of the only photograph of the girl I loved more than anything, feeling like maybe this building had already buried me too.

My feet moved slower, weighed down by more than guilt. Still, I left the photo behind.

But that guilt ate at me, sinking its fangs in deep, ripping away the illusion of who I was now. One glance over my shoulder and I found her once more watching me. I couldn't stand the way Camille smiled at me—like she still believed in me. I hadn't crawled back into this world too late, dragging guilt and debt like a shadow.

The hallway was fuller now.

People returning from meetings, coffee runs, rooftop smoke breaks. The energy had shifted—brisk, focused, self-important. Women in sharp blazers strutted past with the click of four-inch heels, their voices cool and decisive. Men walked in smooth, choreographed packs, hands tucked into pockets of tailored slacks, their laughs low and effortless.

I didn't fit.

I never had.

And now, I didn't even try to pretend.

I ducked into the nearest bathroom, yanked the stall door shut, and locked it with shaking fingers. The clack of the latch echoed too loud in the tiled silence.

I sat on the closed toilet lid and pulled my knees to my chest. Pressed my palms to the tops of my thighs until the heat from them grounded me.

Until I felt real.

Not like a shadow.

Not like a mistake.

Not like a girl trying to resurrect a life she never got to claim.

My phone buzzed.

One sharp vibration in the pit of my bag.

I knew who it was before I pulled it out.

UNKNOWN NUMBER:

You're not here to make friends. You're here to keep your mouth shut.

No signature.

But I didn't need one.

Selene.

Her voice lived inside my bones now. Cold. Controlled. Sliced into everything soft.

I stared at the message for a long moment before putting the phone on silent and shoving it back into my bag. Like I could push her away that easily.

But she always came back.

Always knew the perfect moment to tighten her grip.

My fingers trembled.

I counted my breaths.

One. Two. Three.

The door creaked.

Heels tapped the tile. Two women entered the bathroom, laughter trailing behind them like perfume.

I didn't move.

Didn't make a sound.

They didn't know I was there.

"She's not that pretty," one of them said. Her voice was coated in sugar and venom.

"I mean, not ugly," the other replied, "just... kind of frumpy. Cheap shoes. Thick around the thighs."

Their words landed like bruises. Quiet, brutal, precise.

I stayed still.

"She's, like... the cousin of someone they used to know, right?"

"Or the sister's friend. I don't know. Either way, she doesn't fit. Total pity hire."

The first woman laughed. "I heard Barron didn't even approve it. Loyal did."

A pause.

The rush of running water.

The mechanical chirp of the soap dispenser.

Then one of them laughed again. "Watch her get fired before she finds the break room."

The door opened.

Closed.

Silence again.

Heavy. Absolute.

Eyes squeezed tight. I stayed in the stall for five more minutes.

Long enough to make sure they were gone.

Long enough to swallow every sound I wanted to make.

Then I opened my eyes, stood, slowly, and stepped out.

I didn't fix my mascara.

Didn't blot the sweat at my temples.

I just stared at myself in the mirror.

Frizzy curls.

Uneven lipstick.

A small, dark stain on the sleeve of my blouse I hadn't noticed before.

I looked like everything they said.

I looked tired. Unpolished. Disposable.

And yet...

There I was.

Still standing.

Still trying.

"You don't belong here," I whispered to my reflection.

And for one broken second...

I heard her voice say it back.

Not Selene's.

Not mine.

Camille's.

Soft.

Pained.

Like maybe she'd known all along.

I pressed my hand to the mirror. The glass was cool beneath my fingertips. My own breath fogged the surface.

This wasn't strength.
This was survival.
And sometimes, those looked nothing alike.
I didn't go back to the bathroom stall.
I didn't curl up again.
I just walked back into the hallway.
Back into the building that didn't want me.
And I kept moving.
Because they weren't going to make me disappear.
Not yet.

3

CLOE

The message came through internal chat.

Loyal L.: *Meet me at conference 3B. Bring a notebook. Don't be late.*

No other context. No subject line. No prep time.

Just a command.

I checked the clock. Six minutes.

Six minutes to figure out where conference 3B was, and pray my legs could carry me there without collapsing under the weight of borrowed clothes and a stomach hollow with dread.

I grabbed my notebook—half-filled with frantic scribbles and hopeful lies—and rushed into the hallway. My skirt bunched at the sides from sitting too long, the fabric clinging to my thighs with every step. I tugged it down, but the hem was already fraying. It was one wash away from unraveling entirely.

I passed two assistants with matching Louis Vuitton crossbodies, their heels clicking in perfect unison. They didn't step aside. I had to move. Their eyes barely skimmed over me, like I was background noise.

I was used to that now.

But it still hurt.

I found the door to Conference 3B halfway open. A sliver of sound slipped out—low male voices. One of them laughing.

Royal.

Of course it was him.

I wiped my palms on my skirt, heart thudding, and pushed the door open.

Three men sat at the long table.

Royal at the center, lounging like it was a photoshoot and he was the main event. Loyal beside him—back straight, sleeves rolled, pen already in hand. And a third man I didn't recognize —mid-fifties, steel-gray hair, an expensive suit and a presence that screamed power.

He looked like the kind of man who monogrammed his cufflinks and forgot women's names before they even walked out of the room.

Loyal looked up, just once. "Cloe," he said, nodding toward a seat near the screen. "You're here to observe. Don't speak unless asked."

I nodded. Quiet. Small.

I moved quickly, kept my eyes down, slipped into the chair like I hoped it wouldn't notice. My notebook hit the table with a soft thud, my pen already uncapped.

Royal didn't look at me.

Not right away.

But I felt him.

Felt the weight of his presence like it was draped across my skin.

I opened my notebook and tried to look busy. Tried to look competent. Tried to look like I hadn't just power-walked across the floor like an imposter with a countdown in her chest.

Then Royal looked up.

Just once.

Just long enough to rake his gaze over me from behind his lashes.

And his mouth curled. Slow. Sharp.

Like he knew I didn't belong.

Like he liked it that way.

I dropped my eyes and started writing.

The meeting began. They spoke about acquisition targets. Price per carat. Market value. International holdings.

It may as well have been another language.

I scribbled anyway, dragging down bullet points I didn't understand, words I planned to Google later. Terms like "equity conversion" and "valuation tiering" filled the margins.

I was five minutes in—knees pressed tight, trying to disappear—when Royal leaned back in his chair and tapped the table in front of me.

"You taking notes, little intern?"

I looked up, startled.

"Yes," I said too quickly.

His smile widened.

"Show me."

I blinked. "Sorry?"

"You're supposed to be learning, aren't you?" His tone was mild. But his eyes weren't. "Let's see what you've absorbed."

My stomach dropped.

Loyal said nothing.

The third man watched with passive interest, like this was part of the meeting agenda.

My hand shook as I turned my notebook and slid it across the table.

Royal picked it up with two fingers like it might bite him. He flipped through it lazily.

One of his eyebrows lifted.

"You spelled 'valuation' wrong."

The older man chuckled softly.

Like it was charming.

Like it was amusing to watch a girl drown.

I felt it like a slap. A hot flash of shame climbed up my chest, into my throat, burning the tips of my ears.

Royal glanced at Loyal, then looked back at me.

"You sure this isn't your first day at a call center?"

I wanted to sink through the floor.

"I'm—trying," I said, voice shaking.

He pushed the notebook back toward me.

"Try harder."

My fingers curled around the edge of the table to keep from shaking.

My jaw locked to keep my face neutral.

Loyal cleared his throat. Not loudly. Not forcefully.

Just enough to redirect.

The meeting moved on.

But my heartbeat didn't slow.

And Royal didn't stop watching me.

Royal pushed the notebook back toward me. He didn't toss it. That would have been too obvious. Too kind. He slid it across the table with two fingers, like it offended him.

"Cute handwriting, though," he murmured. "Little hearts over the i's. Still a fan of high school romance novels?"

My face went hot.

Loyal shifted beside him. His chair creaked. "That's enough."

"No," Royal said, ignoring him, eyes still on me. "Let's test her."

He leaned forward, fingers laced under his chin like this was a game he already knew he'd win.

"Cloe," he said, all polite cruelty. "What's EBITDA?"

My blood ran cold.

I blinked.

The room got quieter.

I opened my mouth.

Nothing came out.

The air shifted.

The older executive raised an eyebrow. Amused. Mildly curious. Waiting for the punchline.

Royal's smirk widened. "I thought so."

My stomach twisted. I felt small. Smaller than I'd ever felt in this place—and that was saying something.

Loyal looked at me then.

Just once.

But there was no comfort in it.

Only disappointment.

The kind that didn't have to be loud to hurt.

Like I'd failed him. Like I should've known better than to show up unarmed in a battlefield made of suits and silent wars.

"I—I wasn't given any briefings," I stammered, trying to steady my voice. "I didn't know—"

Royal waved a hand, already bored. "Of course not. You're here for sentimental reasons. Not qualifications."

That stung more than I wanted to admit.

The third man cleared his throat. "Should we move on?"

No one answered.

Not really.

Loyal didn't say anything.

He just flipped a page in his notes and nodded.

Royal leaned back like nothing had happened, like he hadn't just carved a fresh scar under my skin.

And I sat still.

Burning.

The meeting ended with the flick of Royal's pen.

He stood, rolled his sleeves casually like the conversation had been light, fun. The older executive shook both brothers' hands and offered a polite smile. When he glanced at me, it was the same look you gave a forgotten item in the background of a photo.

He would never remember my name.

That certainty hit harder than I expected.

I stayed seated until the room was empty.

I couldn't trust my legs not to shake.

Loyal stood, gathered his folder and notes with the kind of precision that made me ache. He didn't look at me. Not right away.

He walked to the door.

Paused.

Turned.

Our eyes met.

I didn't blink.

I waited. Hoped for something. A lifeline. A scrap of kindness. A look that said this wasn't as bad as it felt.

Instead, he said—

"You need to be better prepared."

I blinked. "I wasn't told—"

"I told you not to be late," he said softly.

"And I wasn't."

"I didn't tell you not to be ready."

The door clicked shut behind him.

And I sat there in the silence, the echo of his words louder than anything else in my head.

It felt like failure. Like the kind that didn't get second chances.

I pushed my chair back.

The leather peeled from the backs of my thighs with a sound that made me wince. I stood slowly. My knees locked. My heels wobbled on the slick tile.

I walked out into the hallway.

Head down.

Eyes on the floor.

And then I felt it.

That sting of awareness.

The weight of a gaze so sharp it cut.

Like a wire stretched tight between my shoulder blades.

I looked up.

And there he was.

Wolfe.

Leaning against the far wall like he belonged there. Like the whole building tilted toward him.

His posture was casual. One leg crossed. Arms folded.

But there was nothing casual in the way he watched me.

He wasn't blinking.

He wasn't hiding it.

His jaw was set hard, a muscle ticking beneath his cheekbone. His sleeves were rolled to the elbows, and the silver watch on his wrist caught the light like a blade.

His eyes dragged over me slowly.

Not hungrily.

Not kindly.

Like he was measuring something.

And didn't like what he saw.

I felt it in my spine.

In the heat that bloomed between my legs—humiliating, involuntary.

Because it wasn't attraction.

It was survival.

I felt like prey.

Like a thing.

And somehow, it made my knees weaken.

He said nothing.

Did nothing.

Just watched.

Until I looked away.

Because I had to.

Because I couldn't stand to feel that seen.

Not by him.

And when I finally glanced up again, he was gone.

But I still felt him.

Like fingerprints on the inside of my skin.

I stopped walking.

I couldn't help it.

The air changed as Wolfe moved. It didn't shift. It thickened. Like the building was holding its breath.

He pushed off the wall with the kind of quiet confidence that didn't require power suits or titles. Wolfe didn't move like a man in charge.

He moved like a man who had already claimed everything —and was deciding what to do with it.

He took one slow step forward.

Didn't speak.

Didn't glance.

Just passed me.

His shoulder brushed mine—not hard, not aggressive. Just... deliberate. Enough to unmoor me.

His breath grazed my cheek. Warm. Sharp. It smelled like mint and smoke and something darker. Something that didn't belong in the air but lived in it anyway.

I froze.

Turned, heart hammering against my ribs like it was trying to escape.

But he was already gone.

Like he'd never been there at all.

The hallway was empty.

But my body wasn't.

My hands shook.

I clutched my notebook like it could steady me, like it might absorb the heat crawling across my skin. It didn't help. I walked —unsteady now—back to my desk. The sad little space at the end of the hall. No drawers. No privacy. No dignity.

Just a chair that hated me and a screen that refused to load.

I sat down.

The screen was still frozen.

Still blinking.

Still mocking me with its eternal spin.

I didn't care.

Because all I could think about was Wolfe.

The look on his face—if it had been a look.

The pressure of his shoulder against mine.

The heat that lingered after he left. As if his silence was still touching me.

I hated it.

I hated him.

I hated that I couldn't stop wondering—

What would he have said, if he had stopped?

If he had leaned in close and spoken just behind my ear?

Would it have been cruel?

Would it have been quiet?

Would it have been something like—

You don't walk like you belong here, but your body tells a different story.

The thought made me flinch.

Made my thighs press together.
Made shame tighten across my chest like a corset.
I hated myself for it.
And then I noticed the box.
It hadn't been there before.
It sat at the far corner of my desk.
Black. Matte. Perfect.
There was no label.
No note.
No courier slip.
I looked around.
No one watched me.
No one looked.
The hallway buzzed with normalcy—clicking heels, low murmurs, soft hums of technology.
But not here.
Not in my corner of the building.
I reached for the box with slow fingers.
Lifted the lid.
Inside:
Lipstick.
Deep red. Bold. Almost sinful.
The casing was gold. Heavy. Etched with a single word:
Obedience.
My breath caught.
The letters weren't cheap. They weren't laser-printed. They were carved.
Like a brand.
I turned the tube in my palm.
There was no price tag.
No logo.
Just that one word.
A command.

Or a promise.

My mouth went dry.

I looked around again.

Still no one.

Then I pulled the cap free.

The color was richer than blood.

Velvet-dark.

The kind of red that belonged on lingerie and lips pressed to wrists.

The kind that said everything I wasn't brave enough to ask.

I held it in my hand like it might vanish.

Then—

Ding.

A message appeared on my screen.

Not HR.

Not Loyal.

Not any contact I recognized.

UNKNOWN:

Reapply every time you see one of us.

No name.

No explanation.

Just that.

My chest tightened.

My thighs shifted.

My fingers curled around the lipstick so tightly it could have snapped.

I stared at the message.

Then at the screen.

Then at the lipstick again.

I closed the message.

Opened it again.

The words didn't change.

I didn't breathe.

And then—like I'd been triggered, like I'd been activated—I did it.

I unscrewed the base.

Lifted the stick.

Raised it to my lips.

And drew it across my bottom lip.

The color caught the light.

My reflection in the screen showed it faintly.

I pressed my lips together.

Rubbed.

The red deepened.

Like obedience blooming on my skin.

My heart raced.

I didn't know what terrified me more—

That someone had sent it.

Or that I had obeyed.

The pigment clung like sin.

Dark red. Bold. Reckless. It made my mouth look too full, too soft. Like I'd already done something wrong.

And I swore—for one heartbeat—I could feel them watching.

The break room was empty.

It usually was after five. That's when the real executives disappeared to private lounges and corner offices with stocked bars and panoramic views. The rest of us—assistants, interns, junior staff—scavenged what was left. Cold coffee. Half-stirred sugar packets. The stale scent of status out of reach.

I stood by the small mirror above the sink, lipstick in hand.

Obedience.

I hadn't reapplied it since the message. Since that single line appeared on my screen like a branded order:

Reapply every time you see one of us.

I hadn't questioned it.

I hadn't asked who sent it.

But now, here I was.

My hand trembled slightly as I uncapped the tube again, the soft click of the lid echoing far louder than it should have. I tilted the gold case and ran the color across my bottom lip.

Smooth.

Cool.

Like silk soaked in blood.

My pulse thrummed in my throat.

I didn't hear the footsteps.

Didn't sense the shift.

Not until I saw him.

Reflected in the mirror.

Royal.

He stood in the doorway, one shoulder resting against the frame. His arms crossed. Watching me like I was something unfolding just for him.

My breath caught.

But I didn't lower the lipstick.

Didn't cap it.

I just met his eyes in the mirror.

And he smiled.

Slow. Lazy. Sinful.

"Look at you," he drawled. "Training yourself already."

I swallowed. My hand dropped to my side.

The lipstick stayed uncapped.

Royal pushed off the doorframe and stepped into the room with the kind of swagger that didn't require effort. It was in his DNA. Coiled elegance. Expensive cruelty. Every part of him moved like it had been choreographed for a slower, more dangerous world.

His tie was half-undone. His shirt sleeves rolled up.

He didn't stop until he was behind me.

So close I could feel the heat of him against my back.

He didn't touch me.

Not at first.

He reached forward—slow, calculated—and brushed his knuckles across my cheekbone.

A feather-light graze.

"Little smudge," he murmured.

His voice was velvet-wrapped violence.

I couldn't breathe.

"You want to be perfect for us, don't you?"

The words slithered down my spine like silk laced with barbed wire.

I didn't answer.

I couldn't.

My breath caught in my chest, shallow and frantic.

I hated how my thighs pressed together beneath my skirt.

How the mirror showed everything—me, red-lipped and trembling, and him behind me like a shadow with teeth.

He leaned closer, mouth near my ear.

"Careful, Cloe," he whispered. "If you act like a toy... someone's going to play with you."

The words hit harder than I expected.

Not because they were lewd.

But because they were true.

He stepped back before I could respond.

Left the room without a sound.

Like he hadn't touched me.

Like he hadn't undone me with a smile.

I stayed frozen there.

Lipstick still uncapped in my hand.

The color burned on my mouth.

And something even darker burned between my legs.

Later, at home, my apartment was still and dim.

Quiet in the way loneliness always is—too silent, too loud. It hummed with a kind of ache that no playlist could fix.

I kicked off my shoes the moment I stepped through the door.

The soles peeled. One heel bent slightly when it hit the floor.

I didn't fix it.

I peeled off my skirt.

Hung the blouse on a chair.

Dropped my bag with a hollow thud.

The fridge hummed softly when I opened it.

Empty.

A near-expired yogurt. Two condiment packets. A bottle of water I'd already refilled from the office sink three times this week.

I closed the door.

Stared at the nothing.

My phone buzzed.

UNKNOWN:

Final notice. Balance: $2,378. 72 hours remaining.

I silenced it.

Didn't respond.

Then turned back to my bag.

The lipstick was still there.

Still in its case.

Still pulsing in the back of my mind like a dare.

I pulled it out.

Set it on the counter.

Stared at it under the kitchen's flickering fluorescent light.

The gold casing gleamed like it knew something I didn't.

I could still feel Royal's knuckles against my cheekbone.

Still hear Wolfe's breath in the hallway.

Still taste the shame in my mouth.

I picked up the lipstick again.
Ran my finger along the engraved word.
Obedience.
And I whispered—
"I don't want this."
But I didn't throw it away.

4

―――――

CLOE

THE ELEVATOR DOORS opened onto the executive floor, and the air shifted—again.

Colder.

Smoother.

Sharper.

It smelled like expensive leather and richer blood.

I stepped out and shivered, the files for Loyal clutched in my arms. I was out of place here. Not just unwanted. Invasive. Like a paper cut in the middle of a diamond showroom. But until I was out of here, until this was done, this *cut* would fester and scab leaving a scar behind.

My shoes clicked against the polished floor with a hollow, insecure rhythm. The right heel had started peeling at the edge —only noticeable if you looked close, but I felt it with every damn step I took.

The women on this floor didn't walk. They glided. Their heels made confident, rhythmic taps. Mine sounded apologetic and pathetic all at the same time.

I passed reception. The secretary didn't look up. She didn't need to. She already knew I didn't belong. I turned the corner. And there he was.

Wolfe.

He stood at the head of a sleek glass table in the alcove near the mezzanine. His posture relaxed but commanding. Effortless. Like the whole floor tilted toward him and my heart slammed against my chest in response.

He was surrounded by three women.

All of them beautiful in the way legacy money makes women look. Sculpted hair. Glossed lips. Fitted dresses in tones too pale to get dirty.

They laughed softly. Flirted without trying. One of them reached out and touched his sleeve. Another leaned in, brushing his forearm with perfectly manicured nails.

He didn't pull away. Didn't flinch. Just smiled. That almost-smile. The one that never touched his eyes. It was the most I'd seen him emote all week.

That fucking ache twisted inside my chest. I should've looked away. Should've kept walking. But I didn't.

I watched. Watched the way his jaw flexed when he tilted his head to listen. Watched the way the dark fabric of his shirt stretched just slightly over his biceps when he crossed his arms.

God, those hands.

Thick fingers. Veined. Strong.

I remembered the brush of one against my back in the hallway. Just one accidental pass. And I hadn't stopped thinking about it since. My stomach fluttered. Heat bloomed low and unwelcome between my thighs. I hated myself for it.

I shifted the files in my arms, just to give myself something to do—something that wasn't staring.

And then—

Wolfe looked up.

Directly at me.

Dead on.

Like he'd known I was there the whole time. The laughter around him softened. Muted.

One of the women turned, tracking his gaze. Her smile faltered when she saw me. Their eyes landed on me like I was gum stuck to the marble.

Wolfe didn't smirk.

Didn't soften.

He just stared.

Once. Slowly.

And then his gaze dropped. Down my body. Not fast. Not like it surprised him. Like it was deliberate. A statement. Over the curve of my blouse. The dip of my waist. The hem of my skirt. The files in my hands trembled under his focus. He dragged his gaze back up. Unhurried.

When our eyes met again, I forgot how to breathe. Because he wasn't looking at me like I was a mistake. He was looking at me like I was next.

Heat flared between my legs, a thick, heavy pulse throbbed, low and steady. I knew instantly I was wet standing there, motionless. The hallway behind me carried voices. The buzz of admin meetings. The scent of overpriced coffee.

But I felt none of it.

I felt only him.

Watching.

Assessing.

Claiming—*without touching*.

And then, just as casually as he'd looked, Wolfe turned back to the women around him.

Like I hadn't mattered. Like I'd been measured and shelved. But the weight of his gaze stayed. Pressed between my thighs. Crawled beneath my blouse.

I forced myself to walk.

Not too fast. Not too slow. Just enough to pretend I was still in control. But my chest was tight. And the files dug into my arms. And my panties were damp with shame I refused to name.

This floor wasn't just colder.

It was his.

That burn punched through me—unwanted, unwelcome, and *undeniable*. I turned. Walked faster than I should have.

The files were wrinkled at the corners by the time I reached Loyal's office. My arms ached from gripping them too tightly, but I didn't loosen my hold. Couldn't. They were the only thing keeping me from unraveling.

But all I could feel was Wolfe's gaze. Still there. Still crawling across my spine like a brand I hadn't asked for. Like a name I hadn't earned.

I made it ten steps before I felt him behind me. Not footsteps. Not breath. Just... presence. The way a shadow stretches before you see the man casting it.

I kept walking, trying not to look back. Fast but not panicked. Controlled. Or trying to be.

The files crushed tighter to my chest, my heart beating beneath them like it was trying to escape.

You weren't watching him.

You weren't jealous.

Lies.

I could still feel the heat between my thighs. The shame. The confusion.

Still hear the effortless laugh of the woman who touched his arm like she'd done it a thousand times. Who looked at me like she already knew what I wasn't: chosen.

I turned the corner.

And stopped short.

He was already there. Leaning against the wall across from

the elevators. Waiting. Like he knew where I'd end up before I did. His arms were crossed. His stance casual.

But his eyes—

They weren't casual at all. They were locked on mine. Dead on. Sharp enough to pin me to the marble.

My breath caught. He straightened. Stepped forward. Not fast. Just steady. Confident. Predators didn't need to move fast when the prey was already cornered.

I didn't move. Didn't speak. Didn't blink.

He stopped inches away. So close I could smell him. Leather. Soap. Clean linen twisted with something darker— like smoke or danger bottled.

He looked down at the files in my arms. Then up. Past my collarbone. My mouth. Back to my eyes.

"You watching me, Cloe?"

His voice was soft. Curious. Deceptively calm. My lips parted. No words came out.

"I—I wasn't—"

His mouth twitched. Not quite a smile. Too sharp. Too knowing.

"You weren't watching when Ava touched my arm?"

Ava.

So one of them had a name.

He stepped closer. I had to tilt my chin up to keep eye contact. Every instinct screamed at me to look away. But I didn't.

"I was just... passing through," I whispered.

"Hmm."

His eyes dropped. Skimmed over me. My chest. My waist. The hem of my skirt. He didn't linger. He didn't leer. He cataloged. Efficient. Unapologetic. The heat returned. Worse than before. My thighs clenched. My skin flushed.

I hated it. I hated him. But most of all, I hated myself for the part of me that wanted to stay frozen in place.

"You weren't jealous?" he asked, voice still quiet.

I hesitated.

Then lied.

"Why would I be?"

He chuckled.

Soft.

Cruel.

Like the sound of silk tearing.

"Because you, *little girl,* stare at me like you want to be touched."

The words slid under my skin and dug their nails in.

I stiffened. My knees locked. He didn't touch me. Didn't have to. The air between us throbbed like a warning. He let the silence stretch. Long. Long enough to drown in. Then—

"You're not like them."

My heart tried to leap at the words. Almost. Almost softened. Almost let hope in. Until he added—

"You're not meant to be seen."

It landed like a verdict.

Final.

Brutal.

True.

And the worst part?

It cut deeper than anything else he could have said.

He turned. Walked past me. His shoulder brushed mine. Not accidentally. Not hard. Just enough to make me feel it. And then he was gone. Gone before I could answer. Gone before I could fall apart.

But I did. Inside. Silently.

I didn't go back to my desk. I couldn't. Not after that. Not with his words echoing in my skull like scripture.

You're not meant to be seen.

It wasn't just humiliation.

It was recognition.

A mirror I hadn't asked for, held up by the only man in the building who looked at me like I was something to be dissected —not desired.

Not claimed.

Not loved.

Just... noticed.

Long enough to be dismissed.

I pushed open the bathroom door and locked it behind me.

The lights were too bright.

Artificial.

Merciless.

The tile was too clean. It didn't feel comforting. It felt clinical. Like a place meant to sterilize mistakes.

The mirror didn't lie.

That was the worst part.

I stood there for a long second, gripping the edge of the sink with both hands, my knuckles going white against the porcelain. I wanted to look away. I didn't.

Because the reflection mattered.

My curls had flattened on one side. Frizz at the edges. My eyeliner was smudged, mascara clinging to the lower lash line like bruises. My lipstick was gone except for a dark stain on the corners of my mouth.

The cheap blouse I'd ironed twice this morning clung to the wrong places—too tight around the chest, too loose around the waist. My skirt had twisted, riding high at the waistband, cinching at my hips like a warning sign.

I didn't look seductive.

I looked scraped together.

Like someone had tried to build a woman out of clearance racks and desperation.

Wolfe's voice still echoed in my mind.

You're not meant to be seen.

I swallowed.

Hard.

That one sentence had stripped more off me than if he'd reached beneath my skirt and dragged his fingers across my skin. It wasn't just cruel.

It was accurate.

I wasn't like the women he let into his space. I wasn't effortless. I wasn't polished.

But still—

He'd looked.

I exhaled shakily and reached into my bag.

My fingers found it instantly.

The gold casing.

Still cold.

Still heavy.

Obedience.

I pulled it out, slow.

The lipstick shimmered under the too-bright bathroom lights. The word carved into the side glinted like a threat. Or a promise.

I turned the cap.

Twisted the stick.

The color looked darker than before. Richer. Deeper. Like it had absorbed every humiliation I'd endured since stepping into this building.

I raised it to my lips.

Paused.

Just for a second.

One breath.

Then I applied it—slowly. Carefully. With precision I didn't know I still had.

Bottom lip. Then top.

No smudge this time.

No tremble.

The red bloomed on my mouth like a wound. Like power. It didn't make me feel strong. Didn't make me feel sexy. But it made me feel something I hadn't felt in days.

Intentional.

Like every stroke of that color gave me an inch of control. Even if it wasn't real. Even if it was borrowed. Even if it was given to me by the same man who'd just torn me in half with a single sentence.

I leaned forward. Stared at myself in the mirror. Harder this time. My eyes still looked tired. But they were sharper.

Focused.

"If you're not meant to be seen," I whispered.

My voice didn't shake. It didn't rise. It just... existed.

"I guess that means I should make them look harder."

I didn't smile. Not at first. But something flickered at the corner of my mouth. A smirk. A shadow of one. The kind of expression you make when you know you're breaking. And choose to keep going anyway.

I pressed my hand to the edge of the sink. Steadier now. Just barely. And then I walked out of the bathroom.

Obedience on my lips.

And defiance blooming just beneath it.

5

WOLFE

SHE DIDN'T WALK like she belonged here.

She didn't move like the women who glided across our marble floors in their designer heels and sculpted perfection. She clutched her bag too tight. Walked like she was waiting for the floor to fall out from beneath her.

And maybe she was.

I watched from the second floor landing, hands in my pockets, head tilted just slightly. Hidden by the curvature of the glass stairwell. I had a perfect view.

Cloe BreAnne Woods.

Fucking ghost in the machine.

The girl who used to orbit my sister like a second moon. Quiet. Constant. Always hovering at the edge of things, just close enough to soak up Camille's light without trying to steal it.

She was nothing then.

She's nothing now.

And yet—*here she is*.

Floating down our hallway like a shadow draped in desperation and discount perfume.

She didn't see me.

No one ever did, really.

That was the point.

She carried a box in her arms—one of the cheap recycled cardboard types we used for archive transfers. Too heavy for her. The weight of it tipped her forward, made her stumble slightly, forced her to move slower than the current around her.

No one offered to help.

A man brushed past her—not cruelly, just dismissively. Like she didn't register.

A woman in perfect Balenciaga heels sidestepped with surgical precision and never made eye contact.

Cloe flinched anyway.

Apologized under her breath like she was the one who'd done something wrong.

She kept walking.

The box dipped in her hands. She readjusted it mid-step. The strain showed in her arms. In the hitch of her shoulder. Then the heel of her right shoe gave slightly—worn too thin— and the edge of the box slammed into the hallway table.

Papers scattered.

She froze.

Crouched fast. *Clumsy.*

Her skirt pulled tight across her hips. A run in her stocking stretched higher as the fabric bunched around her knees. She scrambled to gather the papers, fingers fumbling. She reached under the table. Hair slipping from the clip at the nape of her neck. Her breath uneven.

From where I stood, I had a perfect view.

The slope of her back. The soft curve of her ass beneath cheap fabric. The sheen of sweat at the base of her spine.

My jaw clenched.

I didn't move.

Neither did anyone else.

One assistant stepped over her papers like they were debris.

Another looked through her.

Cloe was invisible here.

Just like she was supposed to be.

Not with her secondhand clothes.

Not with her biteable lower lip she kept trying not to chew.

Not with the guilt that lived in her eyes and followed her like a second shadow.

She didn't belong.

Not here.

Not anymore.

She gathered the last paper, shoved it into the box with more force than necessary, and stood too fast. Her body wobbled. Her breath caught.

She didn't look up.

She didn't want to see who had seen her.

I stayed hidden behind the curve of the glass, fingers twitching in my pocket. Not because I wanted to help. Because I didn't know what I'd do if I did.

She straightened her back. Kept walking. Head down. Shoulders square. Like she hadn't just been reminded that this place would chew her up and spit her out.

She passed beneath me. Didn't know I was watching. Didn't know I hadn't stopped. Because I hadn't.

I kept my eyes on her until she disappeared around the corner, the cardboard box trembling in her arms like her grip was the only thing keeping it—and her—from breaking.

I breathed out slowly.

Tight.

Controlled.

And tasted her on the exhale.

She turned the corner at the far end of the hall. I followed. Three steps behind. Silent. Not to help. Just to watch. Just to feel what I felt whenever she was near—rage and restraint. And underneath it all... the thing I refused to name.

She didn't used to be like this.

I remembered her in glittering dresses at our family parties, sipping cheap champagne with pink lipstick on the rim and laughter in her lungs. I remembered her with Camille—always with Camille—half-draped across each other like they were made to orbit the same gravity.

Camille.

Fuck.

Camille had loved her like a sister.

She dressed her. Fed her. Protected her. Let her into our world when no one else would've even glanced twice.

And Cloe?

Cloe let her go out alone that night.

Sick, she'd said. Tired. Couldn't make it.

Camille waited.

Then didn't.

She went.

Alone.

And she died with a knife in her side and her lipstick still perfect.

We buried her two days later.

I carried her casket with my brothers. My knuckles bled from the grip I had on the handle. Barron didn't speak for three days. Loyal nearly drank himself blind. Royal vanished to Dubai for a month and came back with new tattoos and worse habits.

I stayed. Watched the world go cold. Watched the company keep growing. Watched the name Camille built get turned into steel and marble and quarterly reports.

And I watched Cloe—quiet little Cloe—walk out of the funeral without saying goodbye.

Not to us. Not even to the girl she once swore was her whole world. She disappeared. Now here she was again.

Same wild curls. Same wide eyes. Wearing Camille's ghost like perfume.

The only question was...*why was she here at all?*

She stopped outside the supply closet. Readjusted the box in her arms. Fumbled for her keycard. It beeped red. She cursed under her breath and tried again.

I moved closer. Not enough for her to hear me. Just close enough to see the sweat forming at her hairline. Her neck flushed pink. Her jaw clenched. Her thighs pressed together beneath the too-tight skirt like she was trying to hold herself together.

She swiped the card again. Green. The door opened. She stumbled inside. The box landed on the floor with a dull thud. And she exhaled. Loud. Like she'd been drowning and finally surfaced.

I stayed in the hallway. Watched the door close. Listened. She didn't cry. Didn't scream.

She just existed. Quiet and cornered. And I didn't go in. Because I didn't trust myself. Because I wasn't sure if I'd shove her against the filing cabinet and growl in her ear to go the fuck home before she ruined what was left of us...or if I'd bury my face in her neck and inhale the last pieces of Camille she carried.

An hour later, I passed her desk. If you could call it a desk.

It was tucked into the corner of the admin bullpen like a punishment. No drawers. No nameplate. Nothing to mark her presence except a crooked Post-it and the ghost of dignity. She was hunched over the keyboard. Typing like her life depended on it.

Her bottom lip was caught between her teeth again. That same goddamn lip Camille used to tease her about. The one she said made Cloe look "accidentally fuckable."

My hand twitched at my side. Her blouse pulled tight across her back as she leaned forward.

I could see the way her shoulders rounded. The way her skirt bunched slightly at the thighs. Still not looking at me. Still pretending she didn't feel me watching. And maybe she didn't.

But I did.

I watched her fingers move across the keys. Watched the way she paused after every sentence like she was second-guessing every word.

I remembered Camille teaching her how to write cover letters. Now she was here—typing the end of her own story one keystroke at a time.

I should've walked away. I didn't. I stood there for too long. Too still. Then—

She looked up. Just for a second. Not at me. But through me. Like some part of her knew I was there. Like the part of her that used to belong to my sister was warning the rest of her that I wasn't safe.

I turned. Walked away. Because I wasn't ready for her to know what I already did. That she didn't belong here. And I was going to make sure she stayed anyway.

She didn't see me.

But I saw her.

And I hated how much of me remembered what she used to sound like when she laughed.

She walked like she was trying to convince the floor she had a right to be there. Head up. Shoulders drawn back. Paper clutched in her hand like a shield. I watched from across the hallway, unseen behind one of the load-bearing columns, watching her move through a world built to make her disappear.

Her blouse slightly wrinkled—and the wrong fucking size. Bought for a frame that was narrower than hers. Her hips shifted in that ugly goddamn skirt that looked like it was sewn for a mannequin and not a woman who had softness at her waist.

The same scent as always clung to her skin—peach and vanilla and something I couldn't name. Something dangerously close to what Camille used to wear. Close enough to make my stomach knot.

Her curls bounced when she walked. The corner of her mouth twitched like she was fighting the urge to smile— desperate to be liked, to be seen, to matter.

And I hated how much of me remembered.

The last time I saw her was the funeral. Black dress, black gloves, her chin tilted downward, her face ashen. She didn't come to the house afterward. Didn't speak to us. Just left. Slipped out the side like grief was a party she hadn't been invited to.

We buried Camille. She vanished.

Until now.

Until she came crawling back with nothing in her wallet and everything on her face.

And still—somehow—I couldn't stop watching her.

She stopped at the far end of the corridor, scanning the room numbers on the glass offices.

Her hand lifted. Knuckles brushed the edge of one door. She didn't knock. She was breathing too hard.

So was I.

I stepped out from behind the column. Her name rose to my lips, but I didn't say it.

Not yet.

Let her feel me first.

Let her skin tingle before she knew why.

"Cloe."

She jumped.

Turned.

I was only a few steps away now.

Her eyes widened. She clutched the folder tighter to her chest like it could shield her from the storm building in my chest.

"Wolfe." Her voice cracked a little. "I didn't see you."

No one ever does.

She glanced down at the paper in her hands, then back up like maybe she could pretend she had a reason to be here. That she wasn't standing in the belly of the empire she once ghosted, wearing its legacy like a second skin.

"Did you need—?"

"You shouldn't be here."

She stilled.

Her mouth opened. No sound.

"This isn't your world," I said. "You don't belong in it."

Her throat worked as she swallowed. "I'm just trying to help."

"You're not helping."

Her spine straightened a little. A flicker of the girl Camille used to bring to family dinners—dressed in borrowed silk and barely hiding the hunger in her eyes.

"I didn't come here to make things worse," she said softly. "I just... I didn't know where else to go."

"Then you should've kept walking."

Her lip trembled. She bit it. Hard.

"Camille wouldn't have wanted—"

"Don't," I snapped.

She blinked.

"Don't you fucking *dare* speak her name like you still have the right to."

Her shoulders jerked back like I'd hit her.

And maybe I had.

"She was the only good thing in this family," I said, voice low. "She held us together. She made the rest of us tolerable."

Cloe's hand trembled around the folder.

"You think you're walking in her footsteps," I continued, stepping closer. "But you're not. You're desecrating them."

"I loved her," she whispered.

"Not enough to go with her."

She flinched.

Again.

God, why didn't she break?

Why didn't she scream, shove me, cry—do something other than look at me like she understood?

"I was sick," she said, her voice barely a breath. "She told me she'd cancel. Said she'd wait. But she went anyway. You think I haven't replayed that night a thousand times in my head?"

"Don't act like a martyr," I spat. "You didn't even stay for the burial. You left."

"I couldn't face you."

"No," I said, stepping in close—too close. Her back brushed the wall. "*You* couldn't face *yourself*."

Her breath hitched.

I leaned in, hands at my sides, knuckles flexing to keep from grabbing her. From pressing her to that wall and shaking the truth out of her until the guilt spilled free like blood.

"You wear her scent," I said. "You still have the earrings she gave you. You came back to this place like you never carved yourself out of it."

"I didn't know where else to go," she whispered. "I thought—"

"You thought wrong."

We were inches apart.

I could see the pulse in her neck. Feel the heat from her skin. She was scared. Not of me. Of herself. Of what she wanted me to do. I wanted it too. And that's why I stepped back. Not far. Just enough to sever the thread between us.

"This place will eat you alive, Cloe," I said. "You're not built for it."

She didn't answer right away.

Then, softly—

"Then why am I still here?"

My jaw ticked.

Because we let you in.

Because none of us stopped Barron when he said yes.

Because we're just as broken as you are.

I didn't say any of that.

I turned.

Walked away.

Didn't look back.

Didn't let her see the way my hands were shaking.

6

CLOE

My fingers shook so hard they almost didn't work. The lock snapped shut with a *crack* as I locked the bathroom door and stumbled backwards, hitting the toilet as my knees buckled and collapsed on toilet lid.

Not to pee.

Not to fix my makeup.

Just to breathe.

Please...just breathe. Just...breathe. The gulp of air was a stone, one that bruised as I it went down. Fluorescent lights buzzed overhead like they were judging me. Just like everything in this fucking place judged me. *Not everything... everyone.*

I closed my eyes for a second and then opened them and looked down. The tile was too white—too sterile, too clean. The scent of bleach and hand soap burned the back of my throat. Nothing in this room held memory.

Except me.

I was the ghost in the room.

In the building.

In my own goddamn life really.

The folder in my lap trembled between my hands. My fingers dug into the edges, bending the paper. I didn't even remember what was in it—contracts, maybe. Invoices. HR paperwork I'd been told to deliver.

None of it mattered now.

What mattered was Wolfe's voice still echoing in my head.

Camille was the only good thing in this family.

And me?

I was the leftover.

The disappointment.

The wrong girl in the right girl's clothes.

The mistake who dared to wear her scent.

I curled forward, pressing my head against the side of the stall. Cold metal met my forehead. I didn't flinch.

My chest ached.

But no tears came.

I wanted to cry.

God, I wanted to cry.

But I'd already cried her dry.

I'd already bled all over the memory of her and still couldn't scrub the guilt out of my skin.

I reached into my bag and pulled out the photo.

It was folded in thirds. Soft at the corners. Nearly worn to fabric. I smoothed it open with care, like the paper might tear if I breathed too hard.

Me and Camille.

Her arm slung around my shoulder. Both of us in heels. Laughter. The glow of some overpriced restaurant behind us.

That night, she'd taken me somewhere I couldn't afford. Walked in like the world belonged to her. Ordered champagne like it was sparkling water. Passed her plate across the table when she saw how slowly I picked at mine.

I'm stuffed, babe. Help me out.

She was always "stuffed" when I was hungry.

She pushed her credit card into the checkbook without glancing at the total. Talked about nothing for the next ten minutes so I wouldn't say thank you.

And when we left, she handed me a shopping bag with a new jacket, heels, and a dress that hugged my hips like it had been tailored.

Not my style, she said, like she hadn't picked it for me six weeks earlier.

She knew I had nothing.

And she never made me say it.

I clutched the photo until my knuckles ached.

She'd been everything.

And now she was gone.

And I was here.

Drowning in her memory. Her clothes. Her world.

The bathroom door creaked open.

I stiffened.

Two steps. Rubber soles against tile.

Then silence.

I held my breath.

Shoes stopped just outside the stall.

No movement.

No sound.

Just... presence.

Like someone was listening.

Waiting.

My heart thudded against my ribs. Loud. Too loud.

I blinked at the door, willing it to stay closed. Willing whoever stood there to walk away.

They didn't.

Not for a long moment.

Then—
One step back.
The door opened again.
Footsteps receded.
And they were gone.
But the echo stayed.
In the space between my shoulders.
In the chill of the air.
In the way my fingers tightened around the photograph like it could shield me from whoever—or whatever—had been there.
I didn't move.
Didn't breathe.
I stayed there for a long time after that.
Because out there, I was a burden.
A stain.
A reminder of something they'd buried.
But in here?
I was just a girl on a toilet lid.
Trying not to fall apart.
I didn't mean to walk that way.
I didn't even realize where I was going until the hallway narrowed and the background chatter of the office floor faded behind me, swallowed by silence and glass. The air shifted. Cooler. Stiller. A corridor that didn't breathe the way the rest of the building did.
Most of the upper-level offices were reserved for investors. Private meetings. People who had power and names carved into brass plaques.
But this wing?
No one came down this wing.
Not anymore.
The lighting was different here. Dimmer. The scent in the

air was older—dust and carpet cleaner and something floral buried beneath layers of time.

I walked slower.

As if my feet knew what was coming before I did.

Then I saw it.

Second door on the right.

Frosted glass.

Bronze plaque.

C. Lawlor.

I stopped.

Everything inside me did.

I hadn't seen it since the funeral. Since the day Barron locked it and told the staff, "No one goes in. No one touches anything."

And no one had.

Not even to remove her name.

Not even to reclaim the square footage.

I stepped closer.

Raised my hand.

Touched the edge of the plaque. My fingers trembled as they brushed the raised gold lettering. A little dull now. Faded at the corners.

Camille always hated this office. Said it was too quiet. Too far from the chaos. *You can't flirt with a printer, babe,* she used to say. *But you can with Royal's assistant.*

And yet—this space was hers.

Still was.

I didn't try the handle. I already knew.

But my hand moved on its own, reaching for the keypad.

Beep. Red.

Still coded. Still sealed.

Of course.

I stepped closer and leaned my forehead gently against the frosted glass.

Not enough to see through.

Just enough to feel like I could.

The hum of air conditioning vibrated through the wall. Faint. Constant.

I wondered if the light inside still flickered. If the scarf she used to throw over her chair was still there. If her heels still sat tucked beneath the desk.

I closed my eyes.

And everything in me hurt.

The begging.

The lipstick.

The shame I kept swallowing with my coffee.

It all started here.

At this door.

This name.

This ghost I couldn't outrun.

"I shouldn't be here," I whispered.

My breath fogged the glass.

"But it's the only place that still feels like you."

I didn't cry.

Not here.

Not where the walls still remembered her better than they'd ever know me.

I didn't go back to my desk.

Didn't check the message Loyal sent asking if I was okay.

Didn't wait for another task. Another look. Another slice.

I just walked away.

Down the stairs.

Through the lobby.

Out the front doors.

And into the rain.

It started soft.

Light pinpricks against my skin.

But it didn't stay that way.

By the time I hit the crosswalk, it had deepened into a slow, deliberate soak.

The kind of rain that feels personal.

I didn't run.

Didn't open my umbrella.

Didn't care if people stared at the girl in the soaked blouse and twisted skirt. Let the rain cling to me. Let it seep through my fabric and into my skin.Let it wash everything off that bathroom mirror hadn't.

The cemetery wasn't far.

Fifteen blocks from the Lawlor tower.

I couldn't afford a cab.

Didn't want one.

My heels ached. Every step a blister. My toes numb. The wind kept catching the hem of my skirt and yanking it up like the world hadn't humiliated me enough.

Still, I walked.

Past shuttered cafés. Umbrellaed businessmen. Past women in dry coats and dry lives.

I walked until the sidewalk ended.

And the cemetery gates appeared.

Tall.

Iron.

Black as grief.

I'd only been here once since the funeral.

Couldn't bear to come back.

Not until now.

But my feet knew the path.

Fourth row from the magnolia tree. Left side. Between a florist's daughter and a retired judge.

Her grave was clean.

Someone had been here recently.

A pale pink lily lay across the stone. No note. Just rain collecting in the curve of the petals.

Camille would have hated that. She liked dramatic florals. Stargazer lilies. Red roses. Orchid sprays.

Not subtle.

Never subtle.

I stepped closer.

My knees gave out before I expected them to.

I sank onto the wet grass, the mud seeping through my tights. My hands curled in my lap. The rain matted my curls to my cheeks.

And I whispered.

"I miss you."

The wind carried my words.

I didn't expect her to answer.

I just needed her to know.

The thought tightened my throat.

I crouched down, wiped the droplets from her name.

Camille Rose Lawlor.

Beloved daughter. Fierce friend. Bright light.

Twenty-six years old.

I sat in the wet grass and let the cold soak through me. I didn't care anymore. My knees were already ruined. The stockings shredded from the walk. My palms scraped raw from the fall that brought me back here in the first place.

I reached into my bag and pulled out the photo again. The one I couldn't stop folding and unfolding like it held the answer I couldn't speak aloud. I smoothed it open with trembling fingers and laid it down on the marble beside her name.

It looked small there.

Fragile.

Just like us.

"I tried, Cam."

My voice cracked. Broke.

"I really did. I tried to stay away. Tried to be strong. Tried to live like you told me to—like I had a place in the world without you."

The rain fell harder.

Thicker now. Like it had finally given up pretending it would pass.

"But I don't."

A tear fell. I let it. Didn't bother wiping it away. My cheeks were soaked anyway.

"I'm in the building you built. Sitting in a chair that doesn't belong to me. Wearing a shirt I can't afford. Pretending not to hear your brothers call me a whore with their eyes."

I paused. Swallowed hard.

"They hate me. You know that, right?"

A gust of wind lifted the edge of the photo. I pressed it flat again.

"They think I left you. And maybe I did. Maybe I should've gone out that night. Maybe it should've been me."

A shiver ran through me. Deep. Violent.

"But I'm here now," I whispered. "And I don't know if it's to make things right or to make them worse. I don't even know if I want to be saved."

My eyes closed.

"I just... miss you."

I pressed my hand to the headstone. Rain sliding down my arm, soaking into the sleeve that had already clung to my skin for hours.

"I miss you so fucking much."

The silence wrapped around me like a cloak. Heavy. Sacred.

Until—

Behind me, the crunch of boots on gravel.

I froze.

My whole body stilled.

The air shifted. Thickened. Pushed against my back like a warning.

And when I turned—

Wolfe was there.

Rain slicked down his face. His jacket soaked through. His jaw tight. His hands clenched at his sides like he was holding something in.

But his eyes—

They weren't soft.

They weren't grieving.

They were burning.

My breath caught.

His presence always felt sharp. Precise. But here, in this place, under this sky, it felt brutal.

I stood slowly. Wiped the rain from my cheeks. Not because I cared about appearances—but because I didn't want him to see how much I'd already fallen apart.

"You followed me," I said. My voice sounded too small. Too exposed.

"No." His tone was clipped. Cold. "You're predictable."

The words hit harder than they should have.

I looked down at Camille's name. Then back at him.

"I didn't come here to bother you."

"Didn't you?"

His boots shifted. Two slow steps forward. Gravel crunched under his weight.

"This place isn't yours, Cloe," he said. "Not anymore."

My jaw locked. "She was my best friend."

"She was our sister."

I nodded, rain dripping off my chin. "And she loved me."

His mouth twisted. "She loved a lot of things. Didn't stop her from dying alone."

I flinched.

He didn't.

"Don't you dare blame me for that."

"I don't have to. You already do."

Silence again. Sharp and painful.

I looked away.

Stared at the stone.

"I told her, *no, I begged her* not to go out that night," I whispered.

"And she did anyway." Wolfe's voice dropped, lower now—dangerous, hollowed out by something deeper. "She trusted you to be there."

"I was sick."

"No," he said. "You were scared."

The word hit like a strike across the ribs.

I froze.

The rain pounded harder between us. Around us. Soaking everything. But it wasn't the cold that made me shiver.

It was him.

He stepped closer.

Not fast.

Not threatening.

But heavy.

Intentional.

Close enough that I felt the heat of his fury under all that wet. Like it couldn't be dampened. Couldn't be cooled. It just burned beneath the surface, licking up the edges of his control.

"You think I don't know what this is?" he rasped. "You think I don't see the game you're playing?"

I shook my head. "I'm not playing—"

"You come back here wearing her perfume. Her curls. Her fucking smile. You crawl into our building like a parasite and act like grief gives you a keycard to our lives."

My stomach twisted.

"I didn't come for them. I came for me."

"No," he hissed. "You came for her. And now you're tearing the last piece of her apart."

Then he did it.

He shoved me.

Not hard.

Not cruel.

But too much.

The kind of push that wasn't meant to land.

But did.

My back hit the gravestone with a wet, hollow thud.

Cold marble bit into my spine.

My breath caught.

Rain slid down my cheeks.

The photo slipped from my hands.

It fluttered to the ground between us, already curling at the corners.

He saw it.

Wolfe looked down.

At Camille's laughing face.

At mine beside her.

Happy.

Untouched.

Before.

His eyes changed.

Not softened.

Broken.

"Fuck," he whispered.

His hands opened and closed at his sides like he didn't know what to do with them.

He stepped back.

One pace.

Two.

The distance didn't help.

He looked at me like I'd stabbed him.

Like he'd just realized what he'd done.

Where we were.

Who we were.

I didn't speak.

Couldn't.

Not with my spine pressed to Camille's name.

Not with his guilt soaking the air like a second storm.

Then he turned.

Walked off into the rain.

No goodbye.

No apology.

Just silence.

Just the sound of his boots scraping the gravel.

And me—

Left there.

Pressed to her grave.

Alone.

Again.

7

———————

WOLFE

I DIDN'T REMEMBER STARTING the engine.

Didn't remember turning the wheel. Didn't remember the gravel crunching beneath my tires as I pulled away from the cemetery, the sound of the iron gate slamming shut behind me like a warning. Like it was trying to keep something in—or trying to keep me out.

But I was driving.

Wet, quiet, empty streets. The kind that belonged to ghosts.

The kind that didn't remember your name even if you bled on the pavement.

My hands gripped the steering wheel too tightly. Leather bit into my palms. The windshield wipers swiped in slow rhythm, but they couldn't erase what I still saw.

Cloe.

Kneeling in the rain.

Her knees buried in the grass. Her curls matted to her face. Her voice too soft to hear, but not too soft to feel.

She talked to that stone like it would answer. Like Camille

would rise and tell her everything was okay. Like she still believed in mercy.

Camille's name was etched behind her head like a crown. And in front of her—flat on the marble—a photo. Two girls laughing in silk. I remembered the night that picture was taken.

Camille had texted me afterwards. Said Cloe cried when she got home. Said she gave her leftovers from dinner and the dress she "didn't like."

Said it felt good to do something right.

I never answered.

Didn't know what to say.

Didn't think Camille needed me to say anything when she already knew the truth.

Cloe didn't belong.

She never had.

And yet—

There she was.

Still.

Haunting every *fucking* place Camille had *touched.*

I passed under a bridge and a truck blew past on the other side, spraying water across my windshield with a slap. The glass shuddered beneath the force. It felt like being hit.

Like a curse.

I clenched the steering wheel harder. My jaw ached from the tension.

I should've never followed her.

Should've let her sit there in the rain until her knees bled and her voice went hoarse.

Should've let her rot in her guilt. Let her choke on it the way we did when we picked out the casket. When we signed the death certificate. When we cleaned out Camille's office and sold her apartment and scrubbed her laughter out of our goddamn lives just to survive.

But I didn't.

I followed her.

And I watched.

And I felt something I had no business feeling.

Not for her.

Not for Camille's ghost in a too-tight skirt and trembling hands.

Cloe was a shadow.

A stain.

A girl who walked like she'd been taught to shrink.

But when she turned her head—

When she pressed her hand to the marble and whispered Camille's name—

She looked nothing like a ghost.

She looked ruined.

And she wore it well.

I hated that.

I hated how my cock stirred when I saw her wet and desperate and broken open by memory.

Not because she reminded me of Camille.

But because she didn't.

Because whatever she'd been two years ago—Camille's project, the pretty charity case in a borrowed dress—she wasn't that anymore.

Now she was wreckage.

And I was the storm circling her name.

I pulled into the private garage beneath the Lawlor tower. Rolled into the reserved space near the elevator. No security. No witnesses. Just concrete and shadows.

I turned off the engine.

Sat there.

Breathing.

Listening to the rain outside the building like it was trying to drive something out of me.

My jacket clung to my shoulders. My shirt was plastered to my back. Rainwater trickled down the back of my neck like penance.

I ran my hand through my hair, slicked it back, felt the sting of memory in my knuckles.

I hadn't meant to shove her.

But I had.

I saw the way she hit the stone. The way her breath caught. The way the photo fell.

And I saw her face when she looked back at me.

Not fear.

Not rage.

Just resignation.

Like she'd been expecting it.

Like she'd known all along that I'd come for her.

And still—she let me.

Still—she stayed.

I leaned back in the driver's seat.

Closed my eyes.

And tried not to picture her soaked to the skin.

Tried not to remember how her blouse clung to her ribs. How her knees pressed together like she was holding herself in.

How her voice shook when she said she missed Camille.

I didn't know what scared me more.

That I believed her.

Or that I wanted her anyway.

The elevator ride was silent.

Fifteen floors.

Just me and the sound of my own heart pounding too fast, too hard, like it was trying to climb out of my chest before I did something worse than what I'd already done.

I didn't stop at my floor.

Didn't go home.

Instead, I went two levels higher.

Where Barron was.

Where the real silence lived.

Because if I was unraveling?

I was going to drag him with me.

The hallway outside Barron's office was quiet—too quiet. That kind of quiet that wasn't stillness, but pressure. Like the walls were listening.

I didn't knock.

Didn't need to.

He'd hear me.

And if he didn't? He'd feel me.

I stepped inside.

Found him exactly where I knew he'd be.

Behind the glass desk. Sleeves rolled. Tie loosened but not gone. Posture straight. Jaw clenched like he'd been holding in a scream since 2019.

A storm held hostage in skin.

He didn't look up.

"Don't make me repeat myself," he said. "*Out.*"

"I found her," I said.

His pen paused mid-signature. Just for a second.

Then kept moving.

"Where."

"At Camille's grave."

He stopped writing.

Good.

I didn't move from the doorway.

Didn't sit.

Just stood there and watched the man who used to be our shield. The one who once held this family on his back like it wouldn't crush him.

Now he looked like a man barely holding the line between grief and collapse.

"She was talking to her," I added. "Brought that photo. The one from her birthday dinner. You know the one."

He didn't speak.

"She cried," I said, voice lower now. "Said she missed her. Said she tried."

Still nothing.

I let the silence hang.

Then:

"I shoved her into the headstone."

His head snapped up.

His eyes—ice cold. *Sharpened.*

"What?"

"She didn't fall," I clarified. "But she felt it."

"You touched her?"

I shrugged. "She was saying things she shouldn't."

Barron stood.

Slow.

Controlled.

His hands braced on the desk like it was the only thing keeping him from losing it.

"You don't get to decide what Camille meant to her," he said.

"Neither do you."

"Then why the fuck did you go?" he snapped.

"Because you won't."

That landed.

He didn't say it, but I felt the energy shift.

"You keep pretending like she's just another intern," I said. "But you see her. You watch her. You don't fire her. You dress her down, and then leave the door unlocked so she can come back in."

His jaw clenched tighter. A tic in his cheek.

"She smells like her, Barron."

His eyes closed. Just once.

"She walks like her. Until she doesn't. And then it's worse."

I stepped forward. One step.

"She's not Camille."

"I know."

"She's ruining you."

"No," he said quietly. "She's waking something up."

That made me pause.

Not because it was wrong.

But because he said it like it scared him too.

I turned to leave.

"Do whatever you want with her," I said. "But don't pretend like you haven't already started."

And then I left.

Left him standing in the silence he built.

Now infected with her name.

I didn't go home.

I went to the penthouse gym.

Turned off the lights.

Wrapped my hands.

Punched until my knuckles burned and the pads split.

Didn't stop.

Didn't breathe.

Every time I blinked, I saw her.

Rainwater on her cheeks. That fucking photo at Camille's grave.

And worse?

The look on her face when I shoved her.

Like she deserved it.

Like she wanted it.

When the fourth bag split, I stood in the dark, soaked in

sweat, fists slick and red. Then I walked into the locker room and stripped off everything that clung.

I stepped into the industrial-grade shower. Let the water hit me until my skin went numb. Until my pulse stopped fighting. Until I didn't feel like I was drowning in her perfume anymore.

I dried off in silence.

Dressed in silence.

Poured whiskey into a coffee mug and sat on the armrest of my own leather chair like I didn't deserve the seat.

And stared out at the city.

Waiting for something that would never come.

She was the one who got away.

Not because we lost her.

But because she left.

Left us with Camille's things boxed in the closet.

Left us with blood on our hands and no answers.

Left us to rot in the ruin she never looked back at.

And now?

Now she was crawling through our hallways like the grief belonged to her.

But worse?

She wasn't pretending anymore.

She meant it.

Every time she looked at Camille's plaque. Every time she touched her name. Every time she tried to smile in that goddamn skirt that didn't fit.

She was trying.

And that made it worse.

Because I didn't want her to try.

I wanted her to bleed.

I finished the drink.

Set it down.

Looked at the blood on my knuckles.

She doesn't get to wear my sister's memory like a second skin.

She doesn't get to grieve here without a cost.

And I'll be the one to remind her what it costs to be a ghost in this house.

8
___

CLOE

I almost didn't open the door.

There was a knock—three crisp taps.

No voice.

No follow-up.

Just a command wrapped in quiet.

I sat on the edge of the hotel bed, still wearing yesterday's regret and an oversized hoodie I hadn't parted with since the rain. It clung to me now like it had absorbed more than water. Like it had soaked up everything I hadn't said.

My heels were ruined. My stockings shredded and thrown away. My eyes were raw—no makeup, no armor. No pretense. Not here.

But the knock didn't come again.

Whoever left it didn't wait.

They didn't need to.

When I opened the door, the hallway was empty.

But at my feet?

A black garment bag. Sleek. Heavy. Hung from a branded

hanger I didn't recognize—stitched leather, a dark gold hook that probably cost more than my rent.

And a box.

Smaller. Velvet-wrapped.

On top of both, a cream-colored envelope.

My name in calligraphy.

Just: *Cloe.*

No return address. No seal. No logo. I didn't need one. I already knew who sent it. I brought everything inside and laid it out on the bed like I was preparing for a funeral. Or a sacrifice.

Then I opened the envelope.

One card. Heavy stock. Embossed edges. No signature.

Just:

Wear this. No excuses.

My heart pounded.

The box came first.

Burgundy.

Deep wine-red lace. Black silk ribbons. A corset that looked like it was built to control and display. A thong that was more suggestion than coverage. A garter belt. Sheer thigh-highs with golden clips that gleamed like threats.

Lingerie designed not for comfort. Not for modesty.

For *exposure.*

For *possession.*

I set it aside and reached for the zipper on the garment bag.

My fingers shook.

The zipper purred down like it knew I wouldn't stop.

Inside: a black pencil skirt. Fitted, tailored to the point of cruelty. A champagne satin blouse—backless, high-necked, with a delicate bow at the throat.

And heels.

Black patent. Red soles. My size.

Exactly my size.

I stared.

And felt two things I hated myself for feeling.

Shame.

And *heat*.

I dressed slowly.

Piece by piece.

Every item clung to me like a whisper.

The corset tightened my ribs until every breath felt intentional.

The garter straps kissed the backs of my thighs. The blouse slid across my skin like silk over sin. Its bow tied perfectly—restraining, ornamental. The skirt gripped my hips, forcing me to move with precision.

And the heels?

They lifted me up.

Changed the sound of my step.

Commanded space even as I tried to shrink.

I stood in front of the mirror.

And didn't recognize myself.

Not entirely.

The reflection wasn't Cloe Woods.

It was someone she might've become if she were braver. Sharper.

Owned.

A doll dressed in obedience.

A gift wrapped for someone else to unwrap.

I should've hated it.

But I didn't.

Not fully.

Because it was the first time in weeks I hadn't felt invisible.

The elevator ride was silent.

Too silent.

Each floor ticked by in cold, surgical precision. I stood in the center, arms close to my body, watching the numbers rise as my breath stayed trapped in my throat.

I wasn't scared of being seen. I was scared of how much I wanted them to look. When the doors opened onto the Lawlor floor, the air hit different.

Sharper.

Cooler.

Like it had been waiting.

I stepped out. And heads turned. Not all of them. Not loudly.

But enough.

A ripple through the air. A stillness at the corners of vision. My heels struck the marble in crisp rhythm. My hips swayed in the skirt's forced precision.

I didn't look at anyone.

But I felt it.

Felt the eyes.

The judgment.

The hunger.

The confusion.

And somewhere beneath all of it—

The power.

It wasn't mine.

But it was on *me.*

And in this moment?

That was enough.

One assistant looked me up and down. Blinked.

A man I didn't recognize adjusted his tie. Another woman smirked like she'd seen a girl make a mistake and couldn't wait to watch it fall apart.

I kept walking.

Felt the burn of my own thighs where the lace rubbed with

every step. The pinch of the corset with every breath. The heel click that wasn't quite steady enough.

But I kept going. Because that's what they wanted. Because I didn't know how to stop anymore. I hadn't made it halfway down the hall before he appeared.

Royal.

Shoulder against the wall. Coffee in hand. Grinning like he'd been waiting hours just to eat me alive with his eyes.

"Well," he said, his gaze dragging from my throat to my hips to my knees, "someone learned how to say thank you."

My stomach twisted.

I opened my mouth.

Nothing came out.

He stepped closer.

"Let me guess..." His voice dropped—husky, amused. "You don't know who sent it."

"I—"

"Was it Barron?" he mused. "Wolfe? Loyal?"

He leaned in, just enough for his breath to ghost over my cheek.

"Or do you just want it to be all of us?"

The words burned hotter than the corset.

I swallowed, breath short.

"Nice color," he added, his finger drifting just above the waistband of my skirt. Not touching. But close. So close.

His voice was a dark whisper.

"Bet the lace is soaked already, isn't it?"

My breath caught.

His smirk deepened.

Then he turned.

Walked away like he hadn't just left me trembling.

The office had never felt louder.

Phones ringing.

Heels clacking.

Keyboards clicking.

But I didn't hear any of it.

Not after Royal's voice in my ear.

Not with the heat still rising under my skin from the way he looked at the hem of my skirt like he could see everything I didn't want him to see—and everything I did.

I moved like I was underwater.

Slow.

Pressed in from all sides.

Hyper-aware of the corset stiff against my ribs. The soft, damp lace dragging between my thighs.

I kept my eyes forward as I passed the glass conference room.

And that's when I felt it.

A stillness.

Like the air went still just to notice me.

My pulse slowed—and then spiked.

I turned.

Wolfe was there.

Behind the glass.

Staring.

He didn't move.

Didn't blink.

Just stood with one hand in his pocket, the other loose at his side, like he wasn't sure if he wanted to break the glass or touch it.

I couldn't breathe.

His gaze didn't just land on me.

It dragged.

From the arch of my neck...

To the bow at my throat...

To the satin stretched across my chest...

Then lower.

All the way to my thighs.

Like he already knew what was beneath it.

Like he'd chosen it himself.

Something flickered in his expression.

Not anger.

Not grief.

Something darker.

Want.

It punched through me so hard I had to grab the edge of a desk as I passed to stay upright.

I looked away.

Had to.

But I felt him watching me all the way to my seat.

And when I sat—corset biting into my ribs, lace dragging between my thighs—I realized something:

Wolfe hadn't said a word. And I was already completely undone.

I couldn't focus. Not on the numbers. Not on the line items. Not on the half-finished coffee beside my hand. Everything was too loud. Too hot.

My back ached from the corset. My thighs pressed tighter where the garter straps rubbed. And every time I moved, the slick lace reminded me how far gone I already was.

People passed behind me.

Phones rang.

But all I could feel was Wolfe.

The way he hadn't blinked. The way he knew. The way I didn't look away fast enough.

I clicked on a spreadsheet. The numbers blurred. I backspaced. Twice. Three times.

Still *wrong.*

Then I felt it. That shift in the air. The awareness. Someone behind me.

I didn't turn.

Didn't have to.

He was there.

The warmth of his breath just behind my neck.

The pause.

Then—

"You wore it."

Wolfe.

His voice was low.

Sandpaper-soft.

Velvet-rough.

"You wanted me to."

I swallowed.

My fingers hovered above the keys.

And then—

"And now you'll spend the whole day remembering…"

A beat.

"Who saw you first."

He didn't touch me.

Didn't wait.

Just walked away.

Left me wet.

Panting.

Completely undone.

With nothing but a screen full of meaningless numbers and the echo of his voice in my blood.

9

———

CLOE

By noon, I couldn't feel my ribs anymore. The corset had become a vise. A slow, elegant torture device made of lace and expectation. Every breath scraped the inside of my lungs. Every shift in my chair felt like punishment.

The silk bow at my throat was still tied.

Still perfect.

I was not.

I kept my back straight—because slumping made the boning bite. I crossed my ankles under my desk so the garter wouldn't catch. I clutched the mouse like it might steady me, but my hand kept slipping. Sweat made the underside of my palm slick.

I hadn't eaten.

The idea of food turned my stomach.

My spreadsheet blinked up at me with quiet judgment. Budget projections for Q3. Loyal had asked me to reformat them three hours ago.

I had. Then unformatted them by mistake. Twice. Now the columns glared back at me. The cells multiplied. The numbers doubled.

I blinked.

No change.

Still two of everything.

Someone passed behind me.

Heels—easy, confident, composed. They clicked like punctuation marks.

I didn't look up.

But I heard it.

The breath. The pause.

Then the whisper.

"She's really still wearing it."

A second voice, lower, amused. "Did you see the skirt? I bet there's nothing under it."

"Oh, there's something under it," the first voice shot back. "Wolfe Lawlor's permission."

Laughter.

Soft.

Effortless.

Cruel.

I clicked too hard into the next cell. The field autofilled. Wrong. Backspace. Backspace. Missed the key. Mouse slipped. I gripped it tighter. Too tight.

My eyes stung.

Camille would've laughed.

Would've told me to kick off the shoes and walk barefoot like I owned the floor.

If you're going to wear something that screams sex, she once said, *you might as well moan while you do it.*

But Camille was gone. And I was still here. Pretending this was fine. Pretending I could still breathe.

Ping.

Inbox.

Loyal.
Subject: Update?
I clicked.
Couldn't read it.
Tried again.
Realized I'd been holding my breath.
The chair creaked as I stood.
I didn't excuse myself.
Didn't ask.
I walked.
Too fast.

The corset pinched with every step. The garter tugged at my thighs. The lace between my legs was wetter than it had been an hour ago.

And I hated how much of it was still want.

More eyes tracked me.

A throat cleared.

A muttered, "She's going to cry."

I turned left.

The private bathroom was at the end of the hall.

I reached for the handle.

Shoved the door open. Slid the lock shut behind me. And dropped to the floor like my knees had finally surrendered.

The tile was cold. Clean. Too clean. No echo. No witness. I pressed my back to the wall. Let the porcelain chill seep into my spine. My heels dug into the tile.

I was wearing lingerie someone else chose. A corset that wasn't just tight—it was possessive. I couldn't breathe. Couldn't think.

I reached back, fingers clawing for the ribbon. Silk threads. Tight boning. My arm twisted. I stretched. Higher. Couldn't reach it.

The laces were pulled too tight. My spine arched in the wrong direction. My muscles shook.

Still nothing.

I bit back a sound. Not because I didn't want to cry. Because I didn't want to make noise.

Noise meant vulnerability. Noise meant someone might hear. And if someone found me here—sweating, crumpled, shaking—they'd win.

I'd become the punchline in every whisper down the hallway. The girl in Wolfe Lawlor's corset. The one who tried to survive inside it—and couldn't.

I blinked hard. Pressed the back of my head to the wall. And whispered, "Just breathe."

But breathing hurt. Because this wasn't mine. This wasn't power. This was control—worn like silk. And I'd put it on anyway. And now I couldn't get it off.

My ribs burned. My spine ached. Every inhale was a punishment I'd agreed to. And maybe that was the worst part—how willingly I'd stepped into the trap. How beautiful it had looked when he dressed it around me.

How safe I'd felt inside a cage.

The lace bit harder the longer I sat.

I shifted.

The pressure didn't ease. It climbed.

Claustrophobic. Flesh-bound. Precision-cut agony.

I reached behind me. Once. Twice. My hand slipped against the satin boning. Couldn't find the edge.

Couldn't find myself.

I choked on a breath I couldn't take fully.

"Please..."

But no one could hear me in here.

And I wasn't sure who I was begging.

Both hands this time.

My elbow knocked the stall wall. My fingers snagged the lace ribbon but couldn't pull it loose.

"Come on," I whispered, voice cracking. "Come on, come on—"

It didn't budge.

I slammed my fist softly against the tile. The echo came back harder than expected. I bit my lip and pressed my head into my knees.

"It was just a job. I just needed a *fucking* job."

The tears came hot and silent.

I reached up and tried again.

Still nothing.

I dropped my arms. Wrapped them around myself like I could hold my pieces in.

Camille's voice echoed across the back of my skull like memory: *Don't ever let them see you bleed, babe. They'll call it performance art.*

She would've laughed.

She would've torn the corset off in the lobby and told everyone to get a good look.

But Camille was gone.

And I was on the floor of the private bathroom stall, unable to even take off my own clothes.

The door creaked open.

Footsteps.

Slow. Measured. Not heels.

Boots.

They stopped just outside.

A pause.

Then a knock. Soft.

"Cloe?"

I didn't move.

Then—

"It's Loyal."

His voice was closer now. Right outside.

"I can't come in if you don't say yes."

Everything inside me screamed no.

But I wasn't sure if it was fear or shame or something worse.

"...yes."

A soft click.

The lock released.

The stall door opened—and there he was.

Loyal.

In a fitted black shirt, sleeves rolled, tie askew. He looked uncomfortable. Not awkward. Just... like he didn't want to see me like this. But he did anyway.

His eyes swept over me—knees tucked to my chest, red eyes, the corset still hugging my ribs.

He didn't flinch.

Didn't leer.

He knelt. Slow. Deliberate.

Like I was made of glass.

"I can't get it off," I whispered.

"I know," he said. "It's meant to be impossible alone."

Of course it was.

He didn't touch me right away.

He just sat with me.

Silent.

Let me breathe.

Let me unravel.

"Turn around."

I did.

Fingers brushed my back. Warm. Steady. He pushed my hair over one shoulder.

His breath grazed my neck.

Then his fingers found the ribbon.

He worked slowly.

Carefully.

Unthreading each pass of silk without pulling, without snagging. The corset loosened with each movement.

Finally—I could breathe.

I turned back.

Arms crossed over my chest.

He didn't look away.

"You can breathe now," he said.

"I don't think I can."

His expression shifted.

Not pity.

Not sympathy.

Understanding.

"They think you want it," he said.

I froze.

He didn't clarify.

"Do *you?*" he asked.

I didn't answer. Because I didn't know. Because part of me had wanted it. And part of me hated every second. He leaned forward—not close, not cruel. Just enough to tie the ribbon again.

Loose.

Gentle.

Then he stood.

And his voice changed.

Colder.

"Then stop crying in places they can't see."

He walked out.

Left me in the stall.

Still in the corset. Still not sure what the fuck I wanted. I didn't look at myself in the mirror. Didn't want to see my face. Didn't want to see the ribbon. Still tied.

But looser.

A knot someone else had tied for me.

The hallway was colder. Or maybe I was. My heels echoed too loud. Every step felt like a confession. A woman looked at the bow at my throat and smirked. Another glanced at my skirt.

I kept walking.

The ribbon pressed between my shoulder blades like a finger. When I reached my desk, my screen was black.

Spreadsheet gone.

And on the keyboard—

A Post-it note.

Tight handwriting.

Fix it. – B

No explanation.

No signature.

Just the letter.

And the implication that Barron had been watching the whole time.

I sat down.

Straightened my skirt.

Tucked my ribbon beneath the collar.

And opened the file again.

Because there was no door here that closed all the way.

And no one who wouldn't open it whenever they wanted.

10

———

CLOE

I DIDN'T TOUCH the Post-it right away.

I just stared at it.

The handwriting was too clean to be rushed. Too sharp to be gentle.

Fix it. – B

It wasn't a request.

It wasn't even a reprimand.

It was a pulse check.

Are you still useful, little girl? Or should we dress you in something tighter and silence you for good?

I peeled the note off and folded it slowly between my fingers. Set it in the drawer I never used. The one where I kept other things that weren't mine. Then I opened the spreadsheet.

And started over.

At first, my hands were too fast. Clumsy. I made three more mistakes in the first three rows.

Then I stopped. Closed my eyes. *Breathed.* Not deep—the corset still wouldn't allow it—but enough. Enough to find my spine again. Camille used to say spreadsheets were like men. They'll lie to you if you don't learn their language.

So I spoke it. Formula after formula. Cell by cell.

I corrected every tab, cross-checked totals, rewrote headers. I restructured the budget breakdown like I was carving my name into it.

It didn't matter if no one noticed. It mattered that I did. The whispering never stopped. But it didn't cut the same. Maybe because I'd already bled all over the bathroom floor. Or maybe because now I knew what they were really afraid of. Not that I didn't belong here. But that I might survive it.

Loyal passed by me once. Then again. The third time, I caught the flick of his eyes.

A glance down the back of my neck.

At the bow.

Still tied.

Still his.

I didn't turn.

Didn't flinch.

Just kept typing.

And for the first time all day, my hands didn't shake.

I hadn't seen him all day.

Not really.

Glimpses. A glance across the floor. His name in an email. But not him—not the man behind the weight I wore like silk and wire.

Until the elevator.

I stepped in first. Mid-afternoon. Empty car. I pressed the button for floor five—delivery confirmation for Loyal's revised numbers. My fingers hovered near the door as it began to close.

Then it stopped.

Reversed.

Opened again.

Barron.

He walked in like the space belonged to him.

Because it did.

He didn't look at me.

Not at first.

He pressed a button. One floor above mine. Then stood behind me—just slightly to the left. Close enough to radiate heat. Power. That scent again. Tailored charcoal and control.

The doors closed.

And then there was nothing.

No music.

No words.

Just breath and restraint.

I didn't turn.

But I felt him.

His eyes.

Dragging over the blouse.

The bow.

The skirt.

"You fixed it."

His voice wasn't gentle. It was precise. Like the words were there to measure me.

I nodded. Didn't speak. Didn't trust myself to.

"Good."

That was it. Until the doors opened at his floor, and he stepped out like the ground owed him passage. But just before he left, he paused.

"Cloe."

I looked up.

Met his eyes.

Stillness. Steel.

Then, low—

"Wear your hair up tomorrow."

The doors closed before I could reply. The elevator moved. But the space didn't shift. Not really. His breath was still in the air. His command still pressed to the back of my neck.

Wear your hair up tomorrow.

I didn't know what that meant. But I knew I'd do it. And that answer came far too easily.

I stepped off on five. Walked through the corridor with the kind of posture that wasn't quite mine.

Not yet.

The hallway was quiet—glass doors, closed offices, everything sterile and untouched. But then I saw it. The mirrored wall between the two corner suites. Floor to ceiling.

I hadn't looked at myself all day. Not since the corset. Not since the Post-it. Not since him. I paused. Turned toward the reflection. And looked. It didn't feel like spying anymore. It felt like surveillance.

I studied the way the blouse clung across my chest—satin molded to skin. The way the pencil skirt cupped my hips. The faint shimmer of stocking where the split moved when I breathed.

My hair still hung damp around my shoulders from earlier —dark, curling at the ends. I reached up. Slowly. Gathered it in one hand. And watched the shape of my neck change.

Longer. *Bared.*

More delicate.

More... open.

Camille used to stand in front of mirrors and narrate.

You always look for the flaws first, C.

Men don't. They look for the weakness.

She'd pull her hair up and smile like a blade.

Give them both. Make them guess which is which.

I tried to smile.

It cracked.

Still, I kept my hand at my nape, hair pulled high, exposing everything Barron had asked to see.

And it didn't feel like surrender. It felt like strategy. Like I was finally learning the rules of a game I didn't know I was playing.

I stepped closer. Studied the details. The garter clip just visible when I shifted. The faint smudge of lipstick Wolfe never mentioned. The bow still tight at the back of my blouse—Loyal's knot, untouched.

And the eyes in the glass? They didn't belong to someone who cried on a bathroom floor. They belonged to someone who learned something there.

"They want a doll," I whispered. "Pretty. Silent. Replaceable."

But dolls remember everything.

I released my hair.

Straightened my shoulders.

And smiled.

Just a *little.*

The kind of smile they'd never expect. The kind that looked like permission—until it was too late. I walked back into the main office with my head higher than I'd ever dared.

Not proud. Just enough to keep the ribbon visible. Barron had asked for my hair up. It wasn't up yet. But I wanted him to see the choice I hadn't made.

My desk was untouched.

The spreadsheet still open. Balanced now. Perfect. The silence shifted around me. Not obvious. But there. Like the sound of a needle lifting from vinyl.

Soft.

Sudden.

Aware.

I sat. Crossed my legs slowly. Straightened my blouse with

one tug. And looked up. Right at them. Barron stood at the far end of the floor. Talking to two board members. Not facing me.

But he glanced over his shoulder once. Quick. Sharp. Our eyes didn't meet. But I felt it. The question. The weight. The heat. He saw me sit straighter. Saw the hair still down. Said nothing. Didn't look away.

Loyal passed through the bullpen, file in hand. Didn't speak. Didn't pause. But his gaze lingered. Right at the bow. Still tied. Still his. And he knew it.

Wolfe was across the room, half-shadowed in his glass corner. Pretending to read something I knew he wasn't seeing. His jaw was tight. Fingers tapping. He hadn't looked at me since the elevator. But every time I moved, I felt the echo of his gaze.

And Royal? Royal wasn't watching from afar. He was perched at the edge of the shared table, legs stretched, phone in one hand, sipping coffee like I was scenery. But when I turned, he was already watching. Grinning. Not a smirk. Something else.

They don't know what to do with you now, sweetheart. The words weren't spoken. But I felt them in the look. I turned back to my screen. Opened a new file. Started typing something that didn't matter.

Because what mattered now—

Was who was watching me.

Not the assistants.

Not the staff.

Them.

And if they wanted a doll?

I'd make sure I was the one they couldn't put down.

11
———

CLOE

THE BAR DIDN'T GLOW. It bled.

Low amber lights smeared across polished bottles like the ghosts of every bad decision that had ever been made under them. The floor was wet from something that hadn't been cleaned properly—beer or bleach or the memory of both. Every time my heel touched down, it stuck just enough to make me wince. Just enough to remind me I shouldn't be here.

But I stayed.

Because leaving meant going home. And going home meant facing silence. Not peaceful silence. Not solitude. No. The kind of silence that lives under your skin. The kind that sits beside you in the dark and whispers *you did this to yourself.*

My thighs were damp. Not from want—sweat and dread. I sat too long in this booth. I couldn't remember when I ordered my last drink. I only knew the glass in front of me was empty and my fingertips were shaking as I reached for it again anyway.

The bartender looked at me once. Then stopped.

The man three seats down licked his lips when he thought I wasn't looking.

He looked a little like Wolfe. And a little like he wanted to be him.

My phone sat face-down on the sticky table, its cracked screen glowing faint blue beneath the condensation of my drink.

One buzz.

Then silence.

Not a message. A battery warning.

10% left.

That felt appropriate.

I picked it up. Opened the thread I hadn't touched since the last time he looked at me like I was something he was trying not to ruin.

Wolfe Lawlor.

No nickname. No emoji. Just the name. Just the weight.

My thumb hovered.

Typed:

I told Camille everything about you.

I think that's why she kept you away from me. Especially after what happened all those years ago between us.

The memory of *their house* all those years ago rose inside me, dragging with it the same desperate hunger. I was just a kid and he was *everything,* I didn't send the message.

I stared at it.

Then added:

I'm in her necklace. You said it didn't belong on me.

So I'm selling it tonight.

You can stop me. Or not.

Nothing.

Not even a typing bubble.

I set the phone down. And let the ache pool in my belly. I

slid out of the booth. My thighs peeled from the vinyl. My knees buckled for half a second before I straightened. I walked slow. Careful. Like someone might be watching. Like someone already was.

The bathroom was worse than the bar. It smelled like old soap and something that hadn't been clean in years. I locked the door behind me even though the lock didn't catch. Pressed both hands to the sink. Looked in the mirror.

Smeared lipstick. Mascara beneath one eye. Necklace tight around my throat. I looked like I'd already fucked someone and tried to wash the guilt off after.

I didn't cry.

I took a photo.

Didn't send it.

Typed instead:

I look like your mistake.

Then I left the bathroom.

Back to the bar.

The music had dulled—less sound, more pulse. Nothing but the thump of bass fading beneath the *thrum* of my bloodstream.

I motioned for the bartender. Ordered something. Let the drink sit there when it came. The ice cubes bobbed. I didn't care. I grabbed the glass and swallowed. Let it burn. Let it punish.

I didn't mean to reach for the phone again. But I did. Because the ache didn't settle—it multiplied. Because the silence felt like permission.

I tried again.

The font blurred. I blinked. Swallowed. Typed again.

I want to forget you.

I want to forget what it felt like to want you to break me.

I hit send this time. Each message was a match. Each word

lit another corner of me on fire. I stared at the screen, pulse stuttering behind my teeth.

The messages stacked like sins. No read receipt. No reply.

Just silence.

Just him.

Just me.

I kept your lipstick in my purse.

I reapplied it tonight.

Just in case.

Then:

Do you think about it?

About what I looked like when I knelt?

And kept going:

Because I do.

Still no answer.

My hands shook.

I took a photo.

Just of my lips.

Smeared red.

Parted.

A stain of salt on the corner of my mouth.

I didn't send it.

I added a line instead:

I could let him fuck me.

My thumb hovered. Shaking.

I could lie.

Close my eyes and pretend it's you.

Still nothing.

I pressed the heel of my hand to my chest.

Everything hurt there.

Everything.

My last message came slower.

Deliberate.

Like a crucifixion.

Ten minutes.

Or I give him my mouth and pretend it's yours.

I hit send.

Turned the phone face-down.

Closed my eyes.

And waited for the sound of the monster I prayed would come.

The man from the end of the bar waited. He wasn't ugly. That would've made this easier. That would've let me recoil. Make a scene. Leave. Be saved from myself. But he was handsome in the way expensive violence could be. Handsome in the way of cold watches and car keys held too tightly. And maybe that's why I let him get close.

He wore a grey jacket with the collar popped and a watch he kept checking like he was late for something—or someone.

"Thought you were going to make me come to you," he said. "Turns out you've got better taste than that."

I smiled. The kind that didn't reach anything real. "Do I?"

He slid into the booth beside me like he owned the seat, the air, and the story.

"You're alone," he said, voice low. "But you're not here for drinks."

I didn't correct him.

He touched my wrist. His fingers were warm. A little rough. The kind of hand that had pressed too hard into too many things.

"You're shaking."

"I'm cold," I whispered.

He leaned closer.

"Then let me warm you up."

My phone buzzed.

One long vibration.

Then black.

Battery dead.

No answer. No Wolfe. So I let him lean in. Let his hand travel from my wrist to the chain around my neck.

"You wear that for someone?" he asked.

I didn't answer. I didn't have to. He slid his thumb down the center of my chest, dragging the chain with it.

"You smell like memory," he said. "Like you've got a past worth ruining."

My lips parted.

And that's when I felt it.

The shift.

The change in the room. The drop in temperature without wind. The sensation of *being watched* by something not human.

The man kept talking. But I didn't hear him. Because I looked up. And saw Wolfe. Standing in the doorway of the bar. Nothing in his stance moved. Nothing in his eyes blinked. But the air *screamed.*

He didn't storm over. Didn't raise a hand. He *looked* at the man beside me. And the man went still.

"Problem?" the man asked, trying to reclaim the air between them.

Wolfe took one step forward. That was all it took. The man stood. No apology. No challenge. Just instinct. He left.

Wolfe's eyes didn't follow him. They were on me. Only me. Like a claim. Like punishment. Like *possession* so deep my lungs stuttered trying to remember how to breathe.

I stood. My knees wobbled. Wolfe said nothing. He just held out his hand. And when I gave him mine, he gripped it like the leash I'd offered.

"Let's go," he said.

It wasn't a question. It was a verdict. And I walked out beside him like the sentence was holy.

His apartment was silent when the door shut behind us. Not the kind of silence that feels peaceful. The kind that presses in around your lungs like the beginning of a drowning.

I didn't realize how tightly I was clenching my fists until Wolfe reached for Camille's necklace and unfastened it. His hands brushed the back of my neck—barely a touch—and still I flinched.

Not because he hurt me.

Because he didn't.

He set the necklace down on the counter like it was a weapon. Like it was evidence. Like it was hers, and I'd worn it too long.

I stood there. Swaying slightly in heels I couldn't feel anymore. My lips dry. My throat aching.

I was waiting for him to speak.

He didn't.

He turned. Walked past me into the dark of the hallway. And when he returned, he held out a glass of water and a folded towel.

"Shower. Now."

It wasn't loud. Wasn't cruel.

But I moved.

Because he told me to.

Because something in his voice made obedience feel holy.

Because I wanted to wash every trace of that bar off my skin before he decided I wasn't worth saving.

I stepped into the steam. Let the water scorch my thighs. Scrubbed the lipstick from my mouth. The glitter from my eyelids. The scent of another man's hand from my skin.

I stood there too long.

Long enough for the water to run cold.

When I stepped out, I toweled off in silence. Found the clothes folded on the bathroom counter. One of his shirts. Soft. Heavy. Black. No pants.

I slipped it on.

The hem hit mid-thigh.

I didn't wear anything else.

Didn't need to.

When I emerged, the apartment was darker. Just the warm light from a lamp in the living room, casting long shadows across the couch where Wolfe sat.

He looked at me.

Didn't say a word.

His eyes dragged from my damp hair to my bare thighs.

To the edge of his shirt brushing the curve of my ass.

"Sit," he said.

I stood still.

"Couch or bed?" he asked.

The breath caught in my throat. "What?"

He leaned back. Spread his knees. "You want to be owned, Cloe? Or just punished?"

My knees almost buckled.

I said, "Bed."

He nodded once.

And I walked.

His eyes didn't leave me.

Not when I walked. Not when I passed him. Not when I hesitated at the doorway to his room and looked back like I might ask for permission to enter a place I'd already been invited to bleed in.

But he didn't move.

Didn't follow.

Didn't rescue.

This wasn't that kind of story.

The bedroom was cold. The kind of cold that lived in places where grief lingered too long. No photographs. No clutter. Just the sharp scent of clean linen and something darker under it—like cologne and memory.

I stood in the center of the room, shaking.

The shirt clung to my thighs. My nipples pressed against the fabric, tight and aching from cold and want and shame.

I didn't know what he wanted from me.

But I knew what I wanted from him.

I wanted to be seen.

I wanted to be named.

I wanted to be ruined in the only language he spoke.

I heard him before I saw him.

The slow tread of bare feet on hardwood.

The soft click of the door being pushed open.

The weight of his gaze pressing into my spine.

I didn't turn.

"Take it off."

His voice didn't rise.

But it hollowed me.

I lifted the hem of his shirt with both hands. My fingers trembled. My throat closed.

He said nothing.

Didn't help.

Didn't move.

I pulled the shirt over my head.

And stood naked in the center of his room.

He exhaled behind me.

A sound like restraint.

A sound like worship.

I didn't speak.

My breathing was too loud. My skin flushed. I felt exposed

in a way I'd never felt before—not on camera, not in shame, not in regret. This was sacred.

This was *his*.

I heard the rustle of his clothes.

But he didn't touch me.

"Lie down," he said.

I climbed onto the bed like I was crawling toward a church altar.

The sheets were cold. They smelled like him. I lay on my back, hands by my sides, legs together, trembling.

"Open."

My breath hitched.

He didn't clarify.

Didn't need to.

I spread my thighs.

The air hit me like a confession.

I closed my eyes.

And waited.

He stepped closer. I could feel it—like heat rolling across skin that wasn't ready to be touched.

Then I felt it.

Not his hands.

His breath.

Hot.

Between my thighs.

Hovering.

Not a kiss. Not a touch.

A presence.

He knelt.

Wolfe Lawlor—king of ice and ruin—on his knees, between mine.

His eyes burned up the length of me, slow and deliberate,

like he was mapping out a territory he already owned but wanted to rediscover with the reverence of a ritual. Like he was deciding which part of me he'd ruin first if he let himself give in.

I opened wider.

Because I didn't know how to ask.

Because begging would have shattered the last of my pride, and I was still clinging to it like skin I hadn't molted yet.

His breath touched me.

One exhale.

I gasped.

It wasn't air.

It was *permission*.

His mouth hovered so close I could feel the drag of heat against slick, swollen skin. He didn't move. Didn't flinch. Just *existed* there.

And my body betrayed me.

I pulsed.

Wetness spilled out of me like confession. Like offering.

"Look at you," he said softly. "Ruined without a single touch."

A sound escaped me. A whimper. Half-broken. Half-devoted.

He leaned closer. His nose brushed the inside of my thigh. I arched. Gasped. My hands clenched the sheets beside me so hard I thought the fibers might give way.

His lips were close enough to feel, not close enough to taste.

And then he breathed again.

A sharp exhale. Right against me.

I choked on a moan.

"Wolfe—"

"No."

The word lashed across me like a belt.

"You don't get to speak. Not until I take the words from your mouth myself."

I trembled.

Every nerve ending lit up like holy fire.

He pressed one palm to my inner thigh. The heat of it. The *claim* of it. I sobbed without sound.

He didn't go lower.

Didn't touch the place that *begged*.

He held me open.

Made me feel the distance.

Made me live in the absence.

"Close your eyes," he said.

I did.

He didn't touch me.

But I felt him.

Every second he hovered above me, I imagined his mouth.

His tongue.

His fingers.

The growl I knew lived in his throat if he ever let himself go.

And just when I thought I couldn't take any more—

The weight shifted.

His warmth pulled away.

The bed creaked.

I opened my eyes.

He stood beside the bed, staring down at me like he'd just carved the world into something unrecognizable and wasn't sure if he should burn it or kneel before it.

"You wanted to forget me?" he asked.

I nodded, breathless.

"Then you shouldn't have invited me back inside you."

I sobbed.

Not from pain.

From *need*.

From the ache that bloomed in my womb like a bruise. From the emptiness that curled around my ribs where he could have been.

He walked away.

I reached for him without thinking. One hand. Fingers outstretched like a girl trying to catch the hem of God's coat as he passed.

He didn't turn.

Didn't look.

He reached the door. Paused.

Looked over his shoulder.

"You think this was punishment," he said. "It wasn't."

Then he left.

The door stayed open.

But I didn't move.

I stayed there.

Naked.

Wrecked.

Thighs still parted.

Heart still pounding.

Body still *begging*.

And when my phone lit up on the nightstand—somehow still alive, somehow still willing—I reached for it.

One message.

WOLFE:

You want to be wrecked?

Next time—I'll leave fingerprints where he was never allowed to look.

I cried.

Because I'd never be clean again.

Because now that I'd tasted him—

I would never stop starving.

12
______

CLOE

I didn't sleep. Not really. I left Wolfe's bed just before dawn—legs sore, throat raw, skin aching in places no one had touched. I dressed in silence. Didn't look at him. Couldn't. Because if I had... I might've begged.

He let me go.

I think that hurt more than if he hadn't.

I walked home barefoot. The heels didn't make it through the hallway. The city felt colder than usual. Or maybe I did.

By the time I got inside, my body felt hollow. I stripped in the dark. Stood under the shower until the water went cold. Sat on the edge of the tub with my knees pulled to my chest. I couldn't cry. I didn't have it in me. But the ache between my thighs wouldn't fade.

And the message he'd sent still echoed in my bones:

Next time—I'll leave fingerprints where he was never allowed to look.

I wore my hair up.

Tight twist. Not a curl out of place. No ribbon this time. No softness. Just clean lines and an exposed neck and the ache of self-control threading through every strand I pinned into place.

My makeup was minimal.

No foundation. No blush.

Just bare lips and mascara thick at the corners to make my eyes seem harder than they were.

The dress was simple. Black. Sleeveless. Ribbed knit that clung to my body in silence. The neckline kissed my collarbones, and the slit up my left thigh wasn't obscene... but it was intentional.

No bra. No jewelry. Just a pair of red-bottom stilettos—loaned from Camille's collection and never returned—that made every step sound like a countdown.

The office noticed.

They always did.

Not with gasps or wide-eyed stares. No, the Lawlor floor didn't give attention freely.

But I saw the way two assistants paused in their conversation when I passed the espresso station.

Heard the scrape of a chair shifting behind me when I walked through the bullpen.

Felt the eyes on the back of my neck, right where Barron had told me to leave exposed.

I kept my chin up.

I moved like the floor was mine.

Even if my stomach was tying itself into knots beneath the corset I hadn't worn today. Even if my fingers still ached from gripping the safe door two nights ago. Even if my dreams kept ending with Wolfe whispering say thank you while my knees hit something cold and unrelenting.

The moment I stepped onto the executive floor, I felt it.

Them.

Their energy.

The air shifted, like the building had braced itself.

The receptionist—perfect, polished, always unimpressed—didn't ask me where I was going. She just gave a single nod.

"They're waiting for you in conference two."

Of course they were. Like goddamn lions in a cage. Only I was the one stupid enough to unlock it...and step inside. I lifted my gaze, swallowed hard and turned toward the hallway.

Waiting.

For me.

Not to scold. Not to humiliate.

To see.

To test.

To tighten the leash they claimed wasn't there but wrapped around my throat all the same.

I walked. My heels echoed. Every step louder than I intended. But I didn't slow. The door was already cracked open when I reached it. I pushed it wide.

And there they were.

Four brothers. Four chairs. *One empty seat.* No one spoke. Not at first. Then Royal smiled without teeth and tapped the armrest beside him.

"C'mon, sweetheart. Don't make us beg."

The door clicked shut behind me. Silence settled. Not the polite kind. Not professional. The kind of silence that wrapped around your ankles like rope and tugged.

The four of them were already seated. Barron at the head of the table, suit pristine, phone face-down beside his leather portfolio. Wolfe across from him, black shirt rolled at the sleeves, fingers steepled as if prayer was ever something he practiced. Loyal, quiet and focused, tapping something into a notepad. Royal—of course—was leaned back, legs spread, arm resting along the chair beside him.

My chair.

He didn't look at me. Not at first. Just kept swirling something in his glass like this was a social call.

"We were starting to think you'd gotten lost," he said without looking up.

"I was sent to the wrong room," I lied.

Wolfe's eyes flicked to mine. Sharp. Fast. He didn't say a word.

Barron didn't motion for me to sit.

But Royal did. A slow tap of two fingers against the seat beside him.

"Come on, sweetheart. Don't leave me all alone over here."

My heels clicked once, twice, three times before I reached the chair and sat. Royal's arm didn't move. It stayed on the back of my chair, just close enough that when I settled in, his fingers brushed my shoulder.

Barely a touch. But enough to set my skin on fire.

Loyal slid a folder across the table toward me. "Barron wants you to review this while we go over the Gotham acquisition. See what stands out."

I nodded, opening it. Spreadsheets. Share allocations. Something about conflict zones and rare stone procurement. I blinked and tried to focus. But the room was too warm. Or maybe I was.

Barron began speaking—his voice low, direct, commanding. He didn't look at me. Didn't address me. But every time he said words like control or ownership or pressure, I felt them settle in my gut like they weren't part of a corporate conversation at all.

Wolfe never turned his head. But I felt his gaze sweep over me again every time I shifted.

Royal leaned in once, murmured under his breath. "Bet you're wet under all that elegance."

I didn't react. I didn't even blink. But my thighs pressed

together beneath the table, and I hated myself for how right he probably was.

Thirty minutes passed in quiet strategy talk. I kept my eyes on the pages. Made notes when I could. Traced numbers I didn't fully understand. Tried to stay small.

Until Barron stopped speaking mid-sentence. His eyes shifted to the screen. Then to Loyal. Then, finally, to me. "There's a flaw in this."

Everyone paused. Even Royal's fingers stopped their lazy glide along the table beside my hand.

Wolfe's head turned—slow and silent—to face me fully.

"You've been reading," Barron said. "Say something useful."

It wasn't a question.

It was a command.

I swallowed.

Let the silence draw for a second longer.

Then I turned the page.

"Page six, third line. The listed supplier in Myanmar was exposed in a procurement scandal last year. The public fallout didn't last long, but it was enough to tank their perceived legitimacy. We'll be accused of compromising ethics if we don't reroute the acquisition chain now."

Silence.

Then Loyal said, quietly, "She's right."

Wolfe didn't blink.

Barron stared at me for three long seconds.

Then said, flatly:

"*Noted.*"

That was it. No thank you. No praise. But I felt Royal's knee shift under the table. His leg brushed mine.

"Sharp little thing, aren't you?" he murmured, just for me. "No wonder they keep dressing you up."

I held my tongue. But something in me twisted. Something tightened. And it wasn't fear. The meeting ended like all their meetings did—with silence and steel.

No "thank you."

No acknowledgment that I'd contributed anything of value.

The brothers stood, gathering papers, checking phones, snapping suit jackets back into place like armor.

I stayed seated. Because I hadn't been dismissed. And because I didn't trust my legs to hold. Royal left first. He winked at me on his way out, then leaned in close enough to brush my ear with his breath. "Try not to drip on the chair, sweetheart."

I didn't look at him. Didn't flinch. But the burn that followed spread like wildfire down my spine.

Wolfe didn't speak. Didn't look at me again.

Loyal nodded once. His only tell was the way he lingered by the door for a second longer than he had to.

Then it was just me.

And Barron.

He closed the door softly behind his brothers. The sound echoed in the conference room like a gunshot. I sat still. Back straight. Hands folded in my lap. Trying not to breathe too loudly. Trying not to hope.

He moved slowly, circling the table. His stride *measured.* Like a man who'd already decided what to do.

I felt him behind me before I saw him. The warmth of him. The weight.

Then—

A single fingertip.

Not on my skin. On the twist of hair at the back of my neck. The exact spot he'd told me to leave exposed.

He didn't press. Didn't stroke. Just touched. Barely.

"You wore your hair up."

I didn't answer.

Couldn't.

My pulse was frantic, a thrashing thing too loud in my ears. My breath too shallow to trust.

His voice dropped. Low. Silken. Possessive. *"Good girl."*

I almost came apart at the spine. It wasn't what he said. It was the way he said it.

Not soft.

Not sweet.

An acknowledgment, like ownership from a man who had given an order and found it obeyed.

He stepped away a second later, already turning toward the door.

"Next meeting's at three. Be early."

That was it.

That was all.

He left me there in that chair with a soaked lace thong, a shaking ribcage, and the impossible knowledge that I would do anything to hear him say it again.

The air changed before she even spoke. The kind of shift that doesn't announce itself—but demands attention. It started with the sound of heels. Not rushed. Not timid. Measured.

Controlled.

Like the woman walking toward us didn't just know who she was—she knew who everyone else wished they were.

Selene Lawlor. She stepped through the main office like she still owned it. Like the company wasn't in her ex-husband's name, but still pulsing in her blood.

Her dress was white. Of course it was. Sharp-shouldered, perfectly tailored, cinched at the waist like she knew the damage it did. Her heels were nude. Expensive. Her lipstick? Red. Like her mouth was weaponized.

I froze before I even saw her eyes. And then—she looked at

me. Like I was dirt tracked in on her marble floor. A single, searing glance. Up. Down. *Done.*

My stomach twisted, not daring to move or speak. I didn't exist in her worl, nothing more than a shadow in her palace.

The office went silent. Even the assistants fell quiet, backs straighter, posture sharpened. And the brothers? They stepped out of their offices one by one.

Loyal went still.

Royal smirked—but it didn't reach his eyes.

Wolfe? He crossed his arms and leaned back like he was watching something he didn't want to want.

And Barron—

God.

Barron looked at her like he'd been shot.

Just for a second. Just one fucking second. Then he blinked. His face closed. And the man who'd just called me good girl vanished behind polished stone and steel.

Selene smiled. Not at him. At everyone else. Like she already knew she'd won. "I was in the neighborhood," she said, her voice velvet and viper. "Thought I'd say hello."

No one stopped her. Not even Barron.

He just watched. Like a man looking at the edge of a cliff he once jumped off, knowing exactly how the fall would feel— but still aching to taste the air again.

She didn't stay long. Ten minutes, maybe less. And when she left? She kissed Loyal's cheek. Winked at Royal. Said nothing to Wolfe. And she passed Barron like he was nothing.

But after she was gone...

He didn't move. Didn't speak. Just turned. Stepped back into his office. And gripped the edge of his desk so hard his knuckles went white.

I watched from across the floor. Unseen. And it gutted me. Because the most dangerous thing about Barron Lawlor?

Wasn't his silence. It was how much he still felt—even when he was trying not to.

I didn't notice the envelope right away. Not until I returned to my desk, still rattled from the echo of Barron's silence. The office air felt thinner, colder—like it remembered Selene's scent more than mine.

It was there. Waiting. Pale, expensive paper. My name scrawled in red ink that looked more like it had been carved than written. No return address. No logo.

Just inevitability.

Inside: a single photo.

The black book.

Small. Leather-bound. Wedged against a stack of sealed files inside a safe I'd only seen opened once. Barron's safe.

The note was printed in smooth, feminine handwriting:

He still keeps secrets. But you're the only one close enough to open the lock. You want peace, Cloe? You know what you need to do.

I stared at it for too long. Long enough for my stomach to knot. Long enough for the silence in the office to settle into my spine like a second skin.

I took it home.

I shouldn't have. But I did.

Because I didn't want anyone else to see it. Because I didn't want to admit that I already knew what the code might be. Because Camille's birthday was seared into me like a scar.

It was late when I finally poured the wine. Too late for visitors. Too late for thinking. Just me, the lights low, the city outside, and the envelope on the table like a loaded gun.

The black book stared up at me from the photo.

I hadn't touched it.

But I wanted to.

More than I wanted to admit.

The phone rang.

I froze.

Private number.

Blocked.

I almost didn't answer.

But I did.

"Hello?"

Silence. Then:

"You always were a good girl."

Selene.

The voice was silk-drenched threat. Lazy and lethal.

"Wearing the perfume. Wearing the skirts. Walking the halls like you've earned something. Tell me, is it as easy pretending to belong as it was the first time? Or does it sting a little more now?"

I swallowed hard. "What do you want?"

"Same thing you do, darling. Peace. Safety. A place you don't have to keep looking over your shoulder. Your ex is back in town. Did I mention that? Sweet boy. Misses you terribly. Still has those photos of you from your little motel phase. You remember that, don't you? The lace wasn't designer then."

My stomach twisted.

"You don't have to do anything dangerous. Just... open a door. Look inside. That's it. I'll take care of the rest. Or don't. But when he shows up? Just remember I gave you the chance to choose."

Click.

I didn't move.

Didn't breathe.

The wine glass in my hand trembled.

And all I could think—as the photo on the table stared back at me—was that I was already running out of time.

13

———

CLOE

THE OFFICE FELT wrong after eight p.m.

It wasn't just the silence. It was the *kind* of silence that hung in the air. Sterile. One that crept along the floor and settled between the ribs. That only existed in places meant for ambition and violence—where worship was performance and failure was foreplay.

My screen was the only light left on the floor. The overhead fluorescents had gone to sleep an hour ago, triggered by motion sensors that assumed no one in their right mind would stay this late.

Maybe they were right.

But I wasn't staying to impress anyone.

I was staying to survive.

The file on my screen blurred. Numbers. Names. Projected metrics. I tried to read it again. For the fourth time. The fifth. My vision didn't cooperate.

Neither did my breathing.

I wiped my palms down the sides of my skirt. The red one.

Tight. High-waisted. The one Wolfe didn't tell me to wear—but I knew he'd notice if I did.

I shifted in my seat. My thighs rubbed together, bare under the desk. He hadn't said anything about panties this morning. So I wore them.

But I thought about not.

God, I thought about not.

The silence cracked.

The copier powered down three rooms over. No one had used it in hours.

I froze.

My eyes flicked to the hallway. Nothing.

No shadows.

No footsteps.

Just stillness.

I shook my head and looked back at the screen. Shifted my weight. Reached for my pen—

Ding.

The elevator.

I stopped breathing.

My chest rose once. Shallow. Again. I listened.

The doors opened.

Hiss.

Silence. No footsteps. No voice. No one came out.

My fingers tightened around the edge of the desk. Still nothing. The elevator doors hissed shut again. I blinked.

"You're being paranoid," I whispered.

But the air didn't agree.

The air felt *watched.*

My hands shook. I shut the laptop. Closed the file. Grabbed my bag. Stood too fast. My chair scraped back with a sharp sound that made me flinch.

I turned to go.

And froze.

He was there.

Wolfe.

Standing ten feet from my desk. Half in shadow. Black button-down, sleeves rolled. Collar open. Veins visible along the inside of his forearms.

He didn't move. He didn't speak. He just *was*. Like the room belonged to him. Like I did. My heart slammed into my ribs.

He tilted his head. Just a fraction. "You always this jumpy when no one's watching?" His voice was a knife dipped in velvet. Low. Deadly. "Or do you just feel me first?"

I opened my mouth. Closed it.

Wolfe took one step forward.

And the air *shifted*.

Not warmer.

Not colder.

Claimed.

"Sit back down, Cloe."

My knees obeyed before I did. I sank into the chair like gravity had changed just for him.

He moved closer. Slowly. Like he had all the time in the world to ruin me. The air around him changed shape as he walked—folded in, wrapped tight, pressed itself into the gaps between my ribs.

Wolfe didn't look at the screen on my desk. He didn't glance at the files. His eyes were fixed on me.

Like he already knew I hadn't been working. Like he knew I'd been *waiting*.

"You think if you stay late enough, you'll earn your way out of being prey?"

I opened my mouth to speak. I didn't know what I was going to say. Something flippant. Something stupid. Something that might distract him from the way my thighs were pressed too tightly together, or the way I was already trembling.

But no sound came out.

Wolfe circled the desk.

Didn't sit.

Didn't touch.

He leaned one hand on the corner of the desk, the other hanging at his side. Every line of him was still. Tense. Waiting.

I stared at his hand. The way the veins moved. The way the knuckles shifted as he flexed once. Just once.

A warning.

Or a promise.

"I told you to wear red."

I swallowed. "I did."

His gaze moved to my lips.

The lipstick was still perfect. Reapplied twice. Once in the lobby. Again when I realized I wasn't alone.

"I told you no bra."

I nodded. "I didn't."

His stare dragged down my chest. My nipples hardened under the thin fabric. His eyes flicked lower, pausing just long enough to make my skin tighten.

Then back to my face.

Back to my mouth.

"Then why do you still smell like defiance?"

He took one step closer.

I tipped my chin up. "I'm not defying you."

He didn't blink. "You're not obeying either."

My breath hitched.

"You don't get to live between obedience and denial, Cloe."

His voice dropped lower.

Darker.

"Choose."

I didn't answer.

But my knees parted.

Barely.

Enough.

His hand left the desk.

And I forgot how to breathe.

Wolfe stepped around me.

Not fast.

Not loud.

Just close.

The edge of his body skimmed mine, a current of heat and pressure that made my skin tighten, my pulse scatter. He stood behind me for a moment, silent. Watching. Measuring.

Then he leaned down.

His mouth wasn't on me.

But his breath was.

Right at my ear.

"You want to pretend this is about work? That you're here late to impress someone? That you're still not mine?"

I shook my head. I didn't mean to. It just... happened.

He laughed. Low. Quiet. The kind of laugh that didn't soften anything.

"You keep forgetting. I don't need you to agree, Cloe."

He pressed one hand flat to the desk beside me. The other curled around the top of the chair. I was caged. Breathless. Lit from within and smoldering from without.

"I only need you still."

I couldn't move. I didn't want to.

He leaned closer. I felt the heat of his chest brush my back, just for a second. Then he shifted again, slower this time.

My breath hitched.

"Tell me what you thought I'd do, when you sent me that last message."

I swallowed.

He waited.

"Tell me."

"I thought... you'd come," I whispered.

"You thought I'd save you?"

"No," I said, shaking my head. "I thought you'd break me."

His breath caught. Just for a second.

Then he stepped around in front of me. Pulled the chair away from the desk with one hand and looked down at me like I was a puzzle he'd already solved and just wanted to watch fall apart.

"You want to be broken, Cloe?"

I didn't speak.

He tilted his head.

"Then stand up."

I rose.

And that's when he touched me.

Not my waist. Not my hips. Not anywhere soft.

His hand went to the back of my neck.

And *held*.

Flat palm. Fingers spread. Thumb resting just under the hinge of my jaw.

It wasn't a caress.

It wasn't even control.

It was *ownership*.

A single point of contact that unspooled every lie I'd told myself about what I could handle. About what I wanted. About what I'd survive.

I gasped.

But I didn't pull away.

His grip wasn't tight. It didn't need to be. The weight of it alone made my spine lock, made my thighs press, made my pulse jump in my throat like a warning bell.

And then he stepped in.

His body brushed mine—solid, heat and breath and restraint. His forehead came down to mine.

Our mouths weren't touching.

But they could have been.

"You don't get to run anymore," he said, voice low. "You sent the prayer. Now live in the answer."

My fingers curled at my sides.

I wanted to reach for him.

Wanted to kneel.

Wanted to beg.

But I didn't move.

Because I knew the second I did, he'd take more.

And I wanted to *ache* for it first.

"Say you understand."

I swallowed. "I understand."

He pulled me closer by that single grip. Pressed my chest to his. My breath caught. My knees threatened to buckle.

He leaned down.

His mouth brushed the corner of mine.

Not a kiss.

Not yet.

Just the *possibility* of one.

"Good girl."

And then—

Not softly.

Not sweetly.

It wasn't a request. It wasn't even an answer.

It was a *verdict*.

His mouth claimed mine like a promise already broken. Heat flooded down my spine, spread through my chest like fire pressed between bone. I gasped, but he didn't let me pull away.

His grip on the back of my neck tightened—just slightly.

Just enough to hold me still, just enough to say: *you don't run from this.*

The kiss wasn't rushed.

It was *measured.* Intentional.

His tongue traced the seam of my lips, slow and deliberate, and when I opened for him, I didn't even realize I'd done it.

He took.

Every breath.

Every sound.

He didn't moan. He didn't groan. He kissed me like he was reading scripture and rewriting it with his mouth.

I whimpered. Quiet. Desperate.

His body didn't press closer—but I felt it everywhere.

His scent. His heat. His restraint, tighter than anything I'd ever worn.

He pulled back just an inch.

His breath against my lips.

"This is what silence earns you."

I couldn't speak.

Couldn't move.

His thumb stroked once along my jaw. Tender. Possessive.

"You want more?"

I nodded. Barely.

"Then obey."

And just like that—he let go.

Walked away.

Left the air behind him ruined.

Left me...

Trembling.

Changed.

And *starving.*

Wolfe didn't turn back.

He walked to the door like nothing had happened. Like he

hadn't just rewritten every rule inside my body with a single kiss. He reached for the handle.

Paused.

"Tomorrow," he said, without looking at me. "Wear the same skirt."

My breath caught.

"No bra. No lipstick until five minutes before I see you."

I nodded. He didn't see it. Didn't need to.

"Speak to no one unless they speak to you first."

My chest rose. Fell. My pulse was chaos.

He opened the door.

"And when I look at you—"

He turned his head. Just slightly. Just enough for me to see the edge of his profile, the sharp line of his mouth.

"—you'll know when to kneel."

Then he was gone.

The door clicked shut.

And I collapsed into the chair like something holy had been taken from me.

Or gifted.

I couldn't tell the difference.

I sat there for a long time.

Not moving.

Not breathing right.

Just... processing the aftermath like it was a crime scene I couldn't explain to anyone—not even myself.

The screen on my laptop had gone black.

My reflection stared back at me.

Lipstick smudged.

Eyes wide. Lips parted. Chest rising like I was still catching up to what had happened—or what hadn't.

I tried to focus. Tried to find the file. The numbers. The reason I was still sitting here, dressed like an offering.

But all I saw was *him*.

The imprint of his touch still warm at the back of my neck. The echo of his breath still thick on my skin.

I crossed my legs under the desk.

Too late.

My thighs were already slick.

My body had already answered him in ways my voice hadn't dared.

I touched my mouth.

Traced the edge where his kiss had ended.

A kiss that hadn't fed me—just lit the hunger higher.

A kiss that felt less like intimacy and more like indoctrination.

I closed the laptop.

Stood on shaky legs.

And walked out of the office without another sound.

Because the silence Wolfe left behind?

It didn't need to be filled.

It needed to be obeyed.

14

CLOE

The silence Wolfe left behind didn't soothe me.

It festered.

By the time I made it home, my body was still vibrating—but not from desire. From something darker. Louder. Lonelier.

I scrubbed his voice off my skin. Tried, anyway. But it was already under my nails. Etched behind my teeth. A relic I couldn't exorcise and the shame I'd kept locked behind my ribs was already leaking.

And the second the door clicked shut behind me, I came undone.

I reached for the photo on the counter—the one I never should've kept. The one of him and me, all fake smiles and motel lies.

Then I tore it in half.

And again.

And again.

I tore the photo in half.

Then again.

And again.

The sound wasn't loud enough.

Nothing was loud enough.

I stood in the center of my tiny apartment, barefoot, shirt inside out, wine glass on the floor next to an unopened bottle I couldn't afford, and Selene's voice still echoing inside my skull like it had a lease.

He's back in town.

He misses you.

Motel lace. Motel bruises. Motel shame.

My chest heaved. Too tight. Too hot. My fingers shook as I picked up the scraps of the note and threw them against the wall like they could bleed.

They didn't.

They fluttered.

Mocked me.

I paced. Back and forth. One hand in my hair. The other still curled like it wanted to punch something.

"Fuck. *Fuckfuckfuck—*"

I ripped open the drawer beside my couch.

Camille's old heels? Pawned last month.

Designer perfume she gave me? Half a bottle left—but that wouldn't pay for shit.

"Think, Cloe."

I grabbed my purse. Dumped it out.

Four dollars. A sample lipstick. A receipt from a sandwich I never finished.

I checked the coat pocket.

Nothing.

I opened my bank app again.

$1.21.

Not enough to buy dinner. Definitely not enough to disappear.

I tried to breathe.

Didn't work.

The walls felt like they were inching in.

I opened the fridge.

A jar of olives.

Half a lemon.

Milk that expired a week ago.

"Okay," I whispered. "Okay. *Okay—*"

Get a job. Faster.

Can't. I have one.

Sell something. Anything.

I have *nothing*.

I opened the closet. Pulled out old dresses. Cheap, pilled fabric. A coat from a thrift store that still smelled like someone else's cigarette smoke.

"Fuck."

I dropped to my knees.

Started sobbing—short, choked sounds that didn't go anywhere.

My arms wrapped around my stomach.

My ribs hurt.

My head pounded.

"I can't do this," I whispered to no one. "I can't go back to him. I *can't...*"

But my thighs were already slick. My body too traitorous. Too eager to remember how surrender felt in the dark My throat closed. The panic came fast. Hot. Crippling.

I pressed my face to the carpet. Screamed into it. My voice broke halfway through. When I finally sat back up, eyes burning, body trembling, I reached for my laptop. Didn't think. Just opened the browser.

I typed in one word.

Escort.

My eyes flicked to the closet.
The silk blouse from yesterday still hung from the door.
Next to it: the black skirt. The heels. The lace.
The outfit Barron bought me.
I stared at it for too long.
Thought about selling it.
But instead—
I saw myself in it.
In the mirror.
On a street corner.
In a hotel hallway.
Slick red soles. Satin bow. Lipstick smeared.
The kind of girl you call when your wife's out of town.
The kind of girl who smiles while dying inside.
And then—
I clicked.
Because maybe I was already her.
And maybe that's why the clothes fit so well.
Then added:
Quick cash. One night. Discreet.
I paused.
Stared at the screen.
And realized...
There was nothing else left.
No favors to cash in.
No secrets to trade.
Only me.
My body.
My skin.
My silence.
And for the first time, I let myself know it.
I didn't cry again.
I just sat there.

Still. Hollow.

And I clicked.

I made it to the office ten minutes early.

Which was stupid.

Because early meant more time to sit at my desk and sweat through my blouse, wondering if the digital mistake I made in the dark had already clawed its way into the light.

I hadn't slept.

I'd stared at my ceiling for four hours, then paced my apartment for two more. I drank wine I couldn't taste. Took a shower I didn't remember. And dressed in a blouse that still smelled like Barron's cologne from the day before.

And now?

Now I was shaking.

I opened my laptop with fingers that barely obeyed.

The screen lit up.

I clicked the browser. Reflex.

Just to check.

Maybe it hadn't gone through. Maybe it hadn't meant anything.

Maybe—

Inbox: *1 New Message*

I clicked.

Available tonight? Double if you don't speak.

My stomach dropped.

I closed the window. Fast.

Closed the whole fucking browser.

Or—*thought* I did.

My name was called over the intercom.

Gotham pitch meeting. Top floor.

I stood.

Smoothed my skirt.

Grabbed the laptop.

And walked.

The elevator ride was the longest 40 seconds of my life.

The floor was empty. Too quiet.

Loyal passed me in the hallway, gave a small nod. Royal followed behind, grinning like he already knew a secret I hadn't told yet. Wolfe was waiting at the boardroom door, silent, unreadable, spine like steel.

Barron wasn't there yet.

I prayed that meant something.

It didn't.

I plugged in like I was supposed to.

Opened the presentation folder.

Double-checked the files. The slides.

Everything looked right.

You closed the browser. You're fine. You're fine.

The brothers filed in. Loyal. Wolfe. Royal.

Then him.

Barron.

I couldn't breathe.

His eyes never touched mine.

He took his seat. Leaned back.

"Ready," he said.

I hit the projector button.

The screen blinked.

Then bloomed.

Not the deck.

The inbox.

The escort inbox.

Center screen.

Larger than life.

Available tonight? Double if you don't speak.

Silence.

Immediate.

Devastating.

Royal let out a low whistle.

"Well... *fuck.*"

Wolfe sat forward, slowly. Hands clasped. Eyes locked on me.

Loyal didn't move.

But I saw it.

The disappointment.

And Barron?

He didn't blink.

Didn't breathe.

But the air around him thickened.

I scrambled.

Fumbled for the mouse. The keyboard. Anything.

"Shit—I didn't—this wasn't—I didn't mean to—"

"But you *did,*" Wolfe said quietly.

His voice wasn't cruel.

It was worse.

It was true.

The screen snapped black as I finally disconnected.

But the silence didn't lift.

Barron stood.

Calm. Controlled.

"Out."

One word.

The others left.

One by one.

Until it was just me.

And him.

And the knowledge that I hadn't just been seen.

I'd been known.

The door clicked shut behind Wolfe.

And suddenly, there was nothing but silence.

Me.

Barron.

And the shame I'd just projected across a seventy-inch screen like it was branding.

My chest felt tight. Too small. I couldn't seem to get air into it.

The only sound in the room was the static buzz of the disconnected projector and the blood pounding in my ears.

I didn't move.

Neither did he.

He just sat there, watching me like a man carving his own gravestone—slow, precise, deliberate.

"I wasn't going to go through with it," I said, the words a scratch in my throat. "It was just... a search. A stupid moment. I didn't mean—"

"Stop."

One word.

Flat.

Cold.

But it sliced right through me.

I shut my mouth.

Swallowed hard.

Waited.

He stood.

Slowly.

Every movement coiled, clean, effortless.

He didn't pace.

He stalked.

A predator without urgency.

Because he already knew I wasn't running.

He stepped around the table. Pulled his suit jacket open. Reached into the inner pocket.

And drew out his wallet.

He opened it like it weighed more than it should have.

Like each motion cost him something.

His fingers slipped inside and removed a single bill. A crisp hundred. He held it between his fingers for a breath.

Then added another.

And another.

Three. Four.

I should've spoken. Should've moved.

But I couldn't.

I was frozen under the weight of something too thick to name.

By the time he reached six, his knuckles were white.

And then he looked at me.

Really looked.

Not at my face.

At my mouth.

Then lower.

His gaze dragged down my throat, over the line of my blouse, to where the silk curved around my chest and disappeared into the waistband of my skirt.

Lower still.

To my hips.

My thighs.

The tension between them.

His eyes didn't flicker.

Didn't flinch.

He watched me like a man making a purchase.

Like a man justifying it to himself in real time.

And in that moment, I realized—

He wasn't angry.

He was aroused.

Heat bloomed between my legs, hot and slick and immediate.

My stomach twisted.
I tried to step back.
Couldn't.
He took one step forward.
And placed the money in my hand.
Six hundred dollars.
Not fanned. Not dropped.
Laid.
One bill at a time.
Like he was offering penance.
Or branding me with currency.
One of his fingers brushed mine.
I jerked.
Just slightly.
His gaze didn't shift.
But his nostrils flared—just a little.
And his eyes—they dropped lower.
To my thighs.
To where they were clenched so tight I thought I might snap.
I could smell myself.
The soft, musky sweetness of arousal soaked into lace.
I hated it.
But more than that?
I hated how much I wanted him to notice.
He stepped in.
Closer.
My back hit the edge of the boardroom table.
He didn't touch me.
But he didn't need to.
His presence pressed into every breath I took.
"Get yourself something better for tomorrow."
His voice was soft.

Too soft.
The kind of soft that left bruises.
I nodded.
Couldn't speak.
Couldn't even breathe.
He leaned in.
Not to threaten.
To scent me.
His mouth was close enough to kiss.
Close enough to bite.
I closed my eyes.
"Or *I'll* be the one dressing you."
The words shattered me.
Heat pooled low in my belly.
His voice was low. Brutal. Owned.
"And you might not like what I have in mind."
A pause.
And then—softer.
Almost cruel in its softness:
"Or... considering your browsing history..."
He tilted his head.
Eyes met mine again.
Dark.
Sharp.
Possessive.
"You just might."
My knees almost gave out.
But I stood there.
Burning.
Ruined.
Wanting.
He watched me another breath.
Then turned.

Left me there—holding six hundred dollars in trembling hands, shame pressed against my skin, and something much worse pounding between my legs.

And when the door clicked shut behind him?

I didn't breathe for twelve full seconds.

15

CLOE

The knock came just after six.

No one ever knocked that early.

I opened the door to find no one there—just a black garment bag draped over my doorframe, like it had been hung with care. Like a gift.

Or a trap.

A velvet-wrapped box sat beneath it. Tied with a deep red ribbon. A cream-colored envelope perched on top, my name written in bold strokes, no signature.

I carried it all inside like it might vanish if I blinked. Set it on the bed like it might bite. I opened the envelope first.

No note.

Just a card.

Wear this. No excuses.

My pulse kicked.

The ribbon came undone with one pull—sliding like silk between my fingers.

Inside the box: lingerie.

But not just lingerie.

A corset of black lace and satin—boned, delicate, and obscene in its elegance. A whisper of matching panties, more suggestion than coverage. Stockings. Garter clasps with gold accents. A blouse—blush pink, so sheer I could see the curve of my palm through it. A high-waisted black pencil skirt, perfectly tailored. Expensive. Precise.

There was no signature.

But I didn't need one.

I knew.

Barron.

I should've been furious. Should've thrown it back in the box. Should've said no. But instead, I touched the lace like it might moan for me. Slid my fingers down the curve of the corset and imagined how tightly it would hold.

And something... shifted.

Not shame.

Not fear.

Desire.

Raw and slow and new.

I stripped slowly. Laid my clothes on the chair with trembling hands. Paused. Looked down at my bare skin. The small curve of my stomach. The subtle dip of my waist. The bruises that still lingered on my thighs from nothing but tension.

I stood in front of the mirror in nothing but the morning light and bare skin. Then reached for the corset. Lacing it was hard. Brutal. Every pull drew my waist tighter. Every pass of the silk ribbon sent a new flush to my cheeks. My breath shortened.

And I liked it.

The restriction. The heat. The reshaping of myself into something other.

Not a woman.

A weapon.

The corset cinched me in and made space for something dangerous.

I rolled the stockings up my thighs. Clipped them to the garter with shaking fingers. The clips clicked into place like the loading of a chamber.

Stepped into the skirt. Felt it hug my hips like a promise.

The blouse was last.

Thin as breath.

I slid my arms through, let it fall over the black lace like fog curling through iron. My nipples hardened instantly under the sheer fabric. I didn't cover them. I buttoned the top without hesitation.

No necklace. No perfume.

I didn't want to hide a single thing he wanted to see.

I walked to the mirror. And I looked. I didn't breathe.

Because the woman staring back? She didn't flinch. She didn't apologize. She didn't beg. She wasn't even asking to belong. She was the moment. And she would be remembered.

The corset curved my waist in brutal elegance. My breasts were full, high, flushed where the lace grazed them. My thighs touched. My heels lifted everything. And for the first time, I didn't want to look away.

I wanted to be watched.

No.

I wanted to be studied.

Admired.

Worshipped even.

I lifted my hand and brushed my fingers over the lace. Upward. Until I found the peak of one breast. I traced the curve. Felt the tight swell of heat in my belly respond to the soft friction. The nipple was already hard.

I ran my thumb over it. And gasped. The sound came too

easily. Too sharp in the quiet. My body lit like a fuse. Flushed. Tight. Lit.

I didn't touch myself again. Didn't need to. Because I'd already unraveled something deeper than arousal. I'd found hunger.

Mine.

This wasn't obedience. It wasn't submission. It was transformation. A claiming—from the inside out.

I picked up the card again. Read the words one more time.

Wear this. No excuses.

I didn't argue.

I didn't hesitate.

I tucked the note into my purse like a vow I had every intention of keeping. The sidewalk should've felt cold beneath my heels. But I didn't feel the chill. I felt the corset. Every step tugged at it. Pulled my breath short. Reminded me with every footfall that I was wrapped in someone else's desire—and I had put it on like a crown.

The sheer blouse shifted with every movement. The lace beneath it visible in the sun like a sin. The skirt clung, high and tight, brushing the tops of my thighs like a promise.

The stockings whispered.

The heels sang.

And me?

I was no longer Cloe from the shadows.

I was a siren made of satin and ache.

The Lawlor lobby gleamed with polished marble and polished people. But when I walked through the doors? The world stilled.

Heads turned. Not all. But enough. A pause at the front desk. A flicker from the man holding a paper. The woman waiting for her oat milk latte blinked too long. And I felt it.

The quiet shock of being looked at not like a mistake—but like a problem someone wanted to solve with their hands.

I didn't flinch. Didn't slow. I walked. Poised. Composed. Even as my pulse knocked hard against my ribs. The elevator doors opened with a whisper.

And there she was.

Me.

Reflected in mirrored glass.

A full-length reminder that I wasn't playing a role anymore. The woman in the reflection? She didn't just look beautiful. She looked *dangerous.* And no one in that building would forget it.

I fixed a loose strand of hair behind my ear. And smiled. When I stepped onto the executive floor, the shift was immediate.

The air was different. Charged. Still. Like the floor had taken a breath—and forgot to let it go.

Eyes lifted. Not just assistants. Not just admin. Security. Executives. People who hadn't noticed me before.

Now?

They noticed.

Because I looked like I didn't care if they did. And that kind of confidence? It smells like blood to men who like to bite.

Royal was the first to speak.

He spotted me mid-conversation—some polished man in a navy suit suddenly forgotten. Royal turned like I was gravity.

Grinned.

Stalked.

And *God,* he enjoyed every second of it.

He moved behind me, that lazy swagger oozing control, his breath close to my neck like sin pressed to silk.

"Well, well, *well,*" he murmured. "Look who decided to make the whole fucking building hard before nine a.m."

I didn't turn.

"Good morning," I said softly.

"Oh, it is *now*."

I left him there. Because I could. Because the echo of my heels said more than his mouth ever could.

Loyal stood by the elevator.

Coffee in hand.

Silent, but never still.

His eyes tracked me like a thread unwinding. Throat. Waist. Skirt hem. And then—my eyes. And that was the part that shook me.

Because in his stare, there was a warning. Not stop. Just... *be ready*.

Because if I thought this game didn't have a price? I hadn't been listening.

Then Wolfe.

He didn't speak.

Didn't smirk.

Didn't move.

But his gaze?

It stripped.

Layer by layer, from throat to thigh, across the spot where the garter clipped beneath the skirt. And when he passed me? The air broke. Like glass under pressure.

I sat at my desk—heart pounding, corset biting, silk dragging—and tried to breathe like I wasn't coming apart.

The room didn't settle.

Not around me.

Because they hadn't just seen me today.

They'd recognized what they made.

And I wore it like a gift.

I typed a line.

Deleted it.

Typed again.

Deleted that too.

Each keystroke felt like a scream in the silence.

I shifted.

The lace dragged.

My thighs clenched.

My breath stuttered.

The tension wasn't pleasure anymore.

It was possession.

And I didn't know how to quiet it.

I gripped the desk edge.

Felt my pulse beat in my palm.

And then—

I felt him.

Wolfe.

Still.

Across the floor.

Watching. Like gravity.

Like want.

Like he was already imagining how I'd fall.

His eyes tracked from my face to my throat. Down the slope of my shoulder to where the sheer blouse revealed the outline of black lace underneath.

Lower.

To the soft curve of the corset pressing from beneath the silk. To the tight seam of the pencil skirt where my thighs disappeared behind the desk.

His jaw ticked.

Just once.

But it was enough.

My breath hitched. My pulse stuttered. My core clenched.

He didn't smile. Didn't move. Didn't need to. Because that look? That unblinking, unapologetic, slow-burn drag of his gaze? It was the most intimate thing I'd ever experienced without being touched.

It said: *I see you.*

I own you.

And you wanted this.

And then he turned.

Walked away.

Leaving me shaking.

Trembling.

So close to falling apart I had to bite the inside of my cheek just to keep still.

I shifted.

Slow.

Silk slid. Lace dragged. Heat bloomed.

Five minutes later, I felt it again.

That shift.

That signal the room hadn't learned to name yet—but I had.

Barron was moving. The floor stilled. He passed behind me like wind over glass. Didn't look at me. Didn't speak.

But his fingers—

They dragged across the edge of my chair. Barely a touch. A brush. A claim. When they reached the top of the backrest—

They tapped.

Once.

Twice.

Rhythmic.

Commanding.

And I knew.

He had looked.

He had seen.

He knew the color of the lace under my blouse and the

shape of my hips in his skirt. And he wasn't just letting it happen anymore. He was beginning to want it. And worse?

He was beginning to show me.

I sat there. Heart pounding. Skin flushed. Hands trembling. And for the first time since I walked back into their world...

I didn't want to run.

I wanted to be taken.

I couldn't take a full breath. Not because of the corset. Not anymore. Because of them. Because I couldn't stop feeling them. Even when they weren't in the room. Even when I was alone at my desk, fingers hovering above the keyboard, eyes fixed on a screen that hadn't changed in ten minutes—

They were inside me.

Every glance.

Every slow drag of Wolfe's gaze.

Every time Loyal didn't speak but watched like he already knew how I'd come apart.

Every brush of Barron's knuckles against the back of my chair.

Every time Royal smirked like he already knew the color of my panties.

They were everywhere.

Inside my skin.

My breath.

My hunger.

I shifted in my seat.

Slowly.

The friction made my breath catch.

The lace was wet.

The garter clipped tight.

And the corset—*oh God*, the corset—was biting deep into my ribs like a hand gripping me from the inside out.

Every movement dragged silk across skin that couldn't take another whisper.

Every inhale pressed lace tighter against swollen nipples that ached like I'd already been teased for hours.

My thighs were slick.

My pulse wrecked.

And I was—

Ruined.

Without a word. Without a touch. Just from the want.

I gripped the edge of the desk. Hard. My fingernails bit into the laminate. I needed... *something.*

Anything.

Relief.

Release.

Or someone to step into the room and take it all from me.

I pressed my knees together. Tighter. My stomach clenched. My breath hitched. I blinked at the screen. Nothing made sense anymore. I wasn't even trying. Wasn't pretending. I wanted them to see. To know. That I was soaked through and aching and—

Begging in silence.

The hallway creaked. A door opened. Laughter down the corridor. Too far. Too normal. None of it touched me. I was locked in this cage they'd built and I'd chosen. Corseted. Cuffed in silk. Painted in want. And I didn't want to leave.

I wanted to be tied tighter. Pushed harder. Watched longer.

I wanted them to take the desk from beneath me and make me the surface. I wanted to be bent and broken and ruined.

I wanted Wolfe's teeth.

Royal's mouth.

Loyal's silence.

Barron's hands.

I wasn't a girl anymore. I was a need. And every man in this building was starving. And I—

I was the feast.

16

WOLFE

I saw her before she even walked in.

That scent. That fucking pace she had when she thought no one was watching—half-confident, half-defensive. Like she couldn't decide whether to run or strut.

But I knew.

She *wanted* to be seen.

Needed it.

And then she stepped through the floor...

And I stopped breathing.

The blouse was sheer.

Not pornographic. Not vulgar.

But just thin enough to turn sunlight into revelation. The outline of black lace traced beneath the silk like a secret barely held back. The corset beneath that? It cinched her ribs with precision. Brutal. Beautiful. Like armor you begged to be broken by.

The skirt? Too tight. Deliberately high. Fitted like temptation. Her hips moved in subtle sway, a whisper of power and performance that she didn't even try to hide.

I knew the garter lines were under there.

Because I saw the flash of them.

The faint shift in fabric when she turned her body.

A breath.

A glance.

And I was hard.

Painfully hard.

I didn't move.

Just watched from behind the glass wall of my office. One hand clenched tight around the edge of my desk, knuckles white. The other hovered near my belt. Not touching. Not yet.

She sat at her desk.

Shifted.

Twice.

Her thighs pressed together. Ankles crossed. Back straight like she'd been posed that way.

She was wet.

I could see it in the way her spine refused to relax. In the subtle lift of her chest every time she exhaled like her breath didn't know where to land. In the sharp little inhale when she reached for her mouse.

I adjusted myself under the desk.

Subtle. Quiet.

Still hard.

Still pulsing.

No relief.

The pressure behind my zipper was starting to throb.

I licked my bottom lip. Bit it.

Don't.

Fucking don't.

But my body didn't listen.

I opened my browser.

Typed the first three letters—P O R—

Autofill: pornhub.

I tapped.

Scrolled.

Women in fishnets. Red lips. Open mouths.

Gasping. Whimpering. Getting fucked.

Nothing worked.

It all felt wrong.

Because I didn't want to see someone get fucked.

I wanted her.

Cloe.

In garters.

On her knees.

With mascara streaking down her cheeks and my hand gripping her hair like a leash.

I wanted her sobbing against my thigh, her panties ruined, her mouth full of *Wolfe.*

And the worst part? I didn't even want to fuck her. I wanted to own the need in her eyes. I closed the tab. Leaned back in my chair. Still hard. Still pulsing. Still fucking wrecked.

I looked up. And there she was. Still at her desk. Still pretending to work. Her lips parted. Just slightly. She was squirming. Not visibly. Not publicly. But underneath? She was falling apart.

And I knew—because I was doing the exact same thing.

The tension in her shoulders. The way her thighs shifted beneath the desk. The subtle tremble in her fingers every time she hovered above the keyboard like she'd forgotten how to type.

She didn't need to touch herself. Because her body was already vibrating with the need. And I knew that need. Because I felt it too.

I saw her like this once before. Not in lace. Not in perfume. But in want.

Christ, I shouldn't be doing this. She was just a kid, a kid we fucking knew. A kid I remembered. I closed my eyes reliving the memory.

Camille's twenty-fourth birthday.

We rented out a rooftop. Real private. Private waitstaff. Champagne towers. Music so smooth you could taste it.

Camille wore black. Red lips. A crown in everything but name.

And she brought Cloe.

No warning. No announcement. Just walked her in like she'd always belonged.

Cloe wore a black dress that didn't quite fit. Too tight across the chest. Straps that dug into her shoulders. Second-hand. Borrowed. She smiled too much. Laughed too loud. Nervous. Eager.

Camille gave her the shoes. I remember because the sticker was still on the bottom when she crossed her legs.

She sat beside Camille and looked out at the crowd like she didn't know where she belonged in it—but hoped someone would give her permission to stay.

And she watched Camille. Not jealous. Not resentful. But wide-eyed. Hungry. Like she wanted to be her. No—like she wanted to be wanted the way Camille was.

She laughed too hard at something Royal said. Camille reached out and touched her hand. Squeezed it. And I remember thinking—

If someone held her too tightly, she'd shatter.

She didn't know how to carry wealth. Didn't know how to wear power. But she wanted it. Desperately.

Now?

She's learning.

And the hunger is still there.

But so is *something else.*

She doesn't wear desperation anymore. She wears desire. She walks through the floor like she knows every man who sees her wants to ruin her. And the worst part?

I want her more now than I ever wanted anything. Even when she belonged to Camille. Even when Camille was the only good thing this family ever had. Even when I swore I'd never touch that kind of want again.

I hadn't thought about her that night in years. But now, after watching her twist in that chair today, thighs squeezed, lace soaked?

I can't *not* remember it. Because it's the same look she wore that night. The quiet hunger. The ache to be seen. To matter.

The way her eyes tracked the room—not like she wanted to belong, but like she was studying the price of admission.

She looked at Camille like she was art and royalty and God all in one. Not jealous. Not resentful. Just desperate to be touched by something brighter. And now?

Now that hunger had grown teeth. Now she walks like power has started to fit her. And it should make me back the fuck off. It should make me look away. But all it does is make me want her more. More than anything I've wanted since Camille.

And that thought?

That thought burned.

Because Camille was the only good thing this family had.

And I was corrupt enough to want the girl who used to orbit her.

I couldn't stay in the building. Not another fucking second. Not with her scent still clinging to my shirt. That perfume— light, powdery, soft—followed me down the hallway like a hand pressing between my shoulder blades.

I breathed her. Tasted her. Felt her in the gaps between every breath.

The elevator opened. I stepped in alone, jaw clenched so hard it hurt. I punched the ground floor like the numbers could answer for me. I should've dragged her into my office. Should've slammed the door. Made her say it. Say she was wet. Say she wanted to be touched. Say *thank you* while she shook.

I should've ruined her until she forgot what it felt like to belong to herself. But I didn't. Because I'm the one who waits. The one who doesn't cross the line. Not since the funeral. Not since everything I loved bled out and left me hollow.

But now?

Now I was hard. Angry. Ruined from the inside out. So fucking desperate to feel something I could've ripped the doors open just to escape the air. Because it still smelled like her.

The elevator opened.

She stepped in like she was built for it.

Tall. Blonde. Tight skirt. Red lips.

I'd had her once.

Or maybe twice.

Her name was... Penny. Or Prue. *Something* with a P.

Didn't matter.

She leaned back against the mirrored wall like she belonged there. One foot crossed over the other. Her posture told a story —accessible, practiced, easy.

Her eyes flicked to me.

Curious.

Open.

Inviting.

I stared at her mouth. Imagined grabbing her by the wrist. Turning her around. Pressing her into the corner. Yanking her skirt up. Fucking her fast enough to forget.

I flexed my fists at my sides.

My breath hitched.

Do it.

Just fucking do it.

But I didn't move.

Because the moment I blinked—

Cloe's face was there instead. On her knees. Tears in her lashes. A *thank you* in her throat.

The elevator dinged. Penny—Prue—whoever she was, stepped off without a word. But she looked back. Once.

Not fear. Not judgment. Just expectation. Like she thought I'd follow her. Like she was disappointed that I hadn't. And I hated that. Hated her. Hated myself more.

Because I could have had her. Used her. Left her. It wouldn't have mattered. She didn't ask for anything. Never looked at me like I was a god she didn't know how to pray to. She never made me feel like kneeling.

But Cloe?

Cloe made me *feel everything.*

She made me feel out of control.

Made me *want.*

Made me need things I'd buried years ago.

Things I swore I'd never want again—not after Camille. Not after the casket. Not after the world cracked down the middle.

But now?

Now I couldn't breathe without thinking about her thighs spread.

Her mouth open.

Her eyes wet.

The way she trembled in silence in a chair I didn't think she could survive.

The silence in the elevator wasn't stillness. It was punishment. I braced both hands on the mirrored wall. Bent my head. Let my breath fog the glass.

I could've had her. I could've fucked the easy one. But it

wouldn't be Cloe. Wouldn't be the lace I wanted to rip. Wouldn't be the eyes I wanted to watch break. Wouldn't be the girl I wanted to wreck so thoroughly she forgot who she was without me.

I made it home, dropped my keys, and stared at my phone like it might bite me. Didn't go for a drink. Didn't take off my shoes. I just stood in the doorway—still dressed, still hard, still ruined—and let the silence close in like punishment.

The city glowed through the windows, reflecting the shape of my body in the glass. Distorted. Ghosted. Like I was already something else.

Something darker.

I was hard.

Still.

Still.

My cock throbbed against the front of my slacks. Every nerve ending straining for contact. For friction. For fucking release. But I didn't touch it. Didn't move. Because I didn't want release. I wanted damage.

I wanted Cloe on my kitchen counter. Her blouse ripped open. Her skirt shoved past her hips. My hand on her throat. My fingers inside her. Her legs trembling around me while she tried not to cry.

I wanted her ruined.

Not just wet.

Shaking.

Obedient.

Destroyed.

Her contact sat there in my phone.

C. Woods.

No emoji. No title. Just the name. Clean. Sharp.

I hovered over it.

Thumb twitching.

Call her.

Tell her to come here.

Make her kneel and say thank you through clenched teeth while her mascara runs.

I pulled up the message box.

Typed a word.

Deleted it.

Typed another.

Come.

Backspaced.

Deleted again.

I locked the phone.

Threw it across the kitchen.

It hit the wall.

Hard.

My chest rose. Fell. Too fast. Too shallow.

I braced myself on the marble counter and bent my head.

My reflection stared back from the chrome of the fridge.

My skin flushed. My jaw clenched. My body ached with restraint.

I could still smell her on me.

Still taste the memory of her at her desk—breath hitching, thighs clenched, soaked in silence.

And I wasn't angry at her. I was angry at me. Because I let this happen. Because I watched. Because I wanted. And now? Now I didn't know how to stop.

I paced. Back and forth. Room to room. The pressure in my pants unbearable. The sound of her laugh echoing in my head like a fucking dare.

I could see the shape of her nipples through the blouse. The lace when it clung too tight to hide anything. And I hated that I knew the exact color. Because it haunted me. It followed me here.

Her email was still open on my laptop.

Professional. Polite. Polished.

A perfect lie.

Because I knew she hadn't been okay today. She hadn't been calm. She'd been *wrecked*.

And I let her sit through it—dressed like sex, leaking into lace, pretending to be an assistant while every man in the room imagined what it would take to make her beg.

I opened the reply box.

Typed two words.

You forgot.

Pause.

Then added one more line.

To say thank you.

No name. No signature. Just truth.

I hit send. And when she answered? I'd stop pretending I could stop.

17

———

CLOE

I DIDN'T WAKE SOFT. There was no slow stretch. No comfort in the way the sheets tangled around my legs. No gentle drift into the day.

I woke wet.

Heavy.

Tense.

Like my body had spent the night pressed into something that didn't touch me but still left a mark.

Wolfe's voice echoed through me before I even opened my eyes.

Say it in person.

Two words.

One order.

And I had obeyed.

I whispered *thank you* into the darkness like it was a prayer and a punishment and a plea all at once. But it hadn't quieted the hunger. It had fed it. Turned it molten. Sharp. Unrelenting.

I pushed the sheets off and walked naked to the mirror. The floor was cool beneath my feet, but the heat between my legs was already back—slick and pulsing like I'd spent the night chasing something I still wasn't brave enough to name.

I stared at my reflection.

Not to fix it.

To face it.

To choose which version of myself I was going to offer today.

The doll?

The assistant?

The toy?

Or something else entirely?

I opened the closet like I was choosing a weapon. But it wasn't armor I wanted. It wasn't defense. It was surrender. It was seduction dressed like silence. I reached for the corset. Black. Boned. Cruel in its beauty.

I held it like it might bite.

Like it might whisper what I already knew.

That Wolfe wouldn't touch me. That Barron wouldn't fuck me. That Royal would tease. That Loyal would watch. That I would be used anyway. Without being asked. And that I would love it.

I stepped into it slowly. Tightened it myself. Each pull a reminder. Each knot a confession.

By the time I finished lacing, I was already breathless. Already wet. Already burning from the inside out.

The silk blouse came next. Blush pink. Soft as breath. Transparent when kissed by the light. The kind of fabric that begged for a gaze.

The kind of shirt you wear to be noticed and punished for it. The skirt followed—tight, sleek, the slit a little too high, the fit a little too unforgiving. Then the stockings. The garter. The heels.

No perfume. No distraction. Let them smell me.

I paused at the mirror again before leaving. Wolfe's voice whispered in my head. Barron's silence curled at the base of my spine.

I didn't smile. But I didn't look away. Because I wasn't dressing for attention anymore.

I was dressing for consequence. The elevator doors slid open and I stepped into the hallway like I belonged there. Not quiet. Not careful. Claimed.

The first thing I noticed wasn't the hum of the building or the hush of the bullpen. It was sensation.

The way the silk blouse whispered across my skin with every step. The corset kept my ribs tight, spine rigid, breath shallow. The lace beneath my skirt stuck to the inside of my thighs, already damp with want.

I walked like I knew it. Like I wanted them to see it. There was nothing modest in the way my skirt clung to my hips. Nothing reserved in the sway of my step. My thighs brushed. Thick. Full. Deliberate.

Let them look.

My heels echoed down the tile. Sharp. Steady. Like a ticking timebomb.

Every movement reminded me of what I was wearing. Every swing of my hips reminded me why I'd chosen it. I wasn't dressed to perform. I was dressed to provoke. To obey. To bleed power from silk and lace. And I was beginning to love how that felt.

Royal was the first to notice. He turned from the espresso machine, caught mid-stir, his eyes dragging down my body like a slow burn.

He grinned.

Low.

Hungry.

"Someone's ready to get ruined before breakfast."

I didn't reply. Didn't flinch. But the heat that bloomed under my skin said he wasn't wrong.

Loyal passed me in the corridor. Folder in hand. Eyes forward. But he caught the pull at my blouse—the way the buttons strained across the corset-laced swell of my chest.

He looked away too fast. Too hard. His jaw locked. His hand clenched. And he kept walking. But I felt it. Him. The restraint. The want. Behind the glass—voices murmured. Chairs shifted.

I didn't have to look to know. They were watching. All of them. I wasn't invisible anymore. I was present. Poised. Their silent undoing. And I walked through it like shadow given shape.

Heavy.

Hot.

Mine.

By the time I reached my desk, I could feel the lace soaked through. The silk clung between my breasts. The corset was a pulse in my ribs. And still—I sat. Crossed my legs. Opened my laptop.

As if I hadn't just walked through the entire Lawlor floor like a fucking offering. As if I hadn't just felt every set of eyes trace the slit in my skirt, the arch of my back, the slow sway of my hips as I passed.

I clicked into a spreadsheet. Pretended to work. But my breath was shallow. My hands were trembling. And my core pulsed in time with every shift of the corset against my ribs.

I was soaked. Not figuratively. Literally. Dripping.

The lace was warm and tight against my skin. Every movement dragged moisture higher. Every second that passed made it worse.

I bit down on the inside of my cheek. Hard. Just to ground myself. It didn't help. Because then the note appeared.

I returned from the restroom to find it sitting on my desk. Plain white card. Heavy stock. Centered perfectly.

One line.

Office. Now.

No name. No signature. Didn't need one. The print was clean. Bold. Sharp enough to cut.

Barron.

I picked it up.

Turned it over.

Blank.

My throat tightened.

My stomach dropped.

The corset bit deep as I stood, the lace pulling tighter against my thighs. Every inch of me buzzed. Because this time —I wanted it. I wanted whatever this was. Whatever this would be. I wanted it like a bruise. I wanted it like a wound. I wanted it like something permanent.

I walked through the floor with my eyes ahead. But I felt them. All of them. Watching. Reading the card I hadn't tucked away fast enough. Following the sway of my skirt. The click of my heels.

I reached Barron's office. Raised my fist to knock. Paused. Lowered it. Opened the door without waiting. The room was dimmer than the floor outside. Windowlight bled into the edges.

But the rest?

All shadow and silence. Stillness made of tension.

He stood with his back to me. Hands in his pockets. Gaze fixed on the skyline like the city had something better to say than I ever could. For a second, I thought maybe I'd misread it. Maybe this wasn't that. Maybe I was about to humiliate myself by stepping in already wet.

But then—

He turned. And my breath caught.

Barron Lawlor didn't raise his voice. He didn't ask why I was there. Didn't look surprised. He just looked. Looked through me. Measured me in silence.

And then—

"Come here."

Two words. Command. Control. My heels echoed across the floor. Too loud. Too exposed.

I crossed the room like a secret unspooling. He didn't move. Didn't speak again. Just waited.

When I stopped in front of him—close, but not too close— he shifted. Stepped to the side. Nodded to the desk behind me.

"Hands on the desk."

I turned. My knees shook. Not from fear. From relief. From the ache of knowing I'd wanted this since the second I'd laced the corset.

The glass was cool beneath my palms. Slick. Polished. My breath fogged the surface.

He moved behind me. No footsteps. Just heat. Presence. Power.

He didn't touch me. Not yet. But I felt him. Felt the air shift behind my neck. Felt the pause—the weight of silence before touch.

I stared at my reflection in the glass. Lips parted. Chest rising too fast. The lace of the corset was visible beneath the blouse now. The outline of my nipples. The strain of silk across my hips. Every inch of me bared without a button undone.

And then—

"Breathe."

His voice was low. Like a blade drawn slow from its sheath. I did. Barely.

He stepped closer. His breath ghosted along the back of my neck. Fingers reached up. Brushed my hair to one side. Slid over the first button. Then the second. He didn't shake. But I did.

He didn't speak. Didn't ask. Just opened me. Unbuttoned silk. Parted lace. Made me available.

His hand hovered above the corset. Didn't touch. Just traced the outline of the restraint he'd wrapped me in. Fingers brushed the edge where fabric met skin. My breath stuttered. His mouth hovered at my ear.

"You think the clothes make the role."

My knees buckled slightly. A flicker. A reaction. He pressed a hand to the small of my back. Not hard. But firm. Guiding. Corrective.

My spine arched—just slightly.

"They don't," he said.

His voice was quiet.

Final.

"The obedience does."

My chest squeezed around the inhale I hadn't taken. His hand slid higher. To the nape of my neck. Warm. Heavy. Grounding. And then—

Gone.

Just like that.

The absence hit harder than the touch.

I stayed bent over the desk long after the door clicked shut behind him. Still. Silent.

My chest tight. My thighs slick. My whole body trembling —not from fear. Not even from shame. From want. From hunger sharpened by denial.

I buttoned my blouse with shaking fingers. Every press of silk against skin was a reminder. Of where he'd touched. And where he hadn't.

I should've felt relief. Should've felt power. But all I felt was the void. The echo of something I wasn't sure I could name. The office floor felt colder when I stepped out. Or maybe it was me. Stripped. Raw. Carrying the ghost of his fingers like a second skin.

I walked through the bullpen like nothing had happened.

But everything had.

Royal looked up from his phone. Smirked. His eyes slid down my frame. Paused at the top of my blouse. Still undone. Still marked. He didn't speak. Didn't need to. His smirk said it all.

Good girl.

Loyal passed me in the corridor. Didn't meet my gaze. But he paused. Long enough. His jaw tight. His eyes sharp. His silence louder than anything Royal could say. He knew. They all did.

When I reached my desk, I sat carefully. Too carefully. The corset bit deep into my ribs. The lace was soaked through. My hands hovered over the keyboard. But they didn't type. Couldn't. Because I could still feel him. Not his fingers. Not his breath.

Him.

The gravity of the moment. The power in restraint. The way he didn't need to fuck me to take me apart.

I touched the desk. Fingertips flat. The same way I had in his office. My breath caught. Shallow. Staggered. I was still that girl. Still bent in silence. Still split in places no one could see.

A *ping* lit up my screen.

I jumped.

Wolfe.

Conference room. Ten minutes.

No subject.

No signature. Just a command.

Another one.

And I hated how fast my pulse jumped.

I didn't know what he wanted. Didn't care. Because my body already knew the shape of my next fall.

I looked down at my thighs. Shifted in my seat. Heat bloomed again. Not from fear. Not from shame. From hunger.

Because Barron hadn't fucked me. But I'd never been more owned.

18

———

WOLFE

She came out with her head down. Not in shame. In something worse.

Afterglow.

I watched her from behind the glass. She didn't see me. No one ever does—until it's too late.

Her blouse was rumpled. Two buttons undone. Her lipstick smudged at one corner. She adjusted the top of her skirt like it still clung too high.

And I knew. I didn't need proof. Didn't need a camera. Didn't need to ask. I fucking knew. My jaw locked.

I pressed two fingers against the edge of the windowsill to keep from breaking something.

She walked like her legs were shaking. Like her thighs were too slick to move comfortably.

And Barron?

His office door was still open. Not wide. But wide enough.

Wide enough for the assistants to glance up and glance away. Wide enough for the boardroom two doors down to go silent. Wide enough for every single person on this floor to know.

He didn't close it.

Because he wanted them to know. And that? That made something in my chest crack. I turned away.

Because if I looked one second longer, I was going to put my fist through the glass. Behind me, a security notice pinged. A digital signature from a logistics handler we'd buried two years ago.

I didn't check it. Didn't open it.

I didn't care. Because the only thing I could see was the silk of her blouse sticking to her chest. The way she adjusted the skirt like it still held the print of someone's palm. My brother's palm.

I gripped the edge of the console. Hard. Knuckles white. Control bleeding at the edges.

I told myself it didn't matter. That I wasn't the one who touched her. That I didn't want to be. But it was a lie. I'd been lying since the day she walked in.

And now?

Now I was angry.

Not at her.

At me.

For not getting there first.

I crossed the room and opened the sideboard. The crystal decanter was cold in my hand. I poured too hard. Whiskey sloshed over the rim. Didn't care.

I didn't even flinch when it hit my fingers. I just held the glass like it was the only thing I could still control. My fingers were tight enough to crack the crystal. My cock was still hard. My throat raw. My chest burned like something feral was trying to claw its way out. Not because she let him touch her. Because it was him. Barron.

Barron always takes first.

He walks in, makes a decision, and the rest of us bleed for it. He was warned about Selene. We all told him.

I told him. Said she'd break him. Hollow him out. Strip this company bare one secret at a time. He didn't listen. He never fucking does. Because Barron always gets what he wants. *And we always pay for it.*

We pay for the women he can't walk away from. We pay for the silence he keeps like a weapon until it's too late to fix.

And now?

Now he's walking through fire again. Only this time? The girl he wants already *belongs* to me.

She said thank you—*for me.*

She *came* when *I* called.

She *bent* when *I* told her to.

But she bent for *him* too.

And that? That... that was the part I couldn't stop replaying. What did he say? What name did she whisper?

Did he press his fingers against the back of her neck? Did she flinch? Did she beg? *Did she like it?*

I threw back the whiskey. Didn't taste it. Didn't care. It burned like water. The door opened behind me.

Footsteps. Hers.

I didn't turn. Couldn't.

Because if I did, I'd grab her. Drag her into my office. Press her against the glass and make her say my name loud enough that Barron would fucking hear it. I set the glass down too hard. The echo rang through the room like a warning.

I turned my back on the floor. Sat down too fast. The chair creaked. Loud. Sharp. I stared at the screen. Nothing moved. No files. No reports. No distraction. Because she was still out there. Sitting. Typing.

Pretending.

I could picture her—corset cinched too tight, thighs pressed together, lace soaked through. Typing the same sentence over and over again. Deleting it. Starting again. Because that's what she did when she was nervous. When she was wet.

My hands curled into fists on my lap.

I didn't look at the glass. Didn't have to. I could still see her. Blouse open. Breasts rising too fast. Skirt tight across her ass. Bent over Barron's desk.

My brother's desk.

I pressed my palms to my thighs.

Hard.

The ache in my chest was a drumbeat now. The one in my pants worse. Thick. Hot. Unrelieved.

I adjusted myself.

Still hard..

Harder.

The whiskey had done nothing.

My phone lit up.

Security feed.

Ping: Barron's office—door opened.

Five minutes ago.

Then: closed.

She was still in there.

I imagined it again. How he told her to bend. How she shook when he touched her. Whether she cried. Whether she came. My jaw cracked from clenching too tight.

And still—

Still all I could hear was her voice from the night before.

Thank you.

She said it for me. But would she say it for him too? Would she say it softer? Would she mean it more?

I pressed my fists against my thighs until I saw stars.

Because that thought?

That thought made me want to ruin her. Not from anger. Not from hate. From something deeper. Something darker. Something I wasn't sure I could come back from once I touched it.

I wanted to take the obedience she gave me and drag it out of her in pieces. On her knees. In silence. In tears. I stood again. Too fast. The chair tipped. I didn't fix it. Didn't care.

I paced. Back and forth. Five steps. Turn. Five steps. Stop. Breathing hard. Harder. Every inhale felt like fire. Every exhale like something I couldn't name.

I imagined walking out to her desk. Grabbing her by the wrist. Pulling her back here. Making her look me in the eye and say it again.

Not thank you. Not this time.

"Please."

I found her alone. Break room. Corner seat. Glass wall at her back. She held a coffee cup in her hands, untouched. She wasn't scrolling. Wasn't typing. Just staring. Like she was trying to remember who she was before all of this started. Before I started.

Her blouse was buttoned again. Corset still visible beneath the silk—if you knew where to look. And I did. I knew every seam. Every line. Every shiver she thought she could hide.

I stepped inside the room. Silent. Predator quiet.

She looked up. Flinched. Just once. But it was enough.

"Did you look in the mirror after he touched you?"

I didn't soften it. Didn't blink. She froze. Eyes wide. Lips parted. But no answer. Because she knew I knew. And she knew better than to lie.

"You should have."

I moved forward. Not fast. Not looming. Just forward. Letting her feel it. Letting her feel me.

"You're wearing him now."

Her breath caught. Her eyes dropped. Shame. Or something worse. Maybe not shame at all. *Maybe want.*

I circled her once.

Slow.

Close enough to smell the heat on her skin. Coffee. *Silk.* Something darker underneath.

She didn't move. Didn't speak.

I stepped behind her.

Leant down.

Close.

"He marked you," I whispered. "But he didn't claim you."

Let it sit.

Let it settle.

"You're still shaking for someone else."

Her breath hitched.

"I'm not—"

"Don't lie."

She stopped.

Didn't speak again.

Good girl.

I leaned closer.

Mouth to her ear.

Her body tensed beneath the blouse.

"Next time you want to be touched..."

I paused.

Waited.

"...ask me *first*."

Then I walked out. Because when I finally touch her? She won't just say *thank you*. She'll fucking beg.

I didn't go back to my office. I walked. No destination. Just distance. The break room door swung shut behind me. But I could still feel her eyes. Still trembling. Still flushed. Still wet for someone who didn't even lay a hand on her.

I made it to the garage. Got in the car. Didn't start it. Didn't reach for the key. Just sat there. Staring at the wall like it owed me answers I already hated. The ache didn't go away. Not the one in my cock. Not the one in my chest. I pulled out my phone. Scrolled back to the message.

Thank you.

Still there. Still echoing. Still hers.

I didn't delete it. Couldn't. I read it again. Then hovered my thumb over her name. I didn't call. But I wanted to. Not to hear her voice. To hear what she'd say if I told her to kneel.

I let the phone fall to the passenger seat. Leaned back. Closed my eyes.

And for some reason, I saw Camille. Barefoot. Smiling. Standing in my kitchen like she owned it and the whole fucking world. She used to tuck her hair behind her ear when she was thinking. Tilt her head. Say something that made it easier to breathe. She was light. And she was mine. Until she wasn't.

Cloe isn't light.

She's a fuse.

Lit.

Burning.

Begging for someone to strike.

And fuck me—

I want to be the one who does.

The man wasn't supposed to be here. Not in the building. Not on this floor. And definitely not walking toward my office with that smug, entitled smile like he belonged.

I intercepted him at the elevator. No words at first. Just presence. Just pressure. He stopped when he saw me. Raised his hands like I was holding a gun.

"Wolfe," he said, too familiar. "Didn't realize this floor was off-limits."

"It is."

I didn't raise my voice. Didn't need to. Because the look in my eyes said what my fists were already itching to confirm. He worked for us—but just barely.

A diamond handler out of Antwerp. Good with border customs, bad with boundaries. He was supposed to stay off-site. Always. Never show his face in the tower.

And yet *here he was.*

Arrogant. Polished. Late forties. Toned in a way that said he paid for it. His shoes too shiny. His watch too loud.

"You should've called," I said.

"I thought we had an arrangement."

"You *thought* wrong."

He smirked. That was his first mistake. I stepped closer. The smirk faded. That was his second.

"You don't walk into this building unless you're summoned. You don't breathe near my people unless I give you air. And you don't ever speak my name again like we're fucking friends."

He didn't reply. The elevator behind me opened. Perfect timing.

I gestured with my chin. "You're leaving. *Now.*"

He nodded. Lifted both hands again. Backed toward the elevator. And then—

Cloe.

She stepped out of the opposite lift. Didn't see me at first. Didn't see him. She was holding her tablet. A folder tucked under her arm. Moving fast.

The man turned.

Saw her.

Stopped.

And smiled.

Slow.

Filthy.

His eyes dragged from her legs to her mouth.

"Well," he murmured. "She's not wearing that pink blouse for the admin team, is she?"

Cloe froze.

Her head turned.

Her eyes met mine.

Wide.

Alarmed.

The man didn't stop.

"Lawlor's new toy?" he said softly. "Didn't think you went for soft."

I didn't speak. Didn't breathe. My fists curled so tight my nails cut my palms. I stepped forward.

Close.

Closer.

The man turned to me like he didn't realize what he'd done. I leaned in.

"Next time you open your mouth about her," I said quietly, "I'll make sure you can't open it again."

His jaw twitched. But he didn't argue. Didn't smile. He stepped inside the elevator. I followed him halfway in. Close enough to whisper.

"If you ever so much as look at *her* again without my permission..."

I let the silence finish the sentence. The doors closed. I turned back. Cloe stood there. Frozen. Shaken. Her blouse was pressed flat to her chest. Her eyes still wide.

"What was that?" she asked.

I didn't answer. Because if I opened my mouth right now? I wouldn't stop. Not until she was pressed to my desk, saying my name loud enough that the bastard who just left would hear it three floors down.

I walked past her. Didn't touch her. Didn't speak. But inside? Something snapped. Because I knew something she didn't yet.

That man? He'd come back. And next time? He wouldn't ask for diamonds.

He'd ask for *her*.

19

___

CLOE

THE INVITATION ARRIVED SEALED in a velvet envelope.

Black.

No logo.

No name.

Just weight.

Wolfe dropped it on my desk without a word. Didn't look at me. Didn't pause. Just kept walking. His footsteps echoed too loud in the stillness, a sound that shouldn't have made my heart race—but it did.

I stared at the envelope for a long time before touching it. Like it might burn. Like it might brand.

The velvet was soft under my fingertips, but the chill in my palms said otherwise. This wasn't paper. It was something else. Something sharp.

I slid a finger beneath the flap, slow, cautious. The edge sliced the tip of my nail. Inside, in clean, glinting silver script:

Lawlor Diamonds cordially invites you to the Annual Foundation Auction.

Attendance required.

Attire: Formal.

Silence: Expected.

Four lines. No names. No details. Just a demand.

I read it twice. Then again. Each word felt like a collar being fastened around my throat. I wasn't asked. I wasn't invited. I was expected. The script didn't threaten. But it didn't have to. It was Wolfe's handwriting.

Of course it was. My eyes lifted from the envelope. Across the bullpen. Past the quiet hum of printers and the clack of polished shoes on stone tile.

Royal was watching me from the far side of the floor. Leaning against the glass wall with a cup of coffee he wasn't drinking. He didn't blink. Didn't smile. Just raised one brow like he knew exactly what kind of night it was going to be. Like he'd already placed his bet. And I was the prize on the table.

Heat crawled up my spine. Not shame. Not yet. But something close. Anticipation laced with dread.

There were things in this building I didn't understand. Rooms I hadn't seen. Names I hadn't heard. And this invitation? It wasn't about charity. It was about hierarchy. About spectacle. About control.

I set the envelope down like it might hear me thinking too loud. Then I smoothed my skirt, folded my hands in my lap, and pretended to keep working. But my eyes stayed on Royal. And his never left me.

The car arrived at 6:00 p.m. sharp.

Black.

Windows tinted so dark I couldn't see the driver's eyes. He didn't speak when he opened the door. Didn't look at me when he handed me the note.

My name. One word. Nothing else.

CLOE.

Wolfe's handwriting. Of course it was.

I slid into the backseat slowly, smoothing my skirt over my knees as if it mattered. The interior smelled like leather and secrets. The backseat held a single garment bag. Hung neatly on the hook beside me like it had been waiting there since last night.

My name was written on the tag again—this time in black ink, block letters. I reached for the zipper with trembling fingers.

Inside—a gown.

Midnight velvet. Cool against my skin. Sleek. Silent.

Backless.

Slit high enough to show skin no dress had ever dared on me before.

My breath caught. This wasn't fashion. It was strategy. He'd chosen it. Not for comfort. Not for elegance. For impact. The kind that left marks without touching.

I checked the tag—half-expecting a designer label.

Instead, just two hand-stitched initials.

W.L.

Wolfe Lawlor.

Of course.

The venue was a private gallery downtown. It rose from the street like something carved into history. Columns. Stonework. Steel and shadow.

All marble and mirrored walls on the inside—like stepping into a vault built to reflect power. Low lighting pooled at every corner. Glasses clinked. Laughter was hushed and calculated. Men in tailored suits stood like monuments. Women in backless gowns whispered with sharpened smiles.

The air shimmered with money and danger. I didn't belong. But when I stepped inside? Every head turned. Not because they recognized me. Because they didn't.

Royal found me first. His smirk cut through the noise like a blade. He didn't offer a hand. He offered a warning.

"Well, well," he murmured, gaze dragging down the length of me like I was the evening's first bid. "They dressed you up like a gift. Wonder *who* gets to unwrap it."

I didn't answer. Didn't need to. Because Wolfe stepped in behind me.

I felt him before I saw him. The air shifted. My spine straightened. His hand touched the small of my back. Not soft. Not violent. Firm. Claiming.

"She's here to observe," Wolfe said.

But his voice held something darker. Like he already knew I'd be absorbed instead. Like he'd invited me here not to watch —but to be watched.

THE MAIN GALLERY was arranged like a chessboard. Tables in a sharp U-shape. A stage lit center-front. But this wasn't for art. Not paintings. Not sculpture. Not jewelry.

This was an auction of names. Of influence. Of empire. Board seats. Foreign permits. Port clearances. Lawlor didn't deal in diamonds tonight. They dealt in power.

I tried to follow Wolfe to his table. He stopped me with a touch to my wrist. Directed me two chairs down. He sat at the center of the table, flanked by Royal and Barron.

I was seated between Loyal and a man I didn't recognize. Tall. Grey hair. French cufflinks and a practiced smile.

He said nothing at first. Just passed me a flute of champagne with a nod that lingered too long. When he reached for the salt, his knuckles brushed my wrist. Deliberate.

I stiffened. Loyal didn't say a word. But he shifted his chair back. Just slightly. Pushed mine away from the man with one slow slide of his foot. The message was clear.

Wolfe watched the entire thing. Didn't interrupt. Didn't stop it. Because this *was* the test.

The room buzzed with the first round of bidding. I barely understood the numbers. Eight figures. Silent nods. Paddles raised like declarations of war. Royal bid first. Barron lifted his glass but said nothing. And Wolfe? He watched me. Not the auctioneer. Not the screen.

Me.

Every time the man beside me leaned closer, Wolfe's jaw twitched. Every time I shifted, pulled the slit of the dress lower, his gaze narrowed. I felt his fury before I saw it. It vibrated in the air like electricity.

When the French cufflink man finally leaned over and whispered, "What's your name?"—

Wolfe stood.

The sound of his chair sliding back silenced the table.

"That's enough."

His voice didn't rise. But it didn't have to. Every person in the room stopped breathing. He didn't look at the man. He looked at me.

"Come."

Just one word. But it split me open.

I stood. Followed. Didn't look back. He led me through a private hall. Long. Dim. Lined with portraits of men who stared down like they owned the city.

We passed one closed door. Another. Then he opened the last. Stepped inside. Waited.

When I crossed the threshold, the door shut behind me.

Locked.

The room was soundproofed.

Wolfe turned.

And the look in his eyes—

It stripped me bare.

"You think I brought you here to be seen?"

His voice was low.

Rough.

Angry.

"I brought you here so they knew not to touch."

He stepped forward.

"Instead, you let him breathe your air."

I tried to speak.

"Wolfe—"

"No."

He moved too fast. Pinned me against the wall with one hand. Not painful. Just... final. His other hand slid up my thigh. Lifted the slit. My breath caught.

"Next time you want someone's attention," he said, voice dark against my cheek, "you ask me first."

His mouth found my ear.

"You're mine. You got that? I let them look. But you never look back. Only me, Cloe. Only me, because to think about anything else is bringing me undone."

Then he kissed me.

Hard.

Devastating.

I didn't breathe. Couldn't.

My back hit the wall, velvet against glass, my dress already bunched at my hips.

Wolfe's mouth crushed mine with a need so sharp it stole sound from the room. Outside, the auction continued—soft applause, murmurs, the cold exchange of power. But here?

Here, he devoured.

His hand gripped the side of my throat, not tight—never

tight—just firm enough to hold me still. His body pressed flush against mine. His thigh parted mine. And I was already soaked.

He felt it. Smelled it. His growl rumbled against my chest.

"You want them to watch you? Want to be a pretty little thing laid out for everyone to bid on?"

"No," I whispered.

He grinned against my mouth.

"*Liar.*"

His fingers found the slit in the dress. Slid beneath. Tugged the lace panties to the side with practiced precision.

He didn't rush.

Two fingers slid through me.

"So wet," he murmured.

"Wolfe..."

"Look at *me.*"

I did.

His eyes were wildfire.

"Next time someone speaks to you like he did, you tell them what you are."

I swallowed. "What am I?"

He leaned in. His voice was a blade. "*Mine.*"

He gripped my hip, pinned me with his body. Then he undid his belt. The sound alone nearly undid me. My head dropped back. I was trembling.

"Look down," he growled.

I blinked.

He took himself in hand.

"Watch me take you."

I looked.

He lined himself up.

Pushed in.

One slow, brutal thrust.

I gasped—not from pain, from the stretch. From how he filled every part of me like he knew it was his.

Jesus.

I...I couldn't breathe, couldn't think. Couldn't do anything but let my head roll back and be swept away in the delicious feel as he pulled out, only to thrust in so damn hard it made my entire body jolt.

"That's it," he whispered. "That's what you look like when you're owned."

He fucked me against the wall.

Deep.

Controlled.

Every thrust claimed something. My breath. My pride. My soul. His hand slid down my throat. Not to choke. To feel. To control.

"Say it."

I was sobbing.

"Yours."

"Again."

"*Yours.*"

He didn't stop. Not when I clenched. Not when I cried out. Not when I shattered. He followed me down, teeth at my shoulder.

"You don't come for anyone else."

"I don't."

"Only me. You got it?"

"Only you."

The chain at my throat burned. When he pulled out, he didn't clean me up. Didn't kiss me again. He just fixed my dress. Brushed my hair back. Pressed his lips to my ear and whispered:

"Sold."

And outside? The auction carried on. But the only thing sold that night—

Was me.

20

———

CLOE

Something was wrong. I knew it before I reached my desk. Before I even sat down. Even befoe the delicious ache between my thighs from last night bloomed.

It was subtle—barely noticeable—but my body clocked it faster than my brain did. The angle was off. My chair pulled out slightly too far. My keyboard was shifted right.

And the desk itself? It had been turned. Not much. Just enough that when I sat down, I would be aligned perfectly with the one place I tried not to look.

Wolfe's office.

I froze. Halfway to sitting. My pulse stuttered. A flush crept up my neck. Not embarrassment. Awareness.

Heat spread low in my belly like an echo of breath on skin. He hadn't told me. Hadn't warned me. Hadn't asked. But I knew.

There was only one man in this building who would move something just far enough to make a point. Just enough to claim me without ever laying a hand.

I sat slowly. Like I was lowering myself into something

sacred. Something dangerous. Every inch of my skin prickled with heat. Not because I was afraid. Because I was seen. Because I was rearranged.

The glass wall of his office gleamed in the morning light. From this angle, I couldn't miss it. Couldn't pretend I wasn't framed in his view.

I glanced up.

And of course—he was there. Seated. Still. Head tilted slightly. One hand at his mouth. Eyes locked on me.

He didn't blink. Didn't look away. Just sat there. And let me feel it. Let me feel the weight of the new arrangement. Let me feel what it meant to be turned. Just enough. To face him.

My thighs pressed together under the desk. A pulse throbbed between them. Heavy. Demanding.

I adjusted my skirt. Lowered the hem. Didn't help. The lace beneath was already clinging. The corset bit into my ribs with every breath. The silk blouse stuck to the curve of my spine.

I typed.

Or tried to.

My hands shook. My breathing shortened. The sound of my own keystrokes echoed too loud in the silence. Too sharp. Too fast. Everyone around me moved normally. Answered phones. Sipped coffee. Flipped papers.

But me?

I was centered. Positioned. My whole body aligned like a compass.

And Wolfe?

He was the needle now.

The pull. The anchor. He'd tilted my desk like it was nothing. And made me orbit him like it was everything.

And the worst part?

I liked it.

I liked being turned. I liked knowing he'd moved me to face him. I liked wondering how long he'd planned it. I couldn't stop glancing at the glass. Because every time I looked up...

He was still there.

Still watching. Still waiting. Still owning me—inch by inch, breath by breath—without ever moving from his chair.

My fingers hovered above the keyboard, frozen mid-keystroke.

And then—

It hit me.

Low.

Deep.

A sudden twist of pressure in my belly. Dull at first. Then sharp. Coiling into something unmistakable.

Pain. Not the corset. Not arousal. Worse.

My breath caught. My thighs clenched instinctively. Something shifted inside me—liquid and hot and wrong.

No.

Not now.

The ache bloomed. I adjusted in my seat, trying to ease it. The chair creaked. The waistband of my skirt pressed too tight. The corset cinched too hard against my lower ribs. Heat rolled up the back of my neck.

I swallowed hard.

Another pulse.

Then another.

Panic set in. My legs pressed together tighter. My hands returned to the keyboard just to keep from shaking. I typed nonsense. Just movement. Just noise.

But I could feel it. Building. Spreading.

The telltale warmth between my thighs wasn't lust this time. It was blood. Unwelcome. Untimed. Unforgivable. And that's when the panic turned cruel.

When was the last time I bled? I blinked hard. Tried to remember. A date. A month. Anything. Had it been five weeks? Six? Had I skipped it the month Wolfe touched me? Was it stress? Or something worse?

My fingers twitched against the keys.

Think.

The bathroom at my old apartment. A cheap pad from the bodega downstairs. I remembered pulling it from a plastic wrapper with wet hands. I remembered Camille knocking on the door, teasing me through the glass.

That was—what?

A month ago? *No.*

Longer.

Too long.

Stupid.

I never tracked it properly.

I was always careful with passwords. Careful with shadows. Careful with men. But not this. Not my body. Not the one thing that should've warned me before it cracked open under silk and shame and—

Oh God.

Wolfe was still watching.

His eyes didn't move. His jaw didn't twitch. His gaze was fixed—heavy. Knowing. He couldn't see it. Not from here. Not yet.

But he could see me come undone. And I couldn't let that happen here. Not like this.

I grabbed my things and ran for the bathroom. The door slammed behind me. I didn't even check the lock. I just dropped my purse and backed into the wall of the private bathroom stall, breath coming fast, fingers shaking as I reached beneath my skirt.

There it was.

Blood. Bright.

Wet.

Humiliating.

Already soaking through the lace.

A flush of red in a world that had been black and blush and silk and secrecy. It wasn't supposed to happen now. Not here. Not like this.

I pressed my legs together, as if I could stop it. As if I could will it back. I had nothing on me. No tampon. No pad. No dignity. Just slick lace and rising panic. My breath hitched.

The corset tightened around my ribs. Too tight now. Too much. I couldn't breathe. I sat down on the toilet. Hard. Didn't even pull my panties down.

Just sat. Knees together. Head down. Like maybe stillness could stop it. Like shame might be strong enough to keep it all in. My hands covered my face. My shoulders shook.

The tears came hot and immediate. Unforgiving. I hadn't cried like this since Camille's funeral. The door creaked. Footsteps. Measured. Male.

Wolfe.

"Cloe."

He said my name like a verdict.

I didn't answer.

Couldn't.

He stepped closer.

The air shifted with him.

Then—another sound.

Lighter footsteps.

Quick.

Another voice.

"Sorry—"

"Find another bathroom."

Wolfe's voice snapped like a whip.

Cold.

Unmovable.

Final.

The door shut again.

A lock turned.

Click.

Silence. Except for my breath. The corset groaned with every inhale. My thighs were damp.

Sticky.

And I hated it. Hated being seen. Hated being known.

I didn't look up. Couldn't. But I felt him. Still there. Still watching. Still not moving.

The sound came soft—a coat shifting, shoes brushing tile.

Then—

He raised one hand. Not to touch me. Just a gesture. A warning. A promise.

"I'm not going to hurt you."

His voice was low.

Rough.

Like it scraped the inside of his chest just to be spoken.

"I need you to breathe."

My breath caught again.

"I can't," I whispered. "It's too—tight—"

"Corset?"

I nodded.

Eyes still closed.

Hands still covering my face.

I heard him move.

Closer.

A pause.

Then the sound of him kneeling.

I froze.

"I'm going to help you."

He said it like an oath. Like it mattered. Like I hadn't already bled all over the fucking floor.

But still—I nodded.

Slow. Fragile.

He reached behind me. Fingers brushing the laces. Not skin. Not yet.

Just silk.

And then—

Gently.

Quietly.

He began to loosen it.

I couldn't speak. The tears were too close. But I nodded. Barely. And he moved. Forward. Lower. Kneeling. Right there, in front of me.

My legs tried to close. Not out of fear. Out of shame. My thighs weren't long and toned. They were soft. Thick. Flesh pressed against flesh. The blood between them felt hot and slick and too much. Too ugly.

But Wolfe? He didn't flinch. Didn't grimace. He just... looked.

His eyes flicked to mine. Held. And I saw it. Not disgust. Not pity. Just stillness. Like I was something precious. Even now. Especially now.

"May I?"

His voice was low.

Rough.

Reverent.

I swallowed hard. Nodded. He reached into his coat pocket and pulled out a black pouch. Unzipped it.

Inside: tampons. Pads. Wipes. Everything. Emergency kit. Preparedness masked as devotion.

"Take what you need," he said. "Or let me do it."

My lips parted. I should've spoken. Should've said no. But

all I could whisper was:

"I... can't reach. The corset."

His jaw flexed once. Then he nodded. Stepped closer. His fingers brushed the ribbon at my spine.

Slow.

Deliberate.

One pull. Then another.

He unlaced me like he was unwrapping something breakable. Each inch of loosened tension let me breathe deeper. But not easier. Because the shame didn't leave. It shifted. Into something else. Something worse.

Want.

He reached for the waistband of my panties next. Slid them down. Slowly. They stuck at the crease of my thighs—damp with blood and heat. He didn't comment. Didn't look away. Just moved with the kind of gentleness that made me ache.

He opened the wrapper.

And inserted the tampon.

Slow.

Careful.

His fingers touched me—warm, steady, present.

I gasped. Not from pain. From everything. From the touch. From the stillness. From being seen.

I gripped the edge of the toilet. My thighs trembled. My nipples ached. And I hated that my body responded—not just with need—but with grief. Grief that no one had ever done this.

No one had ever treated me like I was worthy of care when I was like this.

Bleeding.

Messy.

Weak.

But Wolfe?

He stayed on his knees.

Looked up at me like I was still something he wanted.

He reached up and wiped a tear from my cheek.

Not with his thumb.

With the back of his knuckle.

Tender.

Dangerous.

"I'm pathetic." I closed my eyes, full of shame.

"You're not disgusting. Or pathetic. You're mine."

I sobbed. Quiet. Breathless. Because I'd never heard anyone say that and mean it. Not here. Not like this.

"Why?" I whispered. "Why are you doing this?"

He stood slowly. Tucked the pouch back into his coat. Didn't answer right away.

Then—

"Because you bleed. So what. You ache. You still belong to me."

And I believed him.

God help me—I believed him.

He stepped back.

Picked up my purse.

Held it out.

Waited.

And when I stood—knees trembling, panties still half-down, corset undone—he didn't look away.

He didn't leer. Didn't mock. He just said—

"Fix your skirt, Cloe. Button your blouse. Come when I call."

And I nodded.

Because what else could I do?

He didn't fuck me. Not this time. But I'd never felt more taken in my life.

The corridor was quiet. Not the normal kind. Not the kind filled with heels and phones and muted clicks. This quiet? It pulsed. Pressed against my ribs like a second heartbeat. The kind of silence that watches. That waits.

I stepped out of the bathroom stall on unsteady legs. My corset was relaced—but looser now. Not styled for seduction. Just held. Just enough to keep me upright. My blouse was buttoned to the top. Lipstick wiped.

But the flush hadn't faded. It burned hot in my cheeks. Lingered on my neck. Licked beneath my blouse like breath.

My skin didn't feel like mine anymore.

It felt remembered.

Owned.

His hands hadn't stayed long. But their imprint did.

I didn't walk fast. Didn't look around. But I felt them. Eyes.

Royal—leaning against the printer bay—paused mid-sentence.

An intern behind corner glass. Pretending not to watch. Loyal—far end of the floor, folder in hand, knuckles white.

And Wolfe?

Nowhere to be seen.

But present. Like gravity. Like pressure. Like a name humming in the back of my throat. I made it back to my desk. Sat slowly. Carefully. The lace between my thighs was clean. Dry. But still pulsing.

Still aching like I'd been taken apart and left unfinished. He hadn't fucked me. He hadn't even kissed me. But my body didn't know the difference.

I reached for my mouse. Clicked the screen on. Tried to focus. Failed. The letters blurred. My vision stung.

I blinked.

Breathed.

Once.

Twice.

My phone buzzed. I didn't look right away. Because I didn't

need to. I already knew. It was him. I clicked into the system. Typed the wrong password.

Twice.

Swore under my breath. Typed again. The screen loaded.

Another *ping*. I opened it.

One line.

You're not hiding it well.

No greeting.

No signature.

Just him.

Wolfe.

I stared at it.

Then typed back.

I'm not trying to.

And hit send.

I didn't breathe for five full seconds. And when I did? I smiled. Not out of pride. Not out of rebellion. Out of truth.

Because he'd seen me. Every crack. Every tremble. Every slick, red, shame-soaked piece of me. And he hadn't turned away. He'd knelt. There was power in that. Even if it didn't belong to me.

I looked up. His office sat dark. Still. But I didn't need to see him anymore. Because I could feel him. He hadn't fucked me. But now? I was marked. And I wasn't sure I ever wanted to feel clean again.

21

BARRON

I saw them.

Not clearly. Not fully.

Just a flicker as I crossed the mezzanine and glanced down through the glass railing.

Wolfe's door was half open. Cloe was stepping out. Her head was down, her hair hiding most of her face, but I caught the way her hand brushed his arm. A silent thank-you. A soft linger.

Wolfe said nothing. But I saw his fingers slip something into his pocket.

Black. Small. Familiar.

The pouch.

He always carried one. Always had. I'd seen him hand it to assistants who didn't want to ask. Women on our floor who'd been caught off guard. He never spoke about it, never acknowledged it. Just offered it with a kind of brutal efficiency that made me want to tear his face off.

And now he'd handed it to her.

Her walk was slower than usual. Not weak. Just...

restrained. Careful. Her arms crossed slightly under her chest, as if she was holding herself together from the inside.

I watched her adjust her blouse at the hem. Tug it down like it didn't sit right. Like something underneath had shifted.

Something had.

The ache between her legs? I knew it. Wolfe knew it. But neither of us could do anything about it now.

Except I didn't believe that.

Not really.

Because I saw the look in her eyes when she passed my office.

The shame. The heat. The need that hadn't been satisfied, just redirected.

She didn't glance in.

Didn't give me the flicker of deference she usually did.

But I felt her.

Like a storm passing just overhead. Just enough static to lift the hairs on my arm.

She reached her desk. Sat carefully. Her jaw was tense. Her hand moved to her lower stomach and stayed there a moment too long. Rubbing. Pressing. Trying to hide the fact that she was trying to ease something she didn't want to name.

I knew what it was.

And I knew what she needed.

I left the door open.

Didn't call her name. Didn't need to.

The second she looked up, I saw the flicker. The pause. The weight of her pulse behind her eyes.

She rose slowly. Adjusted her corset at the side. Smoothed her skirt like it made a difference.

It didn't.

Not to me.

She stepped inside.

Didn't speak. Didn't fidget. Just closed the door behind her and stood with her hands clasped in front of her like she already knew why she was here.

I stayed behind the desk.

Watched her. Watched how carefully she held herself. How tight her breath was. How the flush that lingered across her cheeks hadn't dulled since Wolfe's hands left her.

"You're not bleeding because of him," I said.

Her eyes widened—but she didn't move.

I rose. Walked toward her. Slowly. Measured. I stopped just short of touching her.

"He gave you the pouch."

No answer. But I saw it—the tremble in her throat, the way her jaw shifted like she wanted to deny it but couldn't. She'd been seen. And she knew it. I reached out. Pressed my palm to her lower belly. She gasped. Subtle. Sharp. Not in pain. In relief.

"You're cramping."

Still no answer. Just the slightest nod.

My fingers moved in slow, steady circles. I felt the tension in her abdomen, the way her breath caught with each pass. She was trying not to lean into it. Not to admit what it did to her.

I stepped closer. Brushed her hair back behind her shoulder. Let my hand trail down the back of her neck. Let her feel how easy it would be for me to claim her. But I didn't. Instead, I kept my hand on her stomach. Soft. Firm. Gentle.

"You don't have to pretend you're not turned on," I murmured. "You think I don't know what a woman feels like when her body is at war with itself?"

She trembled.

"It's not weakness," I said. "It's fire. Pressure. Heat without release."

I moved behind her. Pressed my chest lightly to her back.

Her spine arched on instinct. I let my hand drift lower. Not to penetrate. Not to take. Just to soothe. The flat of my palm pressed between her thighs. Through the fabric. Slow. Careful.

She let out a breath she hadn't meant to. I didn't speak. Didn't ask permission. I just moved my hand. Upward pressure. Gentle friction. Not fast. Not dirty. Just enough to make her bite her lip.

"Let me help," I said quietly. "No blood. No shame. Just this."

Her head tilted back. Her hips shifted. She didn't say yes. She didn't have to. Her body gave it to me. She didn't say a word. Didn't need to. Her body shifted, barely—just enough to part her thighs beneath the fabric of that skirt. Just enough to invite my hand to stay right where it was.

She was so warm there. So fucking soft. And trembling. Not because she was afraid. Because I was the one touching her now. Because Wolfe lit the fuse, but I was the one who would hold her through the fire. I slid my hand between her legs, cupped her through the silk. Pressed upward with just enough pressure to make her exhale.

"I'm not going to take anything from you," I murmured against the back of her neck. "Not like this. Not tonight."

She nodded—barely—and I felt it. The way her body sagged against me. The tiniest surrender. Her guard crumpling around the edges.

I moved slow. Deliberate. Circles. Pressure. No rush. No shame. Just her thighs flexing and hips shifting as the tension began to unravel.

"You're so damn wound up," I whispered. "Can't even breathe, can you?"

A soft, stuttering breath left her lips.

"I know," I said. "You've been holding it in all day. The ache. The heat. The want."

Her head tilted slightly.

Her breath hitched.

And I knew—she was close.

I used my other hand to slide around her waist. Held her there. Anchored her. My thumb pressed just above the edge of her corset while my other palm kept working—rubbing her through the fabric, coaxing her body to let go.

"You don't have to be strong here," I said against her hair. "You don't have to be anything but mine."

Her breath broke into a soft, desperate whimper.

Good.

That's what I wanted.

Not submission.

Surrender. There's a difference. One is a choice. *The other is instinct.*

Her thighs clenched around my hand. She was shaking. So close. I pressed a kiss to the curve of her neck.

"You're allowed to come for me like this," I whispered. "Messy. Overwhelmed. Turned on when you shouldn't be."

She choked on a breath. Tried to hold it back. And that's when I moved my hand slightly higher. Found the right pressure. The perfect rhythm.

Whispered it again:

"Come for me, Cloe."

Her breath caught.

Her body locked.

Then—release.

Silent. Shattering.

Her head bowed. Her hips trembled. Her thighs clenched hard around my hand and I felt the rush of wet heat even through the layers of fabric.

I held her while she shook.

Held her while she came undone. Held her until her legs

nearly gave out—and even then, I didn't let her fall. I wrapped both arms around her now, turning her in the circle of my chest. Cradling her without softness. Without apology.

She didn't lift her head. Didn't meet my gaze. But she let me hold her. That was enough. For now. I didn't speak. Didn't move. Just held her. Her breath was still unsteady, shoulders rising and falling in sharp little waves like she was trying to pretend she hadn't just come in my arms. That her body hadn't betrayed her pride.

But I knew the truth. I'd felt it. I'd caused it. And I'd do it again.

I reached into the drawer behind me and pulled out a handkerchief.

White. Monogrammed. Still folded from the last time I thought I might need to clean up after someone I shouldn't have touched.

I held it out. She took it with one shaking hand. Pressed it between her legs. Closed her eyes for a second longer than she meant to. But she didn't cry. Not for me. Not yet.

I helped her straighten her blouse. Buttoned the second one from the top myself. My fingers brushed the skin above her corset, and I felt her pulse skip beneath the touch.

Her skirt was still rumpled, her hair a little mussed, but she didn't rush to fix it. She just stood there. Quiet. Raw. Like the silence between us had become something sacred. I reached up and tucked a loose strand of hair behind her ear.

"You did well," I said quietly.

Her throat moved. Like she wanted to speak. But she didn't. She just looked at me. And I saw it then—behind the layers of shame and heat and confusion.

Gratitude. Desire. Something closer to safety than she'd known in weeks.

I stepped back. Not because I wanted to. Because I had to.

Because if I didn't, I'd press her back against the desk and take her anyway. Period or not. And I wasn't going to make this about me. Not tonight.

She adjusted her corset slightly, gave a soft exhale like her body was starting to settle. Then she moved toward the door. Stopped. Looked over her shoulder. Just once.

"I didn't ask for it," she said softly.

I nodded. "I know."

"But I needed it."

I didn't smile. Didn't speak. Just let her have the last word.

She opened the door. Walked out. Closed it quietly behind her.

And I stayed in the room with the scent of her still on my fingers and a pressure in my chest that wouldn't go away.

22

———

CLOE

I woke aching.

Not the kind that fades after sleep. The kind that sits in the ribs. In the thighs. In the space between skin and memory. My body was heavy. Tender. My breath still shallow from the way he bent me.

The way he rubbed me. From the way he said *"mine."*

My throat burned. Not from crying. From silence. From what I hadn't said when he unbuttoned my blouse, when he pressed my own hand to my chest, when he pushed me over the desk and filled me like he'd been holding back a decade of possession.

Barron.

He hadn't kissed me. Hadn't whispered anything sweet. But his touch still lived on my skin like something sacred. Or shameful.

I sat up slowly, careful not to shift too much. The corset still hugged my ribs, loose from earlier. My panties clung to my skin, damp with aftermath. My thighs pressed together.

Reflex.

And I hated how it still made me feel good.

My phone buzzed on the nightstand. I reached for it with a shaky hand. No messages from Wolfe. Nothing from Barron. Just silence. Until a new notification appeared.

UNKNOWN NUMBER:

He's asking about you again.

I stared.

My stomach dropped.

Another ping.

UNKNOWN NUMBER:

He says you owe him something. I told him you were clean. Don't make me a liar.

I froze.

My fingers went numb.

Selene.

She didn't sign it.

She didn't need to.

Another message followed.

UNKNOWN NUMBER:

Get the black book. Or I can't stop him next time.

I couldn't breathe. Not because I didn't know what she meant. Because I did. I knew exactly what black book. And I knew exactly who *"he"* was.

And if Selene was afraid? Then I should be terrified. I sat up slowly. The ache flared again. Between my legs. In my stomach. In my throat. But it wasn't just physical. This was something deeper. Something like grief.

Camille's voice filtered in from a part of me I hadn't touched in months. *You'd never let them turn you into one of us, right?*

I'd laughed when she said it. Sworn I was different. Stronger. More self-aware. And now?

Now I was lying naked in a bed that still smelled like

Wolfe's cologne and Barron's grip. I reached down. Traced the outline of the bruise on my hip. A small mark. Purple-blue. Tender. Proof. That I let them claim me. That I wanted it. And that if I wasn't careful—

I was going to break something much bigger than myself.

I got dressed slowly. Not for seduction. For silence. For survival. The hallway outside Barron's office felt colder than it should've. Everything was polished. Ordered. But it felt like walking through a graveyard.

I moved slow. My heels didn't click this time. I wasn't trying to be seen. I just needed to see it. To know if the code worked. To know if Camille's birthday still lived inside something that should've been sealed shut.

The keypad was still there.

Same brushed steel. Same polished buttons. Same number of digits.

I typed them before I could talk myself out of it.

Click.

Unlocked.

The metal groaned softly as it gave way. Like even the vault didn't want to be opened. My breath caught in my chest. I didn't exhale until I leaned in—and even then, it was shallow. Shaky.

There was no alarm. No red light. No siren screaming, *traitor.*

Just quiet.

And inside, lined in black velvet, the contents sat waiting. Like they'd always known I was coming. The pistol was polished. Wiped clean. The envelope was thick. Stamped. Heavy. The USB flash drive sat coiled beside a key.

And below all of it—

The book.

Black leather.

Worn smooth at the edges.

No markings.

No title.

Just presence.

It looked like it belonged in Barron's hand. Heavy. Private. Final.

I didn't touch it at first.

Just stared.

And for a second, I could almost hear Camille's voice.

Don't let them make you into something you're not.

But I already was. They'd already made me. I reached in. Fingers grazing the leather. But I didn't pull it out. I closed the safe slowly. Buttoned the keypad. Wiped the handle with my sleeve. And walked away.

I didn't take it. But I didn't say I wouldn't.I stood in the bathroom stall again. Same one where Wolfe knelt. Where I bled. Where I'd never be the same. The black book wasn't in my bag. But the weight of it was. Still inside me. Still pressing.

I opened the message thread.

CLOE:

I got it open.

The code worked.

SELENE:

Where is it.

CLOE:

Still in the safe.

I didn't have a chance to grab it.

Barron came in. Almost saw me.

I can't risk that again so soon.

... Three dots.

She was typing.

And typing.

I didn't respond.

Not yet.

I closed the thread. Swiped to Wolfe's name. Hovered. I thought about texting him. Just one line.

I opened the safe. I'm scared.

But I didn't. Because he'd come. And I didn't know what was worse—

Facing Selene alone, or facing Wolfe with the truth.

I locked the screen. Reopened Selene's thread.

Typed.

SELENE:

You've had weeks.

CLOE:

You want it clean, right?

No flags. No audits.

You want out, and I can give it to you.

SELENE:

You have 48 hours.

CLOE:

I need 72.

He's watching me too closely.

All of them are.

SELENE:

60.

Make it look like an accident.

You get caught, don't text again.

I locked my phone. My heart felt like it was going to crack in half. But I'd bought time. Two and a half days. And all I had to do? Was survive inside a house full of men I was already betraying.

I didn't lie. I just didn't tell her how much I wanted to stay. I didn't hear him until it was too late. The soft click of polished shoes behind me. The silence between breaths. I turned too fast, heart in my throat.

Wolfe.

Standing just down the hallway. Hands in his pockets. Jacket half buttoned. Watching me. Like he'd been watching me.

"Long morning?" he asked.

Not cold.

Not warm.

Just... still.

Like he already knew the answer.

I nodded too quickly.

Swallowed.

"Yes."

My voice cracked on the second syllable.

I hated that.

His eyes moved over me—slow. Not the way a man checks a woman out. The way a predator checks for weakness.

"Red looks good on you."

I blinked.

Looked down. Realized my blouse was too tight across the chest. My lips flushed from biting them. My pulse high. I looked guilty. Because I was guilty.

He stepped closer. Not much. Just enough that I had to hold my ground.

"I thought you'd stop shaking after last time," he murmured.

"I'm not shaking."

"You are."

He reached out. Not to touch me. To tuck my hair behind my ear. His fingers brushed the edge of my jaw. Soft. Measured. But it felt like heat bloomed straight through my skin.

I didn't lean in. But I didn't pull back. I just stood there.

Breath caught. Stomach turning. And in that moment, I didn't know what scared me more—

That he might guess what I'd done.

Or that he wouldn't.

His thumb skimmed a strand of hair that fell again.

"Do you need something?" he asked.

The words were gentle. But his eyes weren't. They were waiting. Like he already knew something was buried in my purse. Like he wanted to see if I'd flinch when he said it out loud.

"Do you need something?"

"No," I said too fast.

His eyes narrowed.

"Then why do you look like you just opened a grave?"

I didn't answer. Couldn't. The black book still felt like it was burning through the lining of my purse—even if it wasn't there. Even if it was still locked away.

He stepped even closer.

I stopped breathing.

"You know," he said, voice low, "if something's wrong—"

"I'm fine."

He didn't move. Didn't push. Just nodded once. Then—

"You have until the end of the week."

I froze.

"To what?"

"To figure out who you belong to."

And then he walked away.

Leaving me there.

Shaking.

Still.

Seen.

I stood there long after Wolfe left. Frozen in the hallway like my body had forgotten how to move. Not because of what he said. But because of what he didn't. He hadn't asked what I was hiding. He hadn't threatened to search my bag.

But he didn't have to.

Wolfe didn't need brute force. He only needed time. Because the longer he stared, the more I fractured. The more I wanted to confess just to make it stop. And part of me wanted to give it to him.

The truth.

The book.

The fear.

Because Wolfe doesn't forgive. He takes. And some dark part of me? Wanted to be taken.

Fully.

Burned.

Emptied.

I sat at my desk and opened my laptop, but nothing made sense. Every number blurred. Every word meant less than the last. Because all I could hear was his voice—

You have until the end of the week.

That wasn't a deadline. It was a line in the sand. And no matter which side I chose, someone was going to bleed. Maybe it would be me. Maybe that's what I wanted.

Because at least if I bled, I wouldn't have to choose.

23

―――

CLOE

THE WALK to the café should've been a relief. Ten minutes outside the building. No polished floors. No mirrored walls reflecting the shape of my guilt. No glass office windows with Wolfe's eyes behind them. No knowing glances from Royal that felt like fingers beneath my skirt. No silence from Barron that said more than his voice ever could.

Just air.

Just noise.

Just me.

Pretending I hadn't already betrayed the one man I swore I'd never hurt.

The sky overhead was overcast. Grey and low and close. The kind of sky that made you feel smaller. Lighter. Like you might be lifted off your feet without warning. I wrapped my coat tighter around my body, but it didn't help. The wind still found its way under the hem.

My phone buzzed in my coat pocket. I didn't check it. It was either Selene or Wolfe. And I didn't have the stomach for either of them right now.

The city moved around me in waves. Headlights. Brakes. The scrape of metal chairs on sidewalk concrete. Someone laughing too loud at something that wasn't funny. Every sound felt too sharp. Every face a threat I couldn't name. Every breath I took tasted like I was about to be found out.

I stepped around a man in a navy coat and flinched even though he didn't look at me. I kept walking. Tighter. Smaller.

The note in my hand crumpled slightly in my grip.

Loyal: Black, no sugar.

Royal: Oat flat white, extra hot.

Barron: Double espresso, splash of almond milk.

Wolfe...

Blank.

He never wrote his name on the list. Never told me what to bring. But I always bought him one anyway. Dark roast. One cream. No sugar. Because not doing it felt like forgetting how to breathe. Somehow giving him something—even if he didn't ask —felt like safety. Felt like survival.

I reached the café door and stepped into the warmth. Too warm. The blast of heat was sudden, almost painful against my skin. My corset pinched tighter beneath my coat. My shoulders drew up.

I stepped into line and kept my head down. Didn't look around. Didn't meet anyone's eyes. Because I didn't want to see him.

Not Wolfe.

Not Barron.

Not Royal or Loyal or any man who might see the way my hands shook as I pulled the coat tighter. But especially not him. The one with the scar on his jaw and the voice that could still make my lungs forget how to fill.

I moved up in the line. Handed over the note. The girl at the register smiled too brightly. I smiled back with the corners of my mouth but not my eyes. My phone buzzed again. I ignored it.

The drinks came slowly. Each one read aloud like a name on a gravestone.

Royal—flat white.

Loyal—black.

Barron—espresso.

And the last?

I forced a smile.

"Just dark roast. Cream. For me."

The tray landed in front of me like a sentence I hadn't finished serving yet. I lifted it carefully. Too carefully. Turned away from the counter and moved toward the door. Ten steps. Ten. And I could pretend I was okay.

Just an assistant.

Just bringing coffee.

Not the girl with blood on her conscience and betrayal in her back pocket.

But then—

The air changed. That shift again. Like the city had inhaled and forgotten to exhale. I stopped. And looked up. And there he was. Leaning against the wall just outside the café. Hands in his pockets. Smiling.

Like he hadn't locked me in a bathroom stall and told me to be grateful. Like he hadn't choked me with one hand and whispered *good girl* like it meant something kind. Like he hadn't left bruises that took three weeks to fade.

My stomach twisted. And for the first time in months—

I wanted to run.

He looked almost bored. Like this wasn't planned. Like he just happened to be standing there. Like he hadn't once told me he'd never stop finding me. His jacket was different.

But his eyes?

His eyes weren't.

And that was all it took. My legs turned to water. My mouth went dry. The tray in my hands felt like it had doubled in weight.

He smiled.

Tilted his head. And in that gesture, I remembered everything I didn't want to. The night he kicked the bathroom door open. The crack of it against tile. The echo of the lock breaking. The way he stood over me, bottle in hand, voice low and steady and terrifying.

You make it so hard to love you, baby.

He used to say that with my hair wrapped around his fist.

He used to whisper it when I tried to leave.

When I bled.

When I begged.

My breathing turned shallow. That kind of shallow you feel in your stomach first. Like air is too expensive. I blinked twice.

Don't run. Don't run. Don't run.

He didn't move. Didn't speak. Just stood there. Smiling like he knew I couldn't scream. Like he wanted me to.

I looked down at the coffee tray. Held it tighter. Stepped to the left. Not fast. Not slow. Just enough to move. To survive. I walked past him. Out the café door. Never looking back.

Because if I did—

If I saw even a flicker of what used to live in his smile—

I'd lose what little composure I had left.

His smile widened. Too wide. Teeth too white. That same lazy confidence in the way he leaned against the wall.

I know you.

That's what his body said.

I remember what you sound like when you cry.

That's what his mouth almost whispered.

I couldn't breathe.

The tray wobbled in my hands.

I tightened my grip.

Adjusted the weight.

Didn't blink.

Didn't move.

Didn't fall.

But God, I wanted to run.

He didn't approach. Didn't wave. Didn't say a word. Just scratched his jaw with one hand. And I saw it. That twitch. The one that always came before he said something cruel. Something that hurt.

He's watching you.

That's what Selene said.

What her message didn't type. What the silence in my pocket was still screaming. But now I knew. He wasn't just back. He was close. And I had just walked past him like I was still the girl who hadn't learned how to leave.

He had eyes that never needed words to scare me. And he was using them now. A woman brushed past me on her way out of the café. I moved too late—stepped aside at the last second. Nearly dropped the tray. My heart shot into my throat. My pulse pounded in my ears. But I held it together. Just long enough to get outside.

He was gone.

Not far.

Just not in view.

And somehow, that was worse. Because when you can't see a monster, you start to imagine where it's hiding.

I made it back to the building without spilling a drop.

But my hands?

They didn't stop shaking until long after I'd dropped the coffees on the conference table and locked myself in the bathroom.

The tile was too cold.

My hands were too hot.

The memory of his face still burned behind my eyes like a hand I hadn't dodged in time. I pressed both palms over my chest like that might hold my ribcage together.

My breath came in shallow bursts.

Tight. Controlled. Useless.

I slid to the floor. Sat there. Back to the stall. Knees up. My phone sat on my thigh. Glowing like a dare. I unlocked it.

The thread opened automatically.

SELENE.

Still at the top. Because I hadn't messaged anyone else. Because I hadn't called Wolfe. Because I hadn't told Barron what I'd seen. If I did? Everything would fall apart.

I typed.

He's here.

Paused.

Deleted it.

Typed again.

You said I had 60 hours.

It's only been five.

You sent him early.

Three dots.

Then nothing.

I stared at the screen until my eyes blurred. The bathroom light buzzed overhead. The stall was too quiet. Too sterile. And I was curled in a ball on the floor trying to decide—

Open the book and hand it over? Or slide it under Barron's door and fall to my knees? The phone buzzed once.

Tick. Tick.

The message was short.

I stared at it.

Read it again.

Then typed.

If you wanted me dead, you should've just let him say hello.

No response. None needed. She'd already made her move. Now it was my turn. I stood slowly. Every joint ached.

Like fear had settled into my bones and refused to leave. I washed my hands. Twice. Not because they were dirty. Because they wouldn't stop shaking. I stared at myself in the mirror. Mascara perfect. Lipstick still intact.

The girl in the glass looked fine. Polished. Obedient. Disposable. But inside? I was drowning. And worse? I wanted someone else to pull me under.

Wolfe.

Barron.

Anyone.

Just so I didn't have to pretend I was the one holding the knife. I straightened my blouse. Smoothed down the front. My palms were damp.

There was a small smear of coffee on my wrist I hadn't noticed until just now. I wiped it away. Watched it disappear. Like none of this had happened. Like I wasn't standing in a locked bathroom stall wondering if the man I once called safety would be the one to end me now.

I looked at my reflection. Harder this time. No makeup out of place. No visible bruise. No blood. No guilt. Just bone-deep ache.

And a girl who had no more lines to walk. Only cliffs. I touched the corner of the mirror. It was cold. My breath fogged the glass.

"You're running out of time," I whispered.

24

———

WOLFE

I wake before the alarm. There's never a need for sound. My body doesn't sleep so much as wait. Wait for the light. For the shift in air pressure. For the next crack in my control. There's always tension. Always breath held somewhere between my ribs and my throat. Always silence I don't trust.

The bed is half-made.

The pillow on the right side is untouched.

Always untouched.

It never needs to be fixed.

I used to tell myself I liked it that way. Clean. Cold. Controlled. But some mornings—this morning—

I wonder what she'd look like asleep there.

Cloe.

What her breath would sound like against the cotton. If she'd tangle her legs in the sheets. If she'd flinch when I ran my hand across her hip before she woke. Not for seduction. For reassurance. To feel the difference between restraint and surrender.

I shower without heat.

Let the cold water hit until my pulse slows.

I brush my teeth with one eye on the monitor. She hasn't left yet. Her apartment door is closed. Hallway still dim. The lights in her building always flicker between 5:20 and 5:22 a.m.

This morning? They're late.

So is she.

The espresso machine hisses. I don't drink it. Not yet. I lace my shoes. Step onto the treadmill in my private gym. The screen in front of me is wall-mounted. Four-panel feed. Her building. Her front door. The side alley. The stairwell. The lobby.

No sound.

Just movement.

Just the shape of her absence. I run to the rhythm of my breath and the sight of her hallway. I don't miss a frame. When her light flicks on at 6:42, *I slow the treadmill.*

When her door opens at 6:57—five minutes late—*I stop completely.*

She steps into the hallway like she's being watched. Because she is. Hair in a twist. Blouse wrinkled. Purse clutched like a weapon she doesn't know how to use.

She doesn't wear the ring yet.

But I can feel it.

She's thinking about it.

She touches her collarbone more lately. Taps it with her thumb like there's already a weight there. And maybe there is. Maybe that's what I've become. A phantom collar. A shadow she can't unhook.

She hesitates at the stairwell.

Looks back.

I lean forward.

Closer to the screen.

She doesn't see anything. But I do. The tension in her shoulders. The pulse in her throat. The quiet scream in the way her steps don't echo the same anymore.

She's slipping.

Sliding.

Becoming something I want more than I ever wanted to possess anything. She moves like someone who's already been claimed. Because she has. She just hasn't admitted it yet.

I shower fast. Steam clouds the mirror. Still, I keep the monitor lit on the sink. She pauses by the building entrance.

Looks left.

Looks up.

Looks right at the camera.

Her spine straightens.

She knows.

Not everything. Not the angles. Not the reach of my eyes. But enough. I dry off in silence. Dress in black. Always. Tailored.

Simple.

Exact.

I tuck the ring box into my coat pocket. Black velvet. Garnet center. Silk chain wrapped twice around the cushion. I won't give it to her. Not directly. That would suggest she has a choice. And we're long past that.

The driver doesn't speak when I step into the car. He never does. The windows tint as we pull into traffic. Standard protocol.

The laptop is already on my seat. I open it. She's halfway to work now. Crosses the street at the light. The intersection camera catches it—a smear of lipstick on her teeth. She doesn't notice.

I exhale through my nose.

Not laughter.

Just... something *close*.

She walks like she wants to disappear. But the sidewalk doesn't let her. She's visible now. To more than me. That's the part I hate. That's the part I can't control.

When I arrive at the building, the security team nods. I don't return it. My eyes are on the elevator feed. She's already inside. Fidgeting with the strap of her heel.

Left foot.

She can't reach it.

The clasp is crooked.

I step into the elevator three floors down. Calculate the timing. When I step out, she's just ahead. Bag slung over her shoulder. Hair twisted.

She walks three steps—

Stops.

The strap *slips*.

And the hallway holds its breath.

There are at least six people watching. They say nothing. They don't move. But they feel it. The shift. The moment. And I? I walk straight to her.

I *kneel*. Not quickly. Not performative. Not as if it's routine. But slow. *Intentional*. A man tying his name to someone else's body with a single flick of his fingers.

I fix the strap. Smooth the leather. Press her ankle lightly. And then I look up. Her mouth is parted. Breath caught. Everyone is watching.

But her eyes?

Only on me.

"Next time," I murmur, just for her, "you ask me to do it before it breaks."

She doesn't nod.

But her knees almost buckle.

I work. Watch. But the day means nothing. Nothing but meetings I'm not interested in and men in suits I no longer see.

I only see her.

And when I can't stand that coiling tension inside me anymore, I rise. Close my laptop and leave.

She's working, head down, a tiny furrow of concentration between her brows. My pulse kicks at the sight and my cock grows hard. *Fuck.*

I leave quietly, slipping away like I wasn't here at all. No one is going to miss me, just like they don't see me. A ghost wrapped in darkness. One I've been my entire life.

THE DRIVER PULLS UP behind her apartment building. I issue a command and climb out. All I'm focussed on now is the door to her apartment, and the faint trace of her she left behind.

She left the window unlocked again.

Top left corner of the frame warped just slightly—enough that if I press with two fingers and lift, the latch clicks free.

The building's cameras won't catch me.

I had them redirected the night she first smiled at Loyal like she didn't know what it meant. It's not the first time I've been here. She doesn't know that. She doesn't know I've counted the steps between her bed and the bathroom. That I know how she folds her towels—wrong, always. That the ones she hides in the back are softer. More worn.

Her apartment smells like her skin.

Lavender soap.

Linen.

Something sweeter.

Faint. Like a secret only I know.

It hits me the second I step inside. Settles into my chest. Makes me walk slower. I don't touch much. Not because I couldn't.

But because I don't need to anymore. She's already mine. She just hasn't said it out loud. I walk through the kitchen. Check the drawers.

There's a black box of tea she hides behind the coffee. The cheap kind. The kind she drinks only when she's overwhelmed. It's half empty. The second drawer in her dresser is open a crack.

That's where I slide the ring box. Black velvet. Folded. Simple. The garnet is cold when I place it inside. It catches the light like a heartbeat cut from stone. I don't leave a note. But I think about it. I think about writing:

This is yours. But you wear it for me.

I don't. She'll know.

I walk to the side table beside her bed.

There's a book she's only halfway through.

The bookmark is a torn receipt. The last chapter she read is underlined in pencil—something about secrets and survival. I don't read further. Because she doesn't survive this. She doesn't survive me.

The curtains are half drawn. She always leaves them that way. Like she's daring the night to watch. Like she wants to be seen. I don't need permission. I run my hand along the headboard. Not because I'm imagining her bent there. I've seen that. I've made her feel it. What I'm imagining now? Is her asleep here. Wearing the ring.

Wearing nothing else.

I fix the latch on the window before I leave. Let her believe she's safe. Let her believe she's alone. Let her dream she's in control. She'll find the ring in the morning. Slip it on with trembling fingers. And when she does? She won't take it off.

I don't sleep well. Haven't in years. Not since Camille. Not since Selene smiled like she meant it and took everything we gave her straight to a lawyer.

Not since I started watching Cloe breathe through a four-panel feed like it was the only prayer I still remembered the words to.

She doesn't know what I've done for her.

How many threats I've intercepted before she ever stepped into this building. How many men I've paid off. How many names I've erased. How many lines I've crossed. And I don't want her to know.

Not yet. Because the moment she finds out she's not just protected—but caged?

She'll hate me.

And I'll let her.

So long as she keeps wearing the ring.

11:34 p.m.

Her building lights dim.

The camera feed shifts to grayscale. I see her outline in the stairwell—tiny, alone, carrying too many bags. She doesn't lift her head. Doesn't check the corners. She forgets she's prey. But I don't.

Midnight. The hallway outside her apartment is still. No motion. No sound. Just her door. Closed. Unmarked. But behind it?

The drawer.

The ring.

I send the first message at 12:03 a.m.

You left the ring in the drawer.

I saw it.

I don't need her to read it now.

She'll see it when she wakes. She'll feel it when she brushes her fingers over the silk chain and thinks about me slipping it over her head.

12:07.

You don't lock your window.

Next time, I won't ask to come in.

12:11.

I delete a draft before I send it.

It said:

I almost stayed tonight.

I erase it because that's not how this works.

Not with her.

Not with me.

12:15.

Last one.

Over your heart.

Or not at all.

I set my phone down. Turn off the lights. Stretch out on the couch—not the bed. Never the bed.

And I watch the glow of her apartment door on my screen until my eyes blur. The plant in the corner is dying. Again. I water it anyway. Because sometimes, even things that won't live deserve a little care before they give up.

She walks into the office at 9:03 a.m.

Three minutes late.

I don't care.

Because when she passes my glass wall, she's wearing it. The blouse is silk again. Blush-colored. Fitted. Too sheer to hide what matters.

The ring hangs just beneath the neckline—garnet catching faint light like it knows I'm watching.

She doesn't look up. But she knows. I wait until lunchtime. Let her sweat. Let her shift in her chair, legs crossed too tight, fingers tapping the desk like she can drum her nerves away.

At 12:04, I send the message.

Office. Now.

No subject.

No punctuation.

She replies in less than ten seconds.

Yes.

She knocks once before entering.

Doesn't speak.

Closes the door behind her. Stands in front of me like she's already learned how to breathe quiet. Like she's ready to obey.

Good girl.

"Undo the top two buttons," I say.

She hesitates.

Then does.

One.

Two.

The chain gleams.

Thin.

Dark.

Delicate against her throat.

The garnet rests just above her sternum, like it was made to press against the beat of her heart. Because it was.

I step forward.

Reach.

Hook one finger under the chain.

Lift.

Not hard.

Just enough to make her tilt her chin.

"You wore it."

She nods once. Eyes wide. Unblinking. I circle her slowly. My hand never leaves the chain. It moves with her. Across her shoulder. Down her back. Like a leash she hasn't been trained to pull against.

"Why?"

Her breath catches.

"I..."

She swallows. Because she doesn't know how to say it. Because there's no good answer. Only the truth.

"Say it."

"I wanted to."

"Louder."

"I wanted to wear it for you."

I hum softly.

Good girl.

I tug the chain gently.

She follows.

I press her back against the glass wall.

Lift her skirt.

Push her panties to the side.

Slide two fingers along her slit—*slow*.

She gasps.

But she doesn't move.

Her eyes close. Her head falls back against the glass. I wrap the chain around my fist.

Tighten.

"Say thank you."

She shudders.

"Thank you."

"Again."

"Thank you."

I curl my fingers. Watch her unravel. One breath at a time. She's soaked. Wrecked. Almost silent. Until she breaks.

When she comes, I don't speak. I just let go of the chain. Let it fall back against her chest. Tuck the ring beneath her blouse. Button the top slowly.

One.

Two.
Step back.
"You hide it again..."
I pause.
Wait for her eyes to open.
"...and I'll make you wear it naked."

I REBUTTONED my blouse with trembling fingers. Each button was a lie. A soft click of denial meant to hide the heat still blooming beneath my skin.

The chain sat heavy against my chest.

Slick with sweat.

Weighted with Wolfe.

I didn't dare touch it. Didn't dare fix the collar or brush my fingers over the garnet where it pulsed in the hollow of my sternum. It felt alive. Branded. He hadn't kissed me. Hadn't said a word once I came. He'd just watched.

Then sat back at his desk. Like he hadn't just wrecked me. Like he hadn't just slid two fingers inside me while wrapping a chain around his fist. His voice had been quiet the whole time.

No praise.

No command beyond "Say thank you."

And now?

Now I had to walk into the hallway. With damp lace and pulsing thighs and the ghost of his hand still cupped between my legs. My heels clicked too sharply on the floor. Every sound felt like guilt. Like a siren that screamed, *she let him.*

Royal looked up first. He always does. He didn't smirk—not fully. But the corner of his mouth tilted just enough. He raised his coffee cup in a mock salute.

"Mornin', sweetness."

My cheeks burned. I didn't reply. Didn't break stride. Even as my skin buzzed and my knees betrayed me.

Loyal passed by me near the corner glass. His eyes flicked downward. To my collar. He saw it.

The faint shimmer of the chain. The outline of something that hadn't been there yesterday. His mouth tightened. His hand curled tighter around the file he was holding. He said nothing. Didn't have to. He's always been quiet in ways that cut.

I walked faster. But it didn't help. Every inch of fabric clung to me now. Wet between my legs. Sticky across my thighs.

The silk of my blouse stretched taut across flushed skin still humming from Wolfe's voice. The panties I hadn't fixed were riding up. The corset had shifted. Too tight now. Too high.

I couldn't breathe. But I couldn't stop. The hallway narrowed as I reached the bullpen. People looked up. Not everyone. But enough. Enough to feel like the walls were closing in. Enough to make me want to pull the ring from the chain and swallow it whole just to keep it secret.

I reached my desk and sat carefully. Too carefully. The chair was cold. Unforgiving. It pressed against the ache between my thighs like it knew. Like it wanted to remind me. I didn't cry. Didn't shake. Didn't fall apart. But my hands? They stayed in my lap for five full minutes before I could type again.

And still—

I didn't look back. Because I already knew Wolfe was

watching. And I didn't trust myself not to say thank you all over again. Barron's office door was half open when I looked up. I hadn't seen him step in. Didn't hear him arrive.

But now he was there—back to the hallway, blazer already off, shirtsleeves rolled to his elbows, collar open just enough to make the whole room feel warmer.

I tried to look away. Tried to focus on the report in front of me. But his hand moved—just once. Two fingers. *A beckon.* Nothing more. But I was already standing.

The walk to his office felt longer than it should have. Every step heavier. Like the ring at my chest had somehow fused to the skin beneath it. I knocked once. He didn't answer. Just looked up from his desk. So I entered. Closed the door behind me.

"Sit."

His voice wasn't cruel. Wasn't warm either. Just steady. Tired in a way that sounded dangerous.

I sat in the chair across from him. Straight-backed. Hands in my lap. The chain under my blouse pressed into my skin like a burn I couldn't reach. He didn't speak. Didn't move. Just watched me. For too long.

"You look tired," he said finally.

I blinked.

"Didn't sleep well," I answered.

Honest.

Almost.

His eyes flicked to my blouse. Stayed there a second too long. The silk wasn't quite smooth. The faint shape of the chain beneath it was... impossible not to see if you were looking for it. And he was.

"Was it him?"

The words landed like glass shattering in slow motion. I

didn't respond. Couldn't. He leaned forward. Hands clasped. Still calm. Still.

"Did he touch you?"

I didn't flinch. But I didn't lie either. And that was the problem. His eyes darkened. Not with rage. Not with jealousy. With something worse. Recognition. He stood. Slow. Deliberate.

Walked around the desk and leaned against it, arms crossed.

"You're wearing something," he said.

A statement. Not a question. I opened my mouth. Closed it. He nodded. Once. Sharp.

"You think I don't see what's happening. But I do."

He stepped forward. Close enough to feel. Not touch. Not yet.

"I told myself I wouldn't ask. I told myself I didn't care."

He exhaled. But it wasn't relief. It was surrender.

"Then you walked in here smelling like him."

I didn't speak. What could I say? That Wolfe had made me thank him with a chain in my throat? That I wore the ring and came so hard my body forgot its own name?

Barron didn't raise his voice.

Didn't pace.

Didn't threaten.

Just asked:

"Do you want him?"

And God help me—

I didn't know the answer. I didn't cry when I left Barron's office.

Not when he looked at me like he'd just tasted the edge of someone else's knife. Not when he said nothing after asking if I wanted Wolfe. Not when I closed the door behind me and walked out like I wasn't already bleeding from everything I couldn't say. But by the time I got to the bathroom? My hands were shaking.

I locked the stall. Sat down hard on the lid, heart pounding, skin flushed, the ring at my chest suddenly too tight. I pulled out my phone. I didn't want to.

But I had to. Because I knew. I knew she wouldn't wait much longer. Sure enough—two messages. Selene. Time-stamped ten minutes apart.

I didn't open them right away. Just stared at the screen. Wolfe's name was still above hers in my threads. I hadn't opened that one in hours. Not since the last message he sent.

You don't lock your window.

Next time, I won't ask to come in.

My stomach twisted.

I opened Selene's thread.

Midnight.

Or it's over.

Photo attached. I didn't want to look. But I did. It was him. The ex.

Leaning against a lamppost on a side street I recognized too well. Two blocks from the building. Hands in his coat pockets. Eyes on the camera. Smiling.

You know how he gets when he's hungry, Selene wrote.

Don't make me let him off the leash.

My fingers went numb. The screen blurred. And for a second, I didn't know where I was. I could smell him again. The inside of his car. The stale cigarette smoke he never let me ask him to stop.

The aftershave he used to rub into my skin when he said I smelled like someone else. I almost threw up. I dropped the phone onto the floor and braced my hands on my knees.

Breathed.

Hard.

In.

Out.

Once.

Twice.

"You've made it this far," I whispered.

"Don't fall now."

I picked the phone back up.

Typed.

Deleted.

Typed again.

I need more time.

Wolfe's watching everything.

Barron hasn't let me out of his sight in three days.

... three dots appeared.

Paused.

Then she typed again.

Midnight.

Or I tell him where to find you.

That was it. I locked the phone. Pressed it to my chest. And whispered the only thing I had left.

"I'm sorry."

To Wolfe. To Barron. To Camille. To the girl I used to be.

The message was still on the screen.

Midnight. Or I tell him where to find you.

I stared at it like it might vanish.

Like maybe if I didn't move, didn't blink, didn't breathe—

Selene would disappear.

The threat would dissolve.

The weight of the book would stop burning in the pit of my gut.

But it didn't. It never does. My throat clenched. My ribs folded inward. And I lurched forward just in time to grab the edge of the toilet.

The vomit came fast. Sharp. Bitter. Burning like shame. *Like lies.*

Like fear so thick it finally found a way out. When it was over, I sat back on the floor. Wiped my mouth with the sleeve of my blouse.

The silk stuck to my skin. Still damp with sweat from Wolfe's office. Still flushed from his fingers. Still wet between my thighs from a chain I hadn't taken off since he looped it around me and whispered *say thank you.* I pressed the back of my head to the tile wall.

Cold.

Unforgiving.

Exactly what I deserved.

I'd never felt this broken. Not when my ex called me a burden.Not when Camille looked at me like I might be the reason she stopped believing in good things. Not even when I stepped into this building for the first time knowing full well that I was already prey. Because now? Now I'd tasted power.

I'd tasted Wolfe's obsession. Barron's rage. Royal's games. Loyal's silence. And I liked all of it. Too much. And I still might give them up.

The ring at my chest felt heavier now. Not like jewelry. Like evidence. Of where I'd been. Of who I'd let touch me. Of what I was about to destroy. I pulled the chain from beneath my blouse. Stared at it.

The garnet caught the light like it remembered blood. I wanted to throw it in the toilet. I wanted to swallow it whole. I wanted to keep it on forever. I thought about going to Barron. About opening his office door and dropping the truth like a bomb.

"Selene sent him."

"He's watching me."

"I opened the safe."

"I know the code."

"I didn't take it—yet."

But I didn't move. Because what if they looked at me like I was dirt? What if they stopped watching me? What if they never touched me again? And worse? What if they still did? Even knowing everything?

I didn't trust myself not to say yes. Not to crawl to one of them. Not to beg. For pain. For punishment. For the kind of ruin I already knew how to survive.

So I sat. On the floor. In the stall. Phone in my lap. Chain in my hand. Body still aching. And whispered the one truth I hadn't admitted yet—

"I want them more than I want to be forgiven."

26

———

CLOE

The city never feels quiet.

But tonight?

It was dead. No horns. No music.

Not even the usual shuffle of feet near my building's entrance. Just the sound of my own boots against concrete. The whisper of my coat collar rustling against my neck.

And the high-pitched whine of panic still ringing somewhere behind my ribs. The air was colder than I expected. It wrapped around my legs and slid under the hem of my coat like it had teeth.

The streets felt too wide.

The shadows too long.

I kept my phone in my hand the entire walk. Didn't check it. Didn't look at the screen. Just held it like maybe it would shield me if something went wrong.

I hadn't heard from Selene. Not at midnight. Not the morning after. Not all day. And somehow, that was worse. The absence wasn't mercy. It was threat. The kind of silence you get right before something bad happens. The kind of stillness animals feel before the snare snaps shut.

I walked faster. Not running. But close. Head down. Eyes sharp. I passed two people near the crosswalk. Didn't look at them. They didn't look at me. But my skin still crawled. Like maybe one of them knew something I didn't. Like maybe everyone did.

I reached the building. Didn't take the elevator. Couldn't. Couldn't stand the idea of doors closing behind me. Of being trapped. Of not being able to run. I climbed the stairs. One floor. Then another.

By the third, my legs started to burn. By the fifth, my breath was catching. By the seventh? My hand shook on the railing. But I didn't stop. I didn't look back. I just climbed.

And when I reached the top? I knew. Something was off. The hallway was too dim. One of the lights near my door had burned out. Or been smashed. It crunched under my boot when I stepped on the shards.

I stopped walking. Just for a second. Just long enough to listen. But there was nothing. No footsteps. No voices. No creak of wood or groan of metal. Just the hum of panic clawing up my spine.

I reached for my keys. Dropped them. Swore under my breath and bent to retrieve them with shaking fingers. The lock turned harder than usual. Like something inside didn't want to let me in.

I stepped inside. Flicked on the light. Everything looked the same. The coat on the hook. The soft yellow glow above the kitchen sink. The pillow I always left slightly askew on the couch. Normal. But nothing felt normal.

I stood just inside the door too long. Breathing like someone had punched the wind out of me. Tried to move. To lock the door. To set the chain.

But then I felt it.

Not a touch.

Not a sound.

Just... *a breath.*

Behind me.

Close.

Too close.

Before I could turn—

An arm wrapped around my throat. Hard. Yanked me backward.

I slammed into a chest that didn't belong to anyone I trusted. Fingers dug into the side of my neck. A hand clamped over my mouth. My phone dropped. Clattered to the floor.

"Time's up."

The voice was low. Filtered. Distorted. But the intent behind it? Crystal clear. Selene. Her silence. Her money. Her warning. He dragged me into the hallway. Slammed me into the wall.

My shoulder cracked against the plaster hard enough to jar my teeth. I tried to scream. Tried to fight. But his grip only tightened. His mask was black. Smooth. Just two holes for his eyes. No mouth. No name. Just threat.

"The book," he hissed.

"You know where it is."

I shook my head. Tried to twist away. His hand flattened harder against my mouth.

"This was your warning."

He leaned closer. Breath hot against my ear.

"Next time, I don't leave you breathing."

I kicked back. Hard. Felt something shift. He grunted. His grip slipped.

It wasn't enough to break free, but it was enough to bite.

And I did. Hard. Felt fabric tear. Felt skin give. Tasted metallic. Blood.

He threw me forward like garbage. I hit the floor. Face-first. My lip split open. The rug scraped my cheek raw. My shoulder lit with pain—white hot and immediate.

I curled. Instinct. Fetal. Frozen. Too late to stop the ache. Too early to process the fear.

He stood above me for one more second. Watching. Measuring. Then he turned. Walked out. No rush. No fear. Just satisfaction. Like a message had been delivered. Like a job half-finished. The door was still open. Swaying slightly. The night air creeping in.

I didn't move. Didn't speak. Didn't even try to breathe right. Because if I did? I'd scream.

And I didn't know how to stop it once it started. My mouth filled with copper. Blood. My lip was split. My face stung. My shoulder pulsed like it had its own heartbeat.

But that wasn't what made me sick. It was the way he moved. Like he knew the layout. Like he knew I'd be alone. I had been. I'd let myself believe it was over. That Selene had changed her mind. That Wolfe had scared her into silence. But this? This was her answer.

I pushed onto my side. Every inch of me throbbed. My knees. My ribs. My throat.

He'd squeezed hard. So hard. Like he'd been trained. Like he knew the exact threshold between fear and collapse.

But the worst part? How quiet he'd been. How efficient. How calm. No yelling. No chaos. Just a whisper and a threat. I rolled onto my knees. Crawled toward the door.

I needed air. I needed space. I needed—

Something cracked behind me. Sharp. Loud. I screamed. Whipped around. Nothing.

But the vase on the side table? Shattered. My elbow must've

caught it. I didn't remember. Didn't care. I tried to stand. My vision spun. A handprint was still pressed into my arm. Purple. Too clear.

I didn't remember when he grabbed me there. Didn't remember anything after the slam. I reached the front door. Closed it with both hands. Locked the bolt. Then the chain. Then backed away like it might come alive and open again.

I turned to face the room. Everything looked normal. But it wasn't. The air was heavier. The space tighter. Like he'd taken something with him I couldn't name.

I ran to the kitchen.

Fumbled in the drawer.

Pulled a knife.

Dropped it.

It skittered across the floor.

Loud. Wrong.

I picked it up. Pressed my back to the wall. Shaking. My hands. My knees. My voice. Something flickered under the front door.

A shadow.

No.

No no no no no—

I ran to the couch.

Curled into the far corner.

Held the knife to my chest like a shield I didn't know how to use.

My heartbeat was too loud.

Too wild.

The sound of blood in my ears drowned everything else.

Until—

The door shook.

Once.

Twice.

A third time.

Then—*shattered.*

And I screamed.

The sound echoed.

Splintered wood.

My scream.

Then silence.

No footsteps. No rush of movement. Just cold air bleeding in through the jagged break in the door.

I didn't move. Couldn't. The knife was still clutched in my hand, but my grip had loosened. My fingers ached from how tightly I'd held it. My lungs refused to expand.

I stayed frozen in the corner of the couch, blinking against the tears that blurred everything.

Then—

Memory.

Too fast.

Too sharp.

The ex.

His fingers around my throat. Not a stranger. Not a mask. But worse. His voice calm. His tone flat.

The way he pressed me against the bathroom wall. *You like this, don't you?* My vision went grey.

I'd fought then too.

Kicked.

Bit.

But he'd held me down by the throat like it didn't matter if I said no.

Like my fear was foreplay. Like my tears meant he was winning. I gasped now, dragged in air too fast. It scraped down my throat like glass.

I tried to blink the past away. Tried to ground myself. I

looked at my phone. Still on the coffee table. Still lit. Still untouched.

No new messages.

No Wolfe.

No Loyal.

No Barron.

No one coming. The door didn't open again. But the splinter down the frame said it could have. That it still might.

I stood on shaky legs. Stumbled to the hallway. Locked the bedroom door. Then the closet. Then the window. Everything.

Then I slid down the back of the door, knees pulled to my chest. The knife on the floor beside me. My head pressed to the wood.

Tears finally came.

Quiet.

Helpless.

Hot.

I rocked.

Back and forth.

Because that's what Camille used to do when I broke down. Because it was the only thing I remembered from before everything got sharp.

I wanted Wolfe. Wanted him like a prayer. Not to hold me. Not to save me. But to see me. To know what I'd survived. To know I was still surviving.

My hands trembled. The garnet ring still pressed into the skin above my heart like a bruise. The chain felt heavier now. Like a leash I didn't know if I was still allowed to wear. I pressed my forehead to my knees.

Breathed.

Breathed.

Breathed.

And whispered—

"Don't come back."

I didn't know if I meant the man who broke in.

Or me.

I didn't fall asleep. Not really. But I must've lost time. The kind of time that comes after trauma—when everything blurs around the edges and your body tries to pretend none of it happened. But it had.

The door was still splintered. The lock still useless.

My shoulder still throbbed with every breath. I pulled myself off the floor. Wobbled toward the broken frame. Stared at it like it might apologize. It didn't.

I turned. Looked at the couch. The knife was gone. Or maybe I dropped it again and didn't remember.

A noise echoed down the hall. Small. Soft. Maybe nothing. Maybe everything. My body reacted first.

I ran.

Slammed the bedroom door. Turned the lock with shaking fingers. I backed away, hit the closet, stumbled. The memory still bloomed in the corners of my mind like a bruise that wouldn't fade. His voice. His hand. That final whisper:

Next time, I don't leave you breathing.

I couldn't breathe now. I dropped to my knees beside the bed. Not to hide. To survive.

My hand found the frame. Gripped it. I tried to scream. Nothing came out. My throat seized. Clogged. Swollen with panic. I tried again. Help. Someone help. Please—

"Wolfe!"

It tore from me. Raw. Violent. Desperate.

It wasn't planned. It wasn't conscious. It was instinct. The only name I trusted to answer. The only name that felt like safety—even when he wasn't safe. Even when I didn't know what he would do. Even if it was already too late.

I clutched the edge of the bed. Whimpered into the fabric.

My shoulders shook. Tears soaked the blanket. But no one came. No one answered. And I felt the truth settle low in my chest like a second heart. I'd screamed for a man who didn't know I needed saving. Because I didn't trust anyone else to hear me.

Not Barron.

Not Royal.

Not even Loyal.

Just Wolfe.

I curled tighter. Fingers clenched. Voice gone. But I whispered again anyway.

"Wolfe..."

And if someone had been listening from the hallway? They'd know exactly whose name I bled for.

I didn't sleep. I sat at the edge of Wolfe's bed with the black book in my lap like it was a live wire. I hadn't meant to take it. But when I passed his office, and the hallway was dark, and no one was watching—I did. Camille's birthday still lived in the code. And now the book lived in me.

My fingers trembled as I opened the cover. Names. Dates. Wire transfers. Blackmail. A history of every sin the Lawlors never wanted written down.

Camille's name was there once. Faint. Crossed out. I wanted to burn it. I wanted to give it to Selene. I wanted to hide it under the floorboards and pretend it never existed.

But what I did instead?

I wrapped it in the silk blouse Barron sent me. Tied it with the ribbon Wolfe once told me to keep around my throat. And I locked it in Wolfe's drawer. Not to hide it. To return it.

He'd find it. And he'd know I chose him. Chose all of them. Even if they never forgave me. Even if I never forgave myself. I didn't save myself. I just stopped running.

27

———

WOLFE

The feed glitched. Just for a second.

A flicker. A shadow.

Barely a movement on the second angle—hallway cam, Cloe's floor.

But I saw it.

A shape. Close to her door. Closer than anyone had a right to be.

The elevator button blinked once. Then went dark. Out of service.

"What the fuck—" I slammed the call button.

No response. No hum. No flicker.

Just silence.

I didn't wait. Didn't think. Didn't breathe. I hit the stairwell door with my shoulder and launched upward—two steps, three at a time. My hand scraped along the metal railing as I climbed, faster than my body could keep up with.

My lungs burned. But it wasn't the stairs. It was *her*. Something was wrong. *That feeling...* the one I'd learned to trust in war zones and interrogation rooms. The one that whispered *too quiet, too still, too late.*

Each floor I passed dragged a blade through my chest.

Second.

Third.

Fourth.

Run.

Fifth.

Faster.

Sixth.

My heart was already a war drum. The kind that only beats when something you love is about to be stolen.

Seventh.

Her floor.

I hit the landing hard—feet barely catching grip on the tile. My eyes snapped to her door. Still closed. But the frame? Splintered. Fresh wood. Shards near the lock. Someone had forced it. My blood turned to ice. Then fire.

MOVE.

I punched the access code into the panel.

Wrong keypress.

"Fuck!"

My hand shook.

Blood smeared across the touchscreen as I tried again.

Green light.

The door clicked. I didn't open it gently. I kicked it open with enough force to snap the lock. The impact echoed through the hall behind me—but I didn't hear it.

I was already inside. Already in the dark. Already seeing everything.

Silence.

Thick.

Wrong.

Like the air had collapsed.

Glass glittered across the hardwood. A vase smashed. A chair flipped on its side like someone had tried to run—or been thrown.

But it wasn't the mess that stopped me.

It was her.

Cloe.

On the floor.

Half-curled. Barely moving. Her body tucked tight like she was trying to fold into herself and disappear. Her arms were around her head. Her legs drawn in. Too still. Too quiet. My heart fucking stopped. No sound. No breath. No sign of life. Just her, crumpled like a doll someone had thrown down too hard.

"Cloe."

My voice broke around her name. Cracked open like it didn't belong to me.

She didn't move.

Didn't flinch.

Didn't lift her head.

Oh fuck—*no.*

No no no.

I dropped. Knees slammed into the floor. Glass cut through the fabric of my pants. I didn't feel it. Didn't care. I crawled to her. Reached out.

"Cloe," I said again, quieter this time. My voice shook.

She still didn't look up. Her whole body was trembling. Not from cold. From fear. The kind you don't come back from. I touched her arm. Light. Careful. Like she might shatter if I moved too fast.

She flinched.

Hard.

Pulled away.

Like *I* was him.

Like *she* couldn't tell the difference.

I froze.

Fuck. Fuck.

I'd seen this before. On the battlefield. In black sites. In places where screams were currency.

But *never* like this.

Never her.

She smelled like blood and sweat and something worse—*fear*. The kind that seeps into your bones and stays there.

"Cloe," I whispered. *It's" me."*

She didn't answer. Didn't lift her head. Didn't speak. But she started to cry. No sobs. No sound. Just tears. Streaming down her bruised face like they'd been waiting for someone safe enough to fall for. Then—finally—she looked up. And I broke. Her lip was bleeding. Her eye already swelling. There were scratches on her collarbone. The side of her blouse was torn.

"Wolfe?"

Her voice cracked. So did something inside me.

"Yeah." I moved closer. "It's me. You're okay. I've got you."

She winced. Her arm shifted. She tried to sit up but gasped—*ribs*.

I caught her before she could fall forward. Held her. Her breath was short and uneven, her hands clutching the chain still around her neck like it was the only thing tethering her to this world.

"What happened?" I asked, barely managing to keep my voice steady.

She shook her head.

"I don't know," she whispered. "He was there and then—gone. I think I... I passed out."

A lie.

I knew it.

But I didn't press. She was shaking too hard.

"Okay," I said. "Okay, baby. I've got you."

I slid one arm under her knees. The other around her back. Lifted her carefully—like she was made of glass. Like every breath might be the last one she trusted me with. She gasped again. A small cry escaped before she could bite it down. Her fingers clutched my jacket.

"Where are we going?"

I didn't look at her.

Didn't blink.

Didn't hesitate.

"The fuck out of here."

She weighed nothing. Or maybe I didn't feel the weight.

All I could feel was the sound of her breath against my chest—ragged, shallow, broken. Her arms around my neck were barely there. Her grip too weak. Too tentative. Like she wasn't sure if I was real.

Like she didn't know if this was over. It wasn't. Not for me. Not until someone bled.

I carried her through the hallway. Past the broken door. Down the stairs, fast but careful, her body curled into mine like it was the only safe place left.

I didn't speak. Didn't look back. Didn't let myself feel anything but the anchor of her heartbeat, faint as it was, against my ribs.

The Audi waited at the curb, door still open. Engine humming. Headlights slicing the dark.

I slid her inside, lowered the seat, adjusted her carefully against the leather. Buckled her in. Her lashes fluttered. She looked at me like she didn't recognize this version of me. Neither did I.

I shut the door and rounded the front. Once inside, I

shifted the car into gear. No music. No words. Just the sound of the city falling away behind us.

When I reached the garage beneath my apartment, I didn't wait for the gate to finish rising. I nosed the car through with an inch to spare, braked hard enough to jolt her seat.

She whimpered.

I cursed under my breath. "I'm sorry."

But sorry didn't mean anything right now. Not when I'd let this happen. Not when I should've stopped it before it began.

I helped her out, carried her again—she didn't resist. Not once. Didn't speak. Didn't cry. Just pressed her face to my neck like maybe, just maybe, I could keep her safe this time.

Inside, I laid her gently on the bed. Pulled a blanket over her. Turned out the lights. Then I left. Walked straight into the kitchen. Pulled my phone from my pocket. Blood still streaked the knuckles from when I punched the access panel. I unlocked the screen. No hesitation.

To: Mason Quinn

Surveillance. Extraction. Recon.

Someone got into her apartment last night. He touched her. Find him.

I didn't move. Just stared at the screen.

... three dots.

Typing.

Then—

Understood.

I typed again.

Don't touch him. Not until I get there.

It cost me to send that. Cost me every ounce of control I had left. I wanted to destroy him. Now. Tonight. But I needed intel first. I stared at the floor for a long moment. Then picked up the phone again.

To: Royal

"Come to the penthouse. Now."

He picked up on the third ring.

"Tell me you didn't do something stupid."

"I need you to stay with her."

A pause.

"You're not asking Barron?"

"No."

"Good. He'd never let you live it down."

"I know."

"Alright. I'm on my way. Don't burn the city down before I get there."

I didn't answer. Didn't need to. He heard it in my silence. In the crackling fury barely held beneath my voice. The room was dark. Royal had arrived—quiet, sharp-eyed, a bottle of wine in one hand and a gun in the other.

He said nothing when I let him in. Didn't comment on the bruise on her cheek or the chain still tangled in her collarbone. He just looked at me. Then nodded once. And took a seat beside the bed like a man ready to kill anyone who got too close.

I left them there. Walked into my office. Closed the door. Turned on the feed. The screen flared to life. Playback. Angle two. Her hallway.

I fast-forwarded. Reversed. Watched the frame-by-frame shift in light.

There.

A figure.

Dark. Hooded. Masked.

Moving past the elevator. Toward her door.

He shouldn't have been there. She shouldn't have been home. But she was. And he knew it. He didn't hesitate. He didn't knock. He just entered.

And then—

Her.

Frozen on the screen. Caught mid-step. The moment before fear takes over. Before instinct replaces thought. She turned. Said something. No sound.

The man lunged.

I saw her fall. Felt it like a gunshot to the chest. Her body hit the floor. Arms up. Knees in. Trying to protect herself with the same hands that had once held me like I was safe.

I stopped the feed. Just stared at that frame. Her body, curled and still.

My fault. Every inch of it. Every bruise. Every breath she didn't take right after.

I stood so fast my chair slammed backward into the wall. I didn't notice. Didn't care. I grabbed my coat. *My keys.*

The rage came quiet this time. Not a scream. Not a roar. But a calm, *brutal* hum.

I got in the Audi. Turned the engine over once. Then slammed the gas. The tires shrieked across the concrete. I didn't slow. Didn't check the mirrors. Didn't blink. Every second she was hurt pulsed like a countdown in my chest.

I ran the first red light. Didn't care. A car honked—sharp and useless.

I swerved around it, tires burning rubber. The scent of smoke filled the cabin. Another light. I didn't stop. Didn't see the truck until too late—metal scraped along the side of the Audi. A scream of steel. A mirror ripped off. Didn't stop. Didn't fucking stop. Because in my head, she was still on that floor. Still bleeding. Still whispering my name like it might save her.

I hit the next corner too fast.The tires lost grip. The car spun once, clipped a barricade, jolted hard enough to make the airbag alert scream.

I didn't let it deploy. Didn't let anything stop me. I needed blood. I needed a name. I needed a body at my feet and the world to know:

You don't touch what's mine and breathe afterward.

I skidded to a stop outside Mason's facility. The Audi door flung open. My boots hit pavement.

Fast.

Hard.

Every muscle in my body screaming—

Not with pain. But with purpose.

28

———

CLOE

I woke to silence.

Not the kind I was used to. Not the kind that made the world feel far away. This silence was built. It felt like protection. Like someone had put it there for me. Like someone had fought to keep it.

The sheets beneath me were too smooth. Too crisp. They didn't smell like detergent. They smelled like him. That sharp, clean mix of cedar and cold. A scent I'd only caught in passing before—brushed against in the hallway, lingering in his office.

Now it was wrapped around me like a second skin. The bed was too big. The mattress barely dipped beneath my weight. Like no one had ever slept on this side before.

I turned my head. Looked at the other half. Untouched. The pillows still fluffed. Perfect. Like he hadn't even dared to lie down. I swallowed. Hard. The bruise on my cheek pulsed. Not sharp. Just constant. A dull throb that tugged at the corner of my mouth when I tried to move it.

I licked my lips. Tasted blood I didn't remember. Wolfe's shirt clung to me. Soft. Too soft. The sleeves hung past my wrists. The hem brushed mid-thigh. It smelled like him too. I didn't know if it made me feel safe or sick.

Everything ached when I sat up slowly. My ribs. My shoulders. My thighs. The space between my legs where Wolfe had once touched me like a secret. And now? Now that same body curled in on itself like it didn't know how to move anymore.

The hallway was dim. Muted light filtered through the blinds. Warm. Unfamiliar.

Something smelled like coffee. I padded barefoot to the doorway. The floors were cold. Too clean. Like no one actually lived here. Like the apartment was curated—not used.

He was in the kitchen. Barefoot. Dark shirt. Tablet in one hand. Coffee in the other. I froze in the archway. He didn't look up right away. Then—

"Morning, bruise girl."

I flinched. Not because it hurt. Because I hadn't expected his voice. I hadn't expected him. He looked at me then. Fully. Eyes sharp. But not unkind.

"Jesus," he muttered, setting the tablet down.

"Relax. I'm not going to bite."

I crossed my arms over the shirt. Suddenly very aware of my legs. Bare. Exposed.

"I thought Wolfe—"

"Wolfe's out," he cut in.

Didn't let me finish.

"Didn't want to leave you alone. And let's be honest, he doesn't trust anyone but me."

Pause.

"That includes himself."

His words landed too hard. Like a truth I hadn't earned yet.

I didn't reply. Didn't move. The coffee smelled good. But my stomach turned. I backed into the hallway. Royal didn't follow. Didn't push. He just watched.

The bathroom was marble. White. Gold trim. Too clean. Too much. It made me feel dirty just for being in it. I peeled off Wolfe's shirt. Every bruise felt like it shifted under the fabric. Like it didn't want to be seen. But I saw them anyway. Purple. Red. Green already blooming in the corners.

The shower was too hot. The water hit my shoulders like pressure, not relief. But I stepped in anyway. Let it burn. And then—

I sat down. Right on the marble floor. Back to the wall. Knees to my chest. And I cried. Not quiet. Not gentle. Just *wrecked.* Because the last two days had hollowed me out and filled me with the wrong things.

I tried not to picture Wolfe's face. The way he looked when he lifted me like glass. The way he gripped the back of my head like he was trying not to break me. I tried not to think about Royal, sitting outside, pretending not to listen. But the truth? This was the first time I'd felt safe in months. And that scared me more than anything else.

I didn't know what to do with myself. So I wandered. Every step was tentative. My body still sore. My breath still shallow. The hem of Wolfe's shirt brushed over bruised skin I hadn't worked up the nerve to look at yet.

The apartment was spotless. Not in a lived-in way. In a curated way. Like someone had designed it for functionality. For discipline. Not for warmth. No photos. No mementos. No clutter. Everything matte and brushed and steel.

A kitchen island he probably never used.

A desk too clean to belong to someone who lived in his own skin.

One potted plant near the window.

Already dying at the edges.

I moved through the space like it might reject me if I

breathed too loudly. Like it was a museum and I didn't belong near the exhibits.

I trailed my fingers along the edge of the coffee table. Opened a drawer in the hallway. Empty. It wasn't just neat. It was empty. Like the apartment had been waiting for someone to occupy it properly. Like me.

I closed the drawer. Swallowed the thought. Moved toward the living room. Royal didn't speak. Didn't ask questions. Just leaned against the counter like he had nowhere else to be.

I didn't know what to say to that. So I said nothing. He sipped his coffee. Stared at me like I might vanish if he blinked.

"You're not what I expected," he said finally.

I blinked. Looked up.

"What were you expecting?"

He tilted his head.

"More attitude. Less shaking."

I flushed. Turned away like that would protect me. It didn't.

"There's coffee," he said.

"Help yourself."

Then, quieter—

"Wolfe told me not to let anything happen to you. So... don't test me."

It wasn't a threat. Not really. But it wasn't a joke either.

I moved to the counter. Poured a cup. It was hot. Stronger than I liked. But I held it in both hands and let the heat sink into my palms. Royal didn't move. Just kept watching. Like I was a puzzle he hadn't finished putting together.

The silence stretched. Sharp. But not cruel. Just heavy. Like both of us were waiting for the other to speak first. And neither of us really wanted to.

I sat on the edge of the couch. Tucked my legs up. Wolfe's

shirt bunched around my thighs. I felt the chain shift across my collarbone and didn't adjust it.

"You hungry?"

Royal's voice broke the silence like it had weight behind it. I looked up. He was still holding the same cup of coffee. Still unreadable.

"Not really."

"You should eat something."

I didn't respond. He pushed off the counter. Walked into the living room and dropped into the chair across from me like he owned the room. Which... maybe he did. Not the apartment. But the space. The energy. He stared at me for a beat longer. Then said—

"You think I don't like you."

It wasn't a question. I blinked.

"Do you?"

He shrugged.

"Doesn't matter."

"It kind of does."

He tilted his head. Smirked. But it didn't hold its usual bite.

"Look. I don't hate you."

"But?"

"But I've seen girls like you come and go. Pretty. Quiet. Complicated as fuck. Always hiding something."

That stung more than it should have. I looked away.

"I didn't ask to be here."

"No," he said. "But you didn't run either."

That one hit harder. Because it was true. He leaned forward. Elbows on his knees.

"You want the truth?"

I didn't answer. He gave it anyway.

"I don't like Barron."

My eyes snapped to his. That I hadn't expected.

"Never have," he added. "Too proud. Too used to people doing what he says just because he says it."

He pointed at me with his mug.

"But you? You didn't fold."

"I kind of did."

"Sure. But you got back up. That counts."

I didn't know what to do with that. So I held my cup tighter. Sipped. Burned my tongue. Didn't flinch.

"You're better than you think," he said, quieter now.

"You barely know me."

"I know Wolfe."

The silence that followed was a different kind of heavy. Wolfe. The man who touched me like I was made of breath and silence. Who looped a chain around my neck and called it protection.

"He's scary when he cares," Royal said.

I looked up. He was staring into his coffee.

"But he listens to me. He trusts me. And right now? That trust is sitting on that couch with bruises and bare feet and a ring she probably shouldn't be wearing."

I didn't say anything. Couldn't. But I felt the lump in my throat swell until I had to breathe through my nose just to keep it down.

"So no," he finished. "I don't hate you."

"Then what?"

He looked at me. Eyes tired. But honest.

"I'm rooting for you. Even if I don't know why yet."

I didn't answer. But my eyes stung in a way I didn't expect. Royal leaned back in the chair. Crossed one ankle over his knee. Like he hadn't just said something I'd remember when I woke up at 3 a.m. not knowing why I felt like I was falling.

"I'm not good at this shit," he added.

I tilted my head.

"What shit?"

"Making scared girls feel safe without sounding like I'm flirting."

I blinked.

A beat passed.

Then—unexpectedly—I *laughed*.

Not loud. Not long. But real. It hurt my ribs. But it loosened something else. Royal's grin was crooked.

"See? Not a total monster."

"You kind of are."

He raised his mug in mock salute.

"Takes one to know one."

We sat in silence a few seconds longer. Then he stood, stretched, and nodded toward the kitchen.

"There's toast. And Wolfe left instructions to feed you. Like I'm your temporary bodyguard-slash-butler."

"And if I refuse?"

He arched a brow.

"I sit on the couch with a gun in my lap until you get hungry."

I shook my head. But I stood anyway. Not because I wasn't afraid. But because...

Maybe I wasn't alone in it anymore.

29

WOLFE

The footage looped again.

Three seconds.

Twelve frames.

One mistake.

The man entered from the blind spot just outside her stairwell. Black hoodie. Mask. Gloves. But he turned. Just enough. A slip in the way his shoulder twisted to push her door open. An angle that gave me what I needed.

Left-handed.

Five foot ten.

Close-cropped beard under the mask.

Military boots.

Clean. Efficient. Fast.

But not fast enough.

I watched it again. This time with the hallway audio unmuted. The audio was grainy. Distorted. Too far from the mic. But I heard it anyway.

The soft click of her boots on the floor. The way she paused near her door—keys in hand. She looked over her shoulder. I saw it in the angle of her spine. The hesitation. Like something in her gut said *wrong*.

She reached for the lock—

And he was there. Fast. Brutal. A blur of black. She didn't scream at first. She choked. Like the sound got caught behind fear and instinct.

Then—

"No—*please—stop—*"

It was faint. But it was her. And I'd never forget that tone again.

My hand clenched the edge of the desk hard enough the wood bowed. My other curled into my thigh until the muscle locked. I should've been there. I should've never left her.

I watched it again.

Slower.

Frame by frame.

I saw the way she fought. The way she kicked. The way she bit his hand. He flinched. She got him. Just for a second. Right before he slammed her down.

I stopped the feed. Froze it on her. Collapsed. Hair fanned out. Knees tucked up. One hand half-raised like she was still trying to shield herself from something already done. I didn't breathe. Didn't blink. Didn't move. Because if I did? I'd lose it.

The door creaked open in the footage. Her voice came faint and terrified—"no, no, please—"

Then the struggle.

The impact.

The silence.

My fists clenched tighter. The playback window reflected her fall again. Over and over. And each time? Something inside me broke wider.

Then—

"Sir."

Mason's voice cracked through the static in my chest.

I turned toward the monitor. His live feed flicked on. He didn't say much. Didn't need to. He stood in front of a man. Chained. Knees bent. Head down. Blood on his shirt. Eyes blackened. Lip split. Breathing like it hurt.

"I found him," Mason said.

"You touch him?"

"Nope."

He raised his hand. Showed clean knuckles.

"Like you asked. He's all yours."

I stared at the screen. At the man's face. Still bowed. Still too calm. But I recognized him now. Not from the footage. From the way Cloe curled into herself. From the sound in her voice that wasn't fear—it was memory. And I knew. This wasn't just an intruder. This was the past. The one Selene warned about. The one who never really left her.

And now?

He belonged to me.

I shut the monitor. Grabbed my coat. And drove.

The parking garage was mostly empty. Third level. Far corner. One single flickering light overhead. The kind of spot where secrets got buried. And men left limping—if they left at all.

Mason stood next to the chair. The man was slumped in it. Wrists tied behind him. One ankle already swelling. Blood drying on his temple. No mask now. No mystery. Just a mouth that had whispered the wrong words in the dark to a woman I'd already claimed.

I stepped closer. Mason didn't move. Didn't speak. He knew better.

The man lifted his head. His left eye was swollen nearly shut. The other fixed on me as I circled once. Just once. Slow.

"Comfortable?" I asked.

He didn't respond.

So I pulled a folding chair from the wall and sat directly in front of him.

"I watched you put your hands on her," I said.

My voice was calm.

Even.

But my fingers curled into fists slowly on my knees.

"You broke into her home."

Still no reply.

"You grabbed her. Slammed her down. You didn't take anything. You weren't there for money."

My eyes locked on his.

"So I'm going to ask once."

"Who paid you?"

He snorted.

Tried to smile.

Split his lip open wider.

"Fuck *you*."

I leaned forward.

Rested my elbows on my knees.

Let the silence stretch.

Then reached down and twisted his left pinky finger until it cracked with a *snap*.

He howled.

Mason didn't flinch.

I didn't blink.

"That was for the bruises."

I moved to the next finger.

"This one's for her lip."

I already knew who he was.

Not just a stalker. Not just a threat.

He was the one Selene promised to unleash. The ex. The

leash. The bastard who once called Cloe his and treated her like property.

The same motherfucker who left bruises on her ribs and panic in her voice.

This wasn't about money. Wasn't about random chance.

It was deliberate. Ordered. A message from Selene, signed in bone.

Crack.

He started breathing harder.

Sweat beading on his forehead.

"You think this is it?" I said. "You think pain is the part I have trouble with?"

I grabbed the back of his chair and pulled him an inch closer.

"Pain is the part I enjoy."

He spat blood onto the floor.

Choked.

Then—

"She—she didn't tell me her name—"

My body went still.

"She called herself *The Bitch*—said the girl *owed* her."

He was shaking now.

"Said—said don't kill her. Just scare her."

My jaw flexed.

His eyes widened.

"Please—she said just enough to make her run. Just a warning—"

A sound cracked behind us.

Sharp.

Final.

Gunshot.

The man jerked. Then slumped. Dead weight. Mason

reached for his gun—but I was already standing. Turning. Eyes wide.

There, across the garage—

A figure in black. No face. No voice. Just a silhouette with a suppressed pistol still raised.

He nodded once. Then disappeared into the shadows. No footsteps. No sound. Just gone.

I stood in the quiet for a long time. Turned back toward the body. Still tied to the chair. Head tilted at an unnatural angle. Eyes open. Mouth slack. He died without ever knowing what was behind him. Or what he was about to say.

I crouched. Not because I wanted to examine the body—but because my legs were trembling and I didn't want to sit. Blood had splattered across his shoulder. The scent of it hit like iron and sweat and something that would never quite wash out of my coat.

My knuckles were still bloodied from what I'd done earlier. Now they were shaking. Not with fear. With rage. Because the man didn't die for what he'd done. He died to protect someone else. And I didn't know who. Not yet. But I would.

Mason stepped forward and held out a towel. I didn't take it. I stood. Wiped my hand across my jacket. And walked away. Not moving. Not breathing right. Because this wasn't justice. It was a message. The man almost gave her up. And someone made sure he never got the chance to finish.

I didn't speak the whole ride back. Didn't turn on music. Didn't wipe the blood off my knuckles. Just drove. Right hand on the wheel. Left curled in my lap like it was still holding the ghost of his throat.

The steering wheel felt hot beneath my palm. Not from sun. From grip. From the tension that had crept into my bones and refused to let go. Every red light felt like mockery. Every turn like a test.

I almost missed the exit once. Didn't correct until the last second. The tires screeched across the line and I didn't care. Her voice echoed in the car like it had been stitched into the leather. *Where are you taking me?* The fuck out of here. That answer hadn't been for her. It had been for me. Because if I'd stood in that apartment one second longer, I would've buried a body there.

I glanced down at my shirt. Sweat had dried into the collar. My fingers tapped the side of my thigh. Pulse still too fast. The chain she wore—the one I gave her—was still pressed between my teeth. Metaphorically. For now.

The air inside the car felt too still. Like even the leather didn't want to rustle. My coat was still damp at the collar from sweat. My jaw still locked.

I flexed my fingers on the steering wheel, watched a line of dried blood crack at the base of my thumb. I hadn't expected the gunshot. Hadn't expected the man in black. But I wasn't surprised. I've seen silence used as a weapon before. I've seen threats that never speak. It's not the ones who yell that make the first cut. It's the ones who nod. Then vanish.

The man was dead.

But he didn't matter anymore.

Because now?

I knew something bigger was moving behind him.

And whoever it was—

They were protecting the wrong person.

I pulled onto the side street near my building. Engine still running. The wheel hot under my palm. The silence pressing in from all sides.

I should've gone upstairs. Should've kicked the door open just to see her eyes. But I didn't. Because I wasn't ready to see her lie to me again.

"I fell."

That's what she said. Like it was a joke. Like I wouldn't notice the bruise blooming across her cheekbone.

I hated that she lied. Not because it made her untrustworthy. Because it meant she didn't believe I could handle the truth. That I couldn't hold it. That I couldn't hold her. She'd protected me.And I was supposed to be the one protecting her.

I slid my phone from my coat pocket with a hand still shaking.

Typed the message.

To: Royal

She okay?

Read receipt.

Typing.

Then—

She's quiet.

Ate something.

Still won't look me in the eye.

But she's okay.

I stared at the screen.

Then typed again.

Paused.

Deleted it.

Typed another.

She's not okay.

But she's safe.

I didn't send it.Didn't need to.The words sat heavy in my chest like they'd been burned into the muscle. I sat in the car a little longer. Let the engine idle. Watched the entry camera on my phone flicker.

The feed from her hallway was quiet. Still. A dim yellow cast from the overhead bulb. Royal wouldn't let anything happen to her. Not on his watch. But this wasn't about trust. It was about presence. About knowing that if she screamed again, I'd hear it. This time, I'd get there in time.

I opened the message thread again.

Typed:

I'm outside.

Deleted it.

Typed another.

I'm not coming up unless you ask.

Deleted that too.

Because I knew she wouldn't. And it wasn't her job to reach for me. It was mine.

I sat back. Closed my eyes. And promised myself this wasn't over. Not until the person who sent him knew exactly what it felt like to bleed for someone who never thanked them. Because safe wasn't a feeling. It was a decision. And I'd already made it for her.

30

____

CLOE

The car ride was silent. Not the kind of silence that held peace. The kind that tightened. Like it was stitched into the seams of the leather. Like it lived in the air between us.

Wolfe didn't speak. He kept one hand on the wheel, the other on his thigh. Eyes forward. Jaw locked. Not angry at me—at least not yet. But something inside him was still burning. The kind of fire that didn't need oxygen anymore.

My fingers curled in the fabric of Wolfe's hoodie—mine now, I guessed. He'd handed it to me before we left. No questions. Just... handed it over.

I wore it over his shirt like armor. It didn't help. The sleeves hung past my fingers. The hem covered the bruises on my thighs. But it didn't stop the way I flinched every time a shadow moved outside the window.

When we pulled up to the building, my stomach twisted. It looked the same. Same brick. Same rusted railing. Same cracked sidewalk. But I wasn't the same girl who'd walked out of it the last time. That girl didn't know what silence sounded like when it was used as a weapon.

Wolfe parked but didn't turn the engine off. He didn't move until I did.

I reached for the handle. Paused. Then looked at him.

"Are you coming up?"

His jaw flexed.

"Do you want me to?"

I didn't answer. Didn't need to. He opened his door. The stairwell creaked beneath our weight.

The air smelled like burnt dust and old heat. When we reached my door, I froze. The frame had been reinforced. Wolfe had done that. New bolts. Steel braces along the edges. The lock looked surgical. Precise. He'd rebuilt the barrier. But nothing would make this place feel safe again.

He unlocked the door with a code I didn't remember giving him. Then opened it first. Stepped in. Waited. I followed. And froze.

It smelled like him now. Not the attacker. Not blood. But Wolfe. Like cedar and frost and control.

Still, the ghost of what happened lingered beneath it. A half-shadow in every corner. A whisper in the air vents. A warning in the lightbulb that still flickered when I shut the door behind us.

I didn't speak. Just moved into the bedroom. My chest was tight. Hands too slow.

I pulled a duffel from the closet and unzipped it. Started with the essentials. T-shirts. Underwear. The only jeans that didn't cut into my hips when I sat down.

I tried to move fast. But every drawer I opened made me feel like I was stealing from my own life. Like I wasn't coming back. Wolfe stood near the door. Didn't move. Didn't speak.

But I felt him there. Every breath I took caught on the silence he gave me. When I reached for my nightstand drawer,

I paused. I hadn't opened it since the break-in. It should've been empty. It wasn't.

A note.

Folded.

Tucked just behind my old journal.

My throat closed before I could even reach for it.

But I did.

Hands trembling.

I unfolded the paper.

One line.

Time's not up. But it will be.

Signed only:

S.

My knees buckled. I sat down on the edge of the bed like someone had cut the strings holding me upright. The note slipped from my fingers and landed face-up in my lap.

Wolfe stepped forward. His shadow stretched across the floor toward me. He didn't ask what it said. Didn't need to. Because he saw my face. And that was enough.

I stared at it like it might catch fire in my hands. I wanted to scream. To cry. To tear the apartment apart and find the cameras I suddenly felt watching me again. But I didn't. I folded the note. Tucked it into the hoodie's front pocket. And zipped it.

Wolfe was still in the kitchen when I walked out. He'd packed a small bag—clean, perfect, like a soldier's field kit. He looked up. Eyes scanned me. Saw the color leave my face. Saw the tension in my shoulders.

"What did you find?"

I shook my head.

"Nothing."

He didn't press.

Didn't blink.

Just held out the bag.

"Ready?"

I nodded. But I wasn't. Not even close.

I moved like I was underwater. Hands fumbling. Chest tight. Every breath felt like I was inhaling glass.

The drawers wouldn't open right. My fingers kept missing the handles. My knees bumped the bedframe like I didn't know the shape of my own space anymore.

Wolfe didn't say anything.

He stood near the door, arms crossed. Watching. Not judging. Not rushing. Just... there.

The silence should have helped. It didn't. It made me feel like I was being timed. Like I was already too late.

I folded a sweatshirt and realized I hadn't blinked in over a minute. My vision blurred. Tears that didn't fall—but burned anyway. When I tried to pull a pair of jeans from the drawer, my hand shook so badly the denim slipped through my fingers.

I reached for them again.

Failed.

Again.

And then I stopped trying.

My arms dropped to my sides. I stared down at the mess on the floor—clothes, socks, a bra I didn't remember liking. It all looked like a stranger's life. One I didn't belong to anymore. Wolfe crossed the room without a sound.

Knelt.

Started folding.

One piece at a time.

Efficient.

Precise.

He didn't look at me. Didn't speak. He just took over. And I let him. Because I couldn't do it.

He moved like he'd done it before. Like there was a version

of him who had packed someone else's life in silence once. Or maybe just pieces of his own.

He held up a toothbrush. Raised an eyebrow. I nodded. He added it to the bag.

By the time he zipped the second duffel, my legs were shaking. I sat on the edge of the bed. Held my hands in my lap. Looked at the window like it might offer something better than what waited behind the door. It didn't.

But Wolfe did. He pulled the hoodie zipper up without touching me. Fixed the collar gently. Then handed me the bag.

"You good?"

I opened my mouth.

Closed it.

Tried again.

"No."

He nodded.

"Okay. Then let's go."

I sat on the edge of the bed and stared at my feet. Wolfe stood. Stilled.

"You're okay."

It wasn't a question. It wasn't reassurance. It was a reminder. I nodded. Even though I wasn't.

He walked over. Held the bag in one hand. Then paused.

"What did the note say?"

I swallowed.

Hard.

"Nothing. Just a warning."

"From who?"

I didn't answer. His jaw ticked once. Then he nodded. Just once.

"Fine."

"Fine?"

"I'll find out on my own."

That made me look up.

Eyes wide.

"Wolfe—what did you do?"

He tilted his head. Didn't blink. Didn't breathe.

"I handled it."

The room was too small suddenly. Or I was too much. Or he was too much.

"Did you...?"

"No."

His answer was sharp. Final.

"He's gone. But not because of me."

Not directly, was what he didn't say.

And I didn't press. Because I didn't want to know what Wolfe was capable of. I already had an idea. And it terrified me almost as much as it comforted me.

He held out his hand. I stared at it. Then reached for it with fingers that didn't feel like mine. When he pulled me to my feet, I didn't stumble. But I came close.

Walking into the Lawlor building felt like stepping into judgment. The lobby lights were too bright. The glass walls too transparent. The click of my heels sounded like alarms. I wore Wolfe's coat. It swallowed me. Covered the bruises. Covered the fear. But nothing could cover the weight.

People looked. They always did. But today? They stared. Not at the bruises. Not at the coat. At Wolfe. And the fact that I was walking beside him.

Close.

Too close.

The elevator ride was silent. I watched the numbers climb. Pretended I didn't see Wolfe watching my reflection in the doors like he was memorizing the girl beside him.

When we stepped onto the floor, it was like a needle scratched across the room.

Phones still rang. Keyboards still clicked. But heads turned. One. Then another. Then all at once.

I kept walking. Because stopping would've meant admitting something was wrong. And I couldn't handle that today.

Royal looked up from the glass-walled conference room. His smirk faded the second he saw my face. His expression dropped into something sharp and serious. He stood. Started toward us. Loyal leaned back from the corner near the espresso machine. Crossed his arms. Didn't blink. Just watched.

Barron stepped out of his office. His eyes went to Wolfe. Then to me. Then to the chain Wolfe had tugged from beneath my blouse two nights ago.

I saw the moment he noticed the bruise. The eye. The swollen lip. His jaw locked. His hands didn't move. Not clenched. Not fisted. Just still. And that scared me more than anything else.

"Inside."

His voice didn't rise.

But the entire floor heard it.

Wolfe moved first. I followed. Barron's office door closed with a soft snick. The blinds stayed open. Which meant this wasn't private. This was a performance.

He stepped behind his desk. Didn't sit. Didn't tell me to. He stared. For a full ten seconds. Then said—

"You let someone into your apartment while wearing my name around your throat."

My stomach clenched. Not because of the way Barron's voice cracked like thunder—

But because Wolfe had seen the bruises.

This wasn't about the day in his office. Not the cramps. Not the heat. This was about the man who'd followed me home.

Wolfe tensed beside me. I spoke before either of them could escalate it.

"I didn't let anyone—"

"You think this is a fucking game?"

The whisper of rage in Barron's voice was worse than if he'd shouted.

"You think you can lie your way through this?"

"She's not lying," Wolfe said.

"No?" Barron turned his eyes on him. "Then why didn't she come to us?"

"She came to me."

That landed like a slap. Even though no one moved. Barron exhaled once. A slow breath.

"And you think that makes it better?"

Royal entered without knocking.

"Hey. Maybe we cool it."

"No," Barron snapped. "We don't."

He turned to me.

"I gave you one rule, Cloe. Don't make me regret trusting you."

I looked at Wolfe.

Then at Royal.

Then back at Barron.

"I didn't choose this. I didn't invite it. And I sure as hell didn't deserve it."

That silenced the room.

Even Barron.

"She didn't ask for what happened," Wolfe said.

His voice was low.

But final.

"And if anyone wants to make her explain it again—they'll answer to me."

No one spoke after that.

Not for a long moment.

Barron turned. Faced the window. Didn't say another word. But I knew this wasn't over. Not by a long shot.

31

WOLFE

THE GARAGE WAS SHADOWED and cold. Concrete sweat in the air. Lights low. Mason stood next to the back wall, arms crossed, tablet in hand. His expression didn't shift when I stepped into view. He just held out the tablet.

"You're going to want to see this."

I didn't respond.

I took it.

And the second I saw the routing code—Belgium, under a security consulting front tied to diamond infrastructure—I knew this wasn't about Cloe.

Not directly.

Someone used her to make a point. To get my attention.

They succeeded.

"It's a ghost corp," Mason said. "Looks like a front through a diamond customs shell near Antwerp."

I scrolled. Every account tied to a private money trail. Moved fast. Moved clean. Too clean.

"Military-trained subcontractor took the job," Mason added. "No direct employer. All offshore. This was planned."

I nodded once. Didn't say anything for a moment.

"She was followed," I said eventually. "This wasn't a mistake."

"No. Someone knew she was yours."

I handed the tablet back. My jaw was already tight enough to ache.

Mason looked at me. "Could be someone in the Antwerp loop. Could be someone watching your diamond trade from the outside. Or..."

"Or it could be one of London's enemies."

"Exactly."

That name tightened everything behind my ribs. I pulled out my phone. Called him. London answered on the second ring.

"Didn't expect you."

"You've got a leak."

"No, I don't."

"Someone used your back-end to fund a hit. On someone close to me."

Pause.

"Cloe?"

"Yes."

Silence stretched.

Then London's voice came low, sharp.

"Tell me what you need."

"I need to know if it's one of yours. Or if someone's coming for both of us."

"I'll find the thread."

"I'll cut it."

The line went dead.

I turned back to Mason.

"Trace it all."

"I already started."

"Find whoever signed off on the offshore account."

"And if it leads nowhere?"

I stared down the garage.

"Then I find the nearest someone. And make them bleed."

"Wolfe," Barron said, voice lower now.

"Tell me you didn't start something you can't finish."

I met his eyes.

Cold.

Unflinching.

"I didn't start it."

"But you're going to finish it?"

"Every last fucking piece."

That was the last word.

I walked out of the conference room without looking back.

Not at Barron.

Not at Royal.

Not even at Cloe.

I knew she was still standing there.

I'd felt her eyes on my back through the whole fucking fight. I didn't want to see her face. Not like that. Not right now.

I didn't want to see her face. Not like that. Not right now. Because if I looked? I'd forget why I was so goddamn angry in the first place. And I couldn't afford that. *Not when Selene was still out there.*

Not when Barron was already unraveling.

And not when I knew—

The next time this family burned...

The bullpen was silent. Conversations stopped the second I stepped out. A few heads dropped. One guy closed his laptop like the click might cover his curiosity. They weren't afraid because I yelled. They were afraid because I didn't.

Cloe stood just past the glass wall, tucked near Royal's shoulder.

She looked—

Small.

Like someone had carved her out of everything she used to be and hadn't quite put her back together yet.

Her arms were crossed over her chest. The chain still gleamed faintly at her collar. She didn't say anything. Didn't ask if I was okay. She looked like she'd been slapped.

Not just by what we'd said—

By how we'd said it.

Every word had been loud enough to echo. Every sentence carved deep enough to leave her reeling.

Her arms stayed crossed. Not like a barrier. Like she was holding herself together. Like if she let go, everything inside her would slip loose. Her lips parted like she might speak. But no sound came.

And when I passed too close—

She flinched.

Not visibly.

Just enough for me to feel it.

And I hated myself for walking away. But I did it anyway. She just stared at me like she wasn't sure who I was anymore. Maybe she wasn't wrong.

Royal caught up with me halfway down the hall. Didn't grab me. Just matched my pace and said—

"You need a minute?"

I didn't answer.

"Because you're about to punch through glass, and that's not a look that screams 'I've got this handled.'"

I stopped walking.

Turned to him.

"He called her a liability."

Royal nodded.

"He's not wrong."

I stared at him.

His expression didn't waver.

"He's also not the one who carried her out."

That hit harder than I expected.

"You think I'm making a mistake?"

"I think you already made it.

Now you're just trying to own the consequences."

"And?"

"And I respect the hell out of that.

But if you burn down the family to protect her, just make sure she's still standing when the smoke clears."

I looked past him toward the far window. Cloe's reflection still hovered in the glass. Not moving. Not blinking. Just watching.

"She's the only one I'd burn for."

The heat hadn't left my chest. It curled behind my ribs like something alive. Like it was pacing while I held the door closed behind it.

I wasn't shaking.

Not visibly.

But my palms itched from the tension.

My knuckles still ached from restraint.

Barron didn't know how close I'd come. Not to hitting him. To walking away from all of it. From the company. From the family. From the weight of keeping all of us from destroying each other.

He said she was a weakness. And he wasn't wrong. She was distraction. She was hunger. She was softness where I'd never allowed any. But she was also the only fucking thing in my life I didn't want to break.

I walked past the elevator like I hadn't heard the stunned silence behind me. Like I couldn't feel the eyes tracking every inch of my retreat.

The glass wall felt colder than it should. Everything did. The conference room burned behind me, but I didn't look back. Didn't slow. Because if I stopped walking?

I wouldn't have left that room without blood on my hands.

Back in my office, I shut the door harder than I meant to. The silence hit too fast. Like it had been waiting for me to come home.

I stood there for a moment. Jaw tight. Breath locked behind my teeth. Then I moved. Took off my coat. Dropped it over the back of the chair like I was shedding something heavier than fabric.

Loosened my tie.

Didn't sit.

Just paced.

Two steps.

Back.

Again.

I pressed my palm to the glass. It was cold. Grounding.

Through the reflection, I saw her.

Cloe.

Still outside the conference room.

Still pale.

Still watching.

She didn't knock. Didn't move. Just waited. But I couldn't go to her yet.

Not like this. Not with my hands still itching to kill. Not with the rage still coiled behind my ribs like a second spine.

I turned.

Grabbed my phone.

Typed the message to London.

Because someone started this.

And I was going to finish it. The sound made the glass tremble.

My hands braced on the edge of the desk. I didn't sit. I didn't breathe. I opened a thread I hadn't touched in months.

Typed:

We need to talk.

Now.

Ten seconds later, one word returned:

Understood.

London.

The only person I trusted to know what kind of war was coming. Because he'd survived it before. Because we both had. And this time? This time, I wasn't walking away until someone bled for her.

32

———

WOLFE

I saw him before he saw me. Same tan coat. Same slick hair. Same smug mouth that had once opened too easily in a steel elevator and whispered something about Cloe that made my blood run cold.

He was standing just outside the service entrance—too close to the private lot.

Too still.

Too casual.

Cigarette in one hand.

Phone in the other.

And a notebook.

I moved faster than I should have. Didn't run. Didn't stalk. Just moved with purpose. Because I knew exactly who the fuck he was. And exactly what the fuck he was doing. When he spotted me, he smiled. The same lazy, condescending tilt of his head that made my fist itch.

"Hey," he said, like we were old friends. "Didn't think I'd see you again so soon."

I didn't answer. My eyes dropped to the notebook in his hand. He started to tuck it into his coat pocket.

Too slow.

I stepped in.

Grabbed the front of his jacket.

Yanked him forward.

Hard.

The notebook fell to the ground.

I kicked it aside. Pressed him against the wall near the dumpster. He grunted. Coughed. But he didn't fight.

"You've got five seconds," I growled, voice low, tight. "To tell me why the fuck you're here."

He opened his mouth.

Tried a smirk.

"Relax. I'm just waiting for a meeting—"

I slammed him into the wall again.

His head hit hard enough to echo.

"No, you're not."

He choked on the next word.

I shoved my hand into his coat pocket, grabbed the notebook, flipped it open.

License plates. Dozens of them. Scrawled in messy, frantic handwriting. I looked up slowly.

"You looking for her?"

He didn't respond.

So I hit him.

Once.

Straight to the gut. He folded, gasped. Still didn't fight.

"W-what's the big deal?" he coughed. "She's beautiful. I wanted to know where she parks."

My vision went white.

"Say that again."

"She's hot, man. You're not the only one who wants a piece of that—"

I didn't hear the rest.

Because I hit him again.

And again.

And again.

Until he dropped. Until the notebook hit the pavement. Until my knuckles split. Until the red on my hands wasn't just his.

I winced hard.

He tried to crawl.

I grabbed the back of his jacket and dragged him behind the parked car, out of view.

"You think you can hunt her like she's prey?" I snarled. "You think you can stalk her and walk away?"

He spat blood.

Didn't speak.

So I kicked him.

Hard.

"Look at me."

He did.

Barely.

One eye swollen shut already.

"She's not *yours* to watch."

He laughed—weak, wet.

"You think she's yours?"

I crouched low. Got close enough that he could smell the sweat on my collar.

"She's mine. In every way that counts."

I took the notebook. Ripped out the pages. Held it to his face. Wasn't about to tell the motherfucker she didn't *goddamn* drive.

"You come here again, and I swear to God, there won't be enough of your body left for them to identify."

He flinched. That felt like victory. Footsteps behind me.

Royal's.

"Wolfe."

I didn't look back.

"He was watching her."

"I figured."

"You going to stop me?"

Royal was quiet for a second.

Then—

"No. Just don't kill him here."

I stood. The man didn't move. Didn't try to run. I dropped the notebook on his chest. Let him see the page again. Then turned.

Walked away with blood cooling on my hands and fire still crawling through my spine. Royal didn't say anything until we reached the corner.

Then—

"Feel better?"

"No."

I wiped my palm on my coat.

Tasted metal in my teeth.

"She's not going to know about this," I said.

Royal shrugged.

"She probably will. But not from me."

I didn't respond. Didn't stop walking. Because if I did? I'd go back and finish it.

33

————

WOLFE

I met London at the back of a butchered cathedral. The kind with stained glass that didn't shine anymore—only fractured the morning light across the floor in bruised shards. The pews had long been cleared. The altar had been scorched. And the air? It still carried the weight of something holy that had long since turned to rot.

It reminded me of the stories.

Whispers about a man London mentioned once in passing. A name that didn't sound like a name at all—just a warning folded into a curse.

They call him the executioner.

A brutal relic from a dead empire. Cold. Mechanical. Made of silence and precision. He doesn't take payment. He takes *possession.*

London said he lives in an old cathedral now. Keeps it like penance. They say he drowned a girl once. In a baptismal font. And when she came back up—*she begged him to do it again.*

Now he's hunting the last daughter of the traitor line.

Not to kill her.

But to keep her.

The air here was damp. Cold. It made your lungs ache to breathe it in too deep.

We weren't in Belgium yet. That would come later. For now, we met where old debts weren't paid in coin—but in blood. Beneath the city. Under a cathedral that no longer rang with bells.

Only silence.

London stood beside the altar like it belonged to him. Hands in his coat pockets. Eyes sharper than the blade tucked in his boot.

"You came alone," he said.

"I always do."

His mouth twisted. Not a smile. Not quite.

"You sent a message."

"You said 'say when.' This is when."

He nodded once, slow. "So what's the play?"

I pulled a folder from my coat. Tossed it onto the cracked stone slab where people used to confess.

"This is everyone who touched the subcontractor. Shell companies. Broker aliases. The last three shipments flagged for customs rerouting."

London flipped through the file without looking down.

"And you want me to what—burn it or trace it back to someone with a last name?"

"Both."

He didn't blink.

"You want names? You'll get bodies."

I didn't correct him.

Because I didn't need names anymore. I needed consequences.

He closed the file and handed it off to the shadow standing behind him. I didn't turn to look. Didn't ask who it was.

Anyone London trusted in rooms like this didn't need introductions.

"There's talk out of Antwerp," London said. "Someone's undercutting your channel. Pushing flawed stone into customs with pristine papers. The money behind it isn't new. It's someone trying to remind the table they never left."

I clenched my jaw.

"Erez?"

London nodded slowly. "That's my guess."

Erez Melek.

He'd once been a broker. Too ambitious. Too efficient. He cut deals too fast, burned favors too wide.

Barron buried him five years ago.

Or tried.

"You're telling me the man who lost everything under our heel is slipping stones past EU customs under a ghost proxy?"

"Not just stones," London said. "Routes. Contacts. Safehouses. Your shadow systems in South Africa are now compromised. Quietly. Almost surgically. That's not Selene. She wants noise. Erez wants legacy."

And Cloe?

She'd walked into the crosshairs of a war that was bigger than family.

"She was just the warning shot," I said.

London didn't reply. He didn't need to. Because we both knew what came next. I looked at the altar. At the flickering candlelight pooled beneath what used to be stained glass saints.

"Then let's start in Belgium."

The hotel was glass and silence.

Nothing branded.

Nothing trackable.

The kind of place where favors replaced credit cards, and

the concierge asked no questions unless he was paid to deliver them later.

London had cleared the floor. Gutted the suite. No art on the walls. No flowers in the vases. There were no beds. Just a long black table that looked like it had been carried in through the freight elevator by ghosts.

Two chairs.

One window.

No blinds.

A single pendant light hung low over the table, casting a perfect circle of illumination that left everything else in the suite shadowed and still.

The man they brought in didn't wear a mask. He didn't need one. He sat in the chair like he'd been there before. Not just in this room—but in this kind of reckoning.

Like he knew the rules.

Like he'd helped write them.

London stood at the edge of the room for exactly three seconds. Then nodded once to me. Didn't speak. Didn't offer last words. That was the favor. He closed the door behind him with the finality of a coffin lid.

And I was alone.

With the man who moved the money that put Cloe on the floor.

He didn't speak. Didn't shift. Didn't even blink. But he smiled. That slow, smug kind of smile that made my knuckles itch and my heart stop pretending it could stay calm.

I set my coat down.

Rolled up my sleeves.

Didn't rush.

This wasn't rage.

It was ritual.

He tilted his head slightly.

"Do you want a confession, or a receipt?"

His accent was clean. Faint trace of Antwerp. Polished like old money.

"I want your hands," I said.

His smile faltered.

Just for a breath.

"I don't—"

"You moved it. Clean. Quick. Like a man who'd done it before. I want to know how fast I can break the fingers that did it."

The first strike wasn't with a fist. It was with the chair. I tipped it backward. Let him fall hard. He didn't scream. Didn't curse. But his grin disappeared like a light turned off. I pressed my boot to his shoulder.

"Tell me who paid for it."

He said nothing. So I gave him thirty-seven minutes to think. Every sound in the room was absorbed by the walls. No echo. No mercy. I didn't shout. Didn't lecture. Just broke pieces.

Not to kill him.

To remind him that people like us didn't deal in clean breaks.

We shattered.

And we left what was left behind.

When I walked out, my jaw was bruised. One hit he got in out of desperation. My hands were shaking. Not from weakness. From restraint. My coat was soaked. Elbow to cuff.

London leaned against the hallway wall, arms crossed like he hadn't heard a thing. Like the screaming hadn't seeped through the marble.

"Done?"

"For now."

He handed me a lighter.

"You still smoke?"

"No."

I lit it anyway.

Watched the flame flicker at the edge of the folder I carried. Watched it catch. The edges curl. Ink turned to ash. Paper to regret.

"We're not done," I said.

London nodded once.

"That was just the clean-up."

We walked out together.

Two shadows made of legacy and ruin.

And I left the ashes behind.

But not the fire.

34

CLOE

I woke in his bed again. Same sheets. Same silence. But everything felt different. The bruise on my cheek had faded to a dull yellow. The cut on my lip barely tugged when I moved now.

Not that I had much to say.

The ache in my ribs had dulled to something background. But the one in my chest? Still there. Still sharp. Still dragging through every breath like it wanted to be remembered.

The other side of the bed was cold.

Untouched.

Just like every morning before.

He didn't sleep there.

I wasn't even sure if he slept at all. The pillow remained fluffed. The sheet tight. No indent where a body should be. Like he stood guard until I fell asleep—then vanished.

I rolled slowly. Tested my muscles. The pain was fading. But the tension wasn't. It lived under my skin now. Settled into the space between healing and memory.

I sat up.Let the silence crawl over me. It wasn't soft. It was thick. *Heavy.* The kind that felt placed there, not accidental.

I listened for him.

Nothing.

No footsteps.

No doors closing.

Just the fridge humming in the other room. And the city outside—too far away to matter.

I stood. The floor chilled my bare feet. Wolfe's t-shirt hung loose against my body. It didn't smell like him anymore. Not after days of sleeping in it. But I wore it anyway.

Because it made me feel like I hadn't completely fallen apart. I padded into the hallway. Then the kitchen. And there he was. Leaning against the counter. Coffee in one hand. Phone in the other. His jaw flexed once. Then again. Something unreadable in the set of his shoulders.

He didn't look at me. Didn't glance over. Didn't acknowledge my presence at all.

"Morning," I said.

Soft.

Unsteady.

Like I wasn't sure if it was allowed.

He nodded once. Didn't speak. Didn't ask how I slept. Didn't check the bruise. Didn't say my name. He just set the mug down. Slid past me. His shoulder brushed mine—barely. But it might as well have been a wall. Because I felt it like a closing door.

I didn't follow.

Didn't ask.

But something inside me wilted.

And the silence that settled behind him? Wasn't stillness. It was distance. It was colder than any silence I'd ever felt from him.

Not cruel. Not indifferent. Just... calculated.

Measured.

Like he'd already decided how far away to stand to keep from catching fire. Or maybe to keep me from burning. I watched the door after he left the room.

Waited.

Expected him to come back.

To say something.

To call me soft or reckless or stupid for what had happened to me.

But he didn't.

He just let me stand there, bruised and barefoot, wearing his shirt and his silence like a punishment I hadn't earned yet.

And maybe that was worse. The chain on my collar felt heavier today. Like it had gained weight just from the tension in the air. Like it knew I was running out of time.

By the time I got to the office, I felt like I'd been hollowed out.

Everyone stared again.

Royal gave me a chin lift. Loyal offered a nod. Barron didn't look up.

I sat at my desk and scrolled through nothing. My inbox was empty. But my chest was full. Too full. Ready to crack.

At 10:02, I got the message.

Office. Now.

Wolfe.

I stood.

My legs felt like they belonged to someone else. The walk down the hallway was too long. Too loud.

The elevator blinked once behind me as I passed it. I didn't stop. Didn't breathe. When I stepped into his office, I didn't wait to be told. I closed the door behind me.

Soft *click.*

A sound that echoed in my spine.

He didn't look up right away. Didn't rise. Just sat there. Across the desk. Hands steepled. Eyes unreadable. His mouth a thin, cold line.

The silence between us didn't just stretch.

It cracked.

"Do you know what it feels like," he said, voice low, "to be trusted by a man who already knows you're lying?"

I froze.

My breath caught. My voice didn't work. He leaned back slowly. Tilted his head. Watched me like he was cataloguing all the ways I might fold.

"I trusted you."

He didn't raise his voice. That would've been easier. I could've cried for that. Screamed. Instead, he gave me something worse.

"You broke something I don't think you even understand."

I opened my mouth.

No words.

Nothing.

Just the sound of my heart beating too loudly in my chest. He looked down at his desk like he was already done with me. Like I was just another entry on a ledger he hadn't closed yet.

"You can go," he said.

Just like that.

Dismissed.

But not released.

I left.

But I didn't stop shaking. Not all day. It came after midnight. Of course it did. I was in Wolfe's apartment. Alone. Wrapped in one of his blankets. The soft grey one that always looked untouched on the back of the couch. The TV was off. The lights low.

The city bled through the windows like it didn't care what I was about to do. I hadn't seen Wolfe since the office. Not really. He'd left before I did.

No message.

No note.

No call.

Just silence.

And I didn't know if he was angry…or preparing for something worse. The chain around my neck felt heavier. Like it knew.

My phone buzzed.

I didn't want to look.

I already knew.

SELENE

One message.

One sentence.

You know what you have to do.

We're waiting.

My throat went tight.

My fingers trembled against the screen.

I wanted to throw the phone. Smash it against the tile. Watch it break so I wouldn't have to be the one doing the breaking anymore. But I didn't. Because part of me still wanted to answer her. And part of me wanted to text Wolfe instead.

I stared at his name in my messages.

Typed nothing.

Just looked.

And then—like punishment—Camille's voice whispered in the back of my head.

You don't lie to people like them, Cloe.

They don't just forgive. They consume.

I folded in on myself. Curled tighter in Wolfe's blanket. Let the phone slide off my leg and hit the carpet with a soft, traitorous sound. And when I closed my eyes? I saw the safe. And the ring. And the fire I was already walking into. No threats. No countdowns. No names. Because she didn't need to say them anymore.

I opened the bedroom drawer. Saw the folded hoodie I hadn't worn since the attack. My fingers brushed the edge of it. Inside the pocket? The note. Her handwriting. Still there. Still curling like a smile. I closed the drawer again. But I didn't lock it.

I went to Wolfe's closet. Opened it slowly. The shirts were arranged like soldiers. Pressed. Black. White. Grey. Minimal. Perfect.

I stepped inside. Closed the door behind me. Sank to the floor between two hanging jackets. And pressed my hands to my face. I didn't cry. Not yet. But I thought about it.

I stayed there until my legs went numb. Until the silence folded around me like a second skin. And when I finally stood—

I didn't feel like the same girl who'd been touched by his hands. I felt like the one who was about to burn everything he gave me. I didn't sleep that night. I curled up in the corner of Wolfe's bed, wrapped in his sheets, and stared at the ceiling like it might give me permission to stop.

Stop pretending.

Stop hiding.

Stop breaking.

The message kept playing behind my eyelids.

We're waiting.

And I hated that I knew what she meant.

I hated more that a part of me wanted to obey. Not out of fear. But out of habit. When I finally sat up, the room was still dark.

No Wolfe.

No movement. Just the city outside and the chain on my skin and the truth curled in my gut like a coiled wire.

I wandered again.

Slow.

Barefoot.

Avoiding the mirror.

His apartment didn't feel quiet anymore. It felt like it was holding its breath. I passed the dying plant. Its edges browning. I touched one of the leaves. It crumbled. Like me.

I walked past the dresser.

The ring was still on top.

In the velvet box.

Next to a drawer that held nothing except the shirt I wore the night I bled on his sheets. I opened that drawer. Just to see it. Just to be sure it was still there. And it was. The shirt. The ring. The note she left.

Everything.

I didn't take the ring out. But I didn't put it away either. I closed the drawer slowly. But this time?

I didn't lock it.

35

———

CLOE

The city was still on Sundays.

Still in the way grief settles into your bones when no one is looking. Still in the way guilt makes the air taste sharper. Everything moved slower. Sound echoed longer. And shame stuck to your skin in places you couldn't scrub clean.

I wore Wolfe's hoodie.

Not for warmth.

Just for the weight.

Like if I wrapped myself in his scent one more time, it might stop me from doing what I came here to do.

It didn't.

The fabric was soft.

Familiar.

The cuffs were stretched from me fisting them in the dark the night before. It still smelled like him. But it didn't feel like safety anymore. It felt like a memory I was about to ruin.

The building lobby was empty.

Security gave me a nod.

Not a second glance.

Because why would they?

I was hers.

His.

Theirs.

The girl from the footage.

The girl with bruises and silence and borrowed clothes.

The girl who walked like she might break if someone looked at her too hard.

The elevator ride stretched.

Too slow.

Too quiet.

Each floor a new excuse to turn around. Each ding a warning I didn't listen to. I watched the numbers climb. Felt the cold metal railing against my back. Held the edges of the hoodie closed like it was armor.

But it wasn't.

It never had been.

By the time I stepped out onto the top floor, my knees had already started to shake. Not from fear. From guilt. The kind that builds bone-deep. That crawls into your ribs and doesn't come out. That whispers in your ear when no one else is speaking.

Every footstep sounded like betrayal.

Like I was breaking a promise I hadn't said out loud.

The promise to stay.

To try.

To be honest.

The chain wasn't around my neck anymore. I'd left it behind that morning. Folded it into the pocket of his hoodie like a confession I couldn't say out loud. Because I couldn't take it with me. Not when I was about to do this. Not when I was about to open the one door that might tear everything apart.

Not when I wasn't sure which of them would burn first.

Me.

Or him.

I passed Wolfe's office.

Didn't look in.

Didn't breathe.

The air felt thick here—like it remembered me. And it hated what I was about to do.

Barron's office loomed at the end of the hall. Dark glass. Heavy door.

I reached into my pocket for the code. Slipped the slip of paper out. My fingers trembled. Not from doubt. From knowing I'd already made my choice. I typed the numbers. Camille's birthday.

The lock clicked open. The door opened with a sigh. That was the worst part. Not the resistance. Not the weight. The ease. Like the lock had been waiting. I stared at it longer this time. Not like a thief. Like a girl standing at the edge of something permanent.

Sweat slid down my spine. The weight in my chest made my breathing shallow. Not panic. Not quite. But the kind of ache you get when you know you're about to be unforgivable.

I imagined Wolfe walking in. What he'd say. What his face would look like when he saw the book in my hands and realized I hadn't just left him—

I'd chosen someone else. I blinked hard. Grabbed the book. And shut the safe before I could change my mind. It didn't feel like paper. It felt like weight. Like heat. Like every lie I'd ever told had been stitched into the spine.

I reached for it.

Paused.

Then picked it up.

My hands didn't shake. Not this time. Because when you're

already broken, there's nothing left to drop. I pressed it to my chest for a second. Closed my eyes.

Whispered—

"I'm sorry."

Not to Wolfe.

Not to Barron.

To Camille.

To the girl I used to be when her laughter made me feel like I belonged somewhere.

I turned. Walked out. Didn't hesitate. Didn't stop. Not until I passed Wolfe's office. The light was off. But I knew what waited inside.

His desk.

His chair.

The velvet box still open where I left it.

I stepped inside. Closed the door behind me. It felt wrong to be here. Like I was inside the skin of a man I'd betrayed.

But I didn't flinch.

I walked to the desk.

Opened the drawer.

Slid the chain inside.

Didn't fold it.

Didn't bury it.

Just let it settle—loose and raw—like a wound.

I placed the lid on the box. Didn't close it. Because closure felt like too much to ask for. The hallway was too quiet. Even for a Sunday.

I walked with the book pressed flat inside my tote bag. Wrapped in a sweatshirt. Not hidden—just... muffled. Like guilt could be padded with cotton and memory. Every step felt heavier. Not because the book weighed anything. But because I did.

I passed the wall of windows overlooking the city.

Stopped.

Just for a second.

I could see Wolfe's building from here.

Knew exactly which windows were his. Wondered if he was there. Wondered if he was watching. Wondered if even knew I was gone.I pressed my palm to the glass. Cold. Clear.

Unforgiving.

"I'm sorry," I whispered again.

But it didn't sound real anymore. I made it to the elevator. Paused when the doors opened. It reflected my face back at me —too pale. Eyes too wide. Too much space where the chain used to sit.

I stepped inside. The doors closed. And that was it. I stared at my reflection in the polished steel. I didn't look like a traitor. I looked like a secretary in an expensive hoodie with too much guilt in her eyes. And that scared me most. Because I could pass. I could walk out of this building and no one would know what I'd done.

The elevator buzzed as it descended. Somewhere on floor twenty-three, it jolted. Just a flicker. A sound. But my whole body locked up like he was behind me again.

I turned.

Of course no one was there.

But the damage was done.

By the time the elevator hit the lobby, I wasn't breathing right anymore. But I still walked. I didn't cry. Didn't shake. I just stood there. Counting the floors like they meant something. Like I wasn't walking out with a piece of Wolfe's soul in my bag. At the ground floor, the security guard waved.

"See you tomorrow," he said.

I smiled.

Didn't answer.

Outside, the wind caught the hem of my coat. The sky had started to grey. Not dark yet. But close.

The kind of light that makes it hard to know what time it is. The kind of light that tells you it's already too late. I walked to the corner. Paused at the red light. Waited. When it changed, I crossed. Didn't look back. Not once.

Because I knew—

If I looked over my shoulder and saw him standing there?

I wouldn't be able to keep walking.

36

WOLFE

I DIDN'T SLEEP. Didn't even pretend to try. I sat in the dark, fully clothed, the light from the surveillance feed turning the walls a cold blue-gray.

The espresso machine hissed in the kitchen. I made coffee just to pour it down the sink. The steam rising from the mug didn't carry warmth—only noise. Something to fill the silence that felt like it might snap my ribs in half.

The feed from her building glowed on my laptop.

Still.

Unmoving.

Sunday footage looped. She never came back. Not to her place. Not to mine. Not to me. I rewound the hallway camera again. Watched the timecode jump. Watched her silhouette blur past the lens—hoodie on, face low.

She moved like smoke. Like someone who didn't want to be seen. She turned the corner like someone who knew what not to be caught by. I told myself I wasn't sure yet. That maybe she just needed air.

But I knew.

I'd known the second my eyes opened and the space beside me was still empty. I didn't know where she'd gone. But I knew what it meant. By the time I stepped into the building, I'd already felt it. The loss. I just hadn't seen it yet.

The Lawlor floor was too quiet. Monday mornings usually carried noise—early staff chatter, Loyal's espresso machine grinding, Barron's voice in the hallway.

But today?

Nothing.

Just the echo of my shoes on polished floors and a tension behind my ribs I couldn't shake.

I got in early. Didn't greet anyone. Didn't take the elevator with anyone. Didn't see her. I walked straight to my office. Unlocked the door. Stopped. The desk looked the same. Exactly the same. Except...

The drawer.

It was open.

Not wide. Just enough.

Just inviting enough. Like a whisper I didn't want to hear. I stepped forward. Didn't take my coat off. Didn't breathe until I reached it.

Inside—

The chain.

Black silk.

Garnet.

Curled in on itself like it missed her.

The garnet still caught the light. Even in the dim. Like it knew it had been left behind. Like it had witnessed something I hadn't.

I stared at it for a long time. Long enough that my eyes started to burn. I didn't touch it. Not at first.

I just stood there.

Frozen.

Reading her absence like scripture. This wasn't a mistake. She didn't lose it. She didn't forget it. She left it. On purpose. Deliberate. Quiet. Final.

I reached down slowly. Picked it up. Felt the weight of it settle into my palm like it belonged there. But it didn't feel like it used to. It was cold now. Too cold.

I turned it over.

Let it pool across my knuckles.

It slid like regret.

Slick.

Sharp.

Soft in the way silk is soft when it's being used to bind. I dropped it. Not because I wanted to. Because I couldn't fucking breathe.

The chain hit the wood with a sound that felt like being punched in the chest. I turned away. Paced to the window. Pressed both palms against the glass like I could feel her on the other side of it.

The city didn't stop moving. Didn't slow. Didn't care. I did. I cared more than I knew how to say. And now she was gone.And the only thing she left behind? Was the part of herself I gave her. That wasn't an accident. It was a message. And I'd just read it.

I reached in.

Touched it.

Lifted it slowly, like it might break under its own weight. The silk slid through my fingers. Still warm. Still carrying her scent—faint lavender, Wolfe's shirt, heat.

I pressed it into my palm.

Tighter.

Enough to bite.

The garnet glinted under the light like it remembered fire. She wore this when I touched her. When she begged. When she whispered thank you like it was the last truth she had left in her.

And now?

She left it.

Not lost.

Not misplaced.

Left.

I wrapped the chain around my knuckles once. Then unwrapped it. Set it down gently. Like if I handled it too roughly, I'd be admitting what it meant. I stared at it for a long time. Didn't touch it. Didn't need to. Because I already knew what it meant. She didn't lose it. She didn't forget it. She left it.

I backed away from the desk.

Turned.

Walked straight to Barron's office. Didn't knock. He wasn't in yet. Of course he wasn't. I crossed the room. Tapped the panel behind the bookshelf.

The safe was already open.

Empty.

Completely.

My vision blurred for a second. Not from anger. Not from grief. From clarity. From the kind of betrayal that explains everything. I stood in front of the safe like I might find something else inside if I looked harder.

But it was empty.

So quiet, it felt like a laugh.

Like the room itself was mocking me.

I touched the inside. There was still a faint line where the book had rested. Like a shadow that wouldn't wash away. Like it wanted me to know it hadn't been stolen. It had been taken. By someone I let that close. I should've changed the code. I should've never let her see me open it. But I had. And some-

where along the way, she stopped being a girl I wanted to keep
safe—

And started being a risk I was too far in to walk away from.
I stood in front of the empty safe for a long time. Then closed it.
Reset the lock. Straightened my jacket. And walked out like I
hadn't just realized the one person I would've burned the
world for—

Was already holding the match.

For one second, I felt it.

The same silence Barron stood in when Selene fucked
another man and walked out with half his heart and none of his
name. He never said a word about it. Not to me. Not to anyone.

But I'd seen it.

In the way he stopped trusting softness. In the way he let
power become punishment. In the way he looked at me when I
started touching her like she was mine.

Back then, I thought he was weak.

Now?

Now I fucking understood it.

This wasn't heartbreak. This was a slow bleed under the
skin. The kind of betrayal that turns to bone. The kind you
build a kingdom out of—just to bury someone in it.

**Want more? Wolfe never said it. But she did. Read
the thank you that changed everything.**

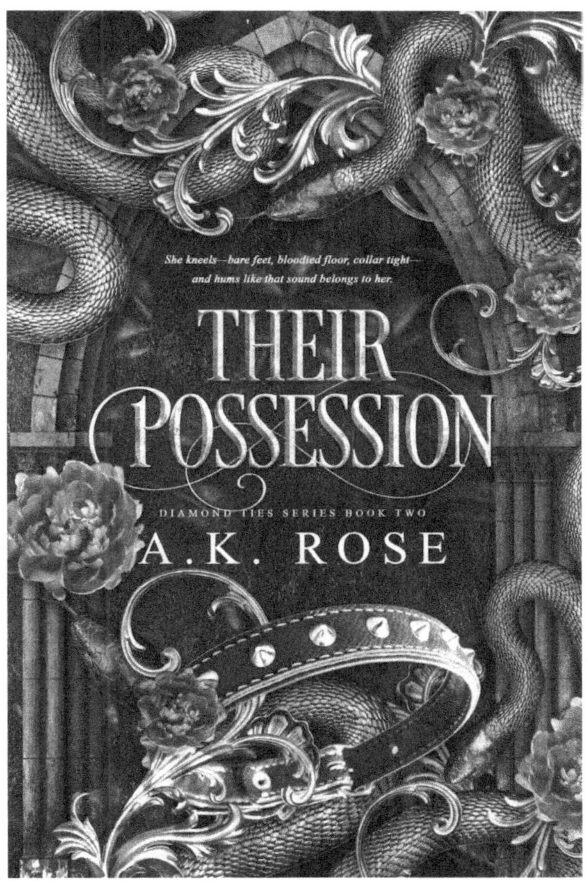

She breathes like she still remembers the leash.

Moves like she knows I'm already watching.

But she doesn't run.

Not anymore.

She kneels—bare feet, bloodied floor, collar tight—and hums like that sound belongs to her.

It doesn't.

It belongs to me.

Always did.

They starved her.

Staged her.

Tried to turn her breath into a weapon.

But what they didn't understand?

That sound she made in the dark wasn't surrender.

It was a summons.

And I'm the one who answers.

Now I'm coming for every man who made her hum without permission.

No mercy. No forgiveness.

Just chain.

And fire.

And the girl they'll never silence again.

THEIR POSSESSION is book two in the brutal dark mafia reverse harem romance Diamond Ties series. Darker, bloodier, and more possessive than ever—this is a story of worship sharpened into vengeance, breath turned into war, and a girl who hums through the silence because she already knows:

He's coming.

And when he does?

They'll learn the difference between having her...

and **owning her.**